TRUST WITH A CHASER

RAINBOW COVE BOOK ONE

ANNABETH ALBERT

To the small town that made me and to everyone who has ever loved a small town

ONE

Mason

When Adam stepped inside the glorified closet I was using as an office, eyes all twitchy and hands wringing a bar towel, I knew I wasn't going to like what came out of his mouth.

"Sheriff Sexy just walked in. He's your problem."

Fuck. I squeezed my eyes shut and took a deep breath. "Please don't call Police Chief Flint that. He might hear, and I'm pretty sure he'd find a citation for you. And I am *not* bailing your ass out."

"You're just worried that one of these days you're going to slip up and call him that." Adam grinned at me. This was an old argument—he'd been calling Flint that stupid nickname since we were in high school. The hard-nosed cop wasn't one to cut teen drivers any slack—especially if they were in any way associated with the name "Hanks." "Anyway, you know he freaks me out. I've got no idea what he wants—all our permits are in order, right?"

"Of course." Standing, I grabbed the folder with the permitting paperwork. I prided myself in the organization I was bringing to the bar and grill that I co-owned with Adam and our friend, Logan. Flint wouldn't find anything to complain about, not with me in charge. "I'll go deal with him. You go back to the bar in case we get a rush."

Adam snorted. Despite it being opening weekend, traffic had been embarrassingly light. We'd worked for weeks transforming the old tavern—a Rainbow Cove institution for decades—into the newly renamed Rainbow Tavern. The gay-friendly bar and grill was our vision for pulling our sleepy little coastal town into the twenty-first century. Logan had crafted a new menu of upscale bar food ready to go, and Adam had innovative drinks specials at the ready. All we needed were customers. And to not run afoul of Nash Flint on our first day of operation.

Flint was a Rainbow Cove institution himself—born and raised here, same as Adam and me, but unlike me, he'd never left, sliding into his father's shoes as police chief and apparently fitting the role as easily as a pair of broken-in jeans. He'd been Officer Flint last time I'd seen him, almost ten years prior.

Guess I could have seen him had I come down for Freddy's trial, something I still felt niggles of guilt over, and I told myself that was why my stomach fluttered on my way out to the tavern's dining room. Unlike Adam, I'd never found Flint particularly...

Sexy. All my thoughts fled as I took in the man sitting in front of the plate-glass window. He dwarfed the small wooden chair, one of dozens that Adam and I had painted bright colors. Broad shoulders stretched the confines of his uniform shirt, biceps bulging under the short sleeves. His cut-glass jaw was firm as ever, as were those hard hazel eyes. But what had been frankly terrifying to my teenaged self made my twenty-seven-year-old libido sit up and take serious notice.

Flint blinked as I approached, head tilting to one side. I'd been getting a lot of that since I'd been back in town. "Mason...Hanks?"

"The one and only." I stuck out my hand. "What can I do for you, Chief Flint?"

He returned my handshake with a sure grip, only a moment's hesitation. I guessed he wasn't all that used to shaking hands with a Hanks. Oh well. I was out to prove to the whole damn town that I wasn't like my father and brothers, and if I had to start with Flint, so be it.

"Nice place you've got here." His eyes swept around the renovated room—restored antique bar on the far wall where Adam wasn't bothering to conceal his nosiness, dance floor beyond that, colorful tables and chairs in the front of the bar, only a handful occupied despite the dinner hour.

"Thanks. Our permits are all in order." I held out my folder. "Liquor license is on top."

He waved the folder off. "Not worried about that."

No? Then why the heck was Flint in my establishment? "Good. We're on the up-and-up. You won't have trouble from us—"

"Glad to hear it," he said levelly, eyes skeptical, reminding me that I was, after all, nothing more than a Hanks. "Cheeseburger?"

"Pardon?"

"That Ringer kid didn't see fit to give me a menu, but I'm trusting you all offer something approximating a burger? Salad, no fries, and an iced tea."

"You want to order?" I was still struggling to keep up with him.

"This *is* a food establishment, right?" He shook his head as if he hadn't expected more from me, and that rankled.

"Of course." I crossed the room in long strides, grabbed an order pad from the bar, ignoring Adam's gaping. As soon as I returned to Flint's table, I added, "Anything you want. On the house."

"None of that." He sighed like my very existence was tiring. "Got my meals from the old tavern for years. They kept a tab open for me."

"We can do the same—"

"Let's see if you can cook first," he said, voice drier than yesterday's toast. "I thought I'd come by, check the place out."

"Appreciated," I said and meant it. Business, any business, was good, but people in Rainbow Cove trusted Flint. If he gave us the seal of approval, more locals might give us a try, make us less dependent on the tourist trade that we were going after. Tourism took a while to build, and our grand plans of making Rainbow Cove an LGBTQ travel destination weren't going to happen overnight. We needed every customer we could get, Flint included, even if he was the unlikeliest of allies.

"You still haven't brought me a menu." He shook his head. "But whatever you've got passing for a burger is fine. Nothing vegan though."

"We've got local grass-fed beef, third-pound patty on a brioche bun with a pesto mayo and local gouda. Or—"

"I reckon that will do fine." Flint always had a bit more country than coastal in his voice. Not Southern, but you could tell he was rural Oregon through and through, and I liked the slow, deep rumble of his words. What I didn't like, however, was the implication in his tone that he wasn't expecting much from us.

"Sure you don't want fries? We have hand-cut sweet potato as an option with a chipotle dipping sauce. As far as salads, I've got side, Caesar, spring berry and pecan—"

"I'm on duty here. Kind of pressed for time. The burger and a side salad are fine. I don't need anything fancy."

Yeah, well, maybe I want to give it to you. I quashed that thought, same as I had the one about how hot he looked in his uniform. Wanting to impress Nash Flint wasn't going to get me anywhere.

"I'll put a rush on it." I made a note on the order pad, not that it was really needed since Logan hardly had a packed house to worry about.

As I walked over to the window to put in Flint's order, I noticed more than one table giving him curious glances. Hell, maybe I was wrong about any business being good business. Last thing I needed was Flint scaring away what few customers we had. Not that he was known as a gossip or anything like that, but he was awfully...old school. Traditional. The last kind of guy you'd expect to find at a gay bar, that was for sure, and even though we were attempting to attract a mixed clientele, he stood out.

Nash

Mason Hanks was trouble. And not the same kind of trouble as his good-for-nothing brothers and father. Hell, even his uncles were a thorn in my side, same as they'd been for my father. The Hanks family was always up to something.

Mason, though, he'd always been a bit different than the rest of the family. A preemie named for being no bigger than a Mason jar, he'd been an asthmatic kid and scraggly teen, nothing like his overgrown bulldog brothers who'd terrorized everyone both on and off the football field. He'd been, well, homely wasn't a very kind word, but it fit. All big teeth and floppy hair and blotchy skin and knobby joints that didn't seem to quite coordinate with each other.

But the man who'd taken my order had nothing, absolutely nothing, in common with that kid, and he was *trouble*. Taller than I remembered—he had to be pushing six feet now, with a sturdy, muscular frame. The "Rainbow Tavern" T-shirt he wore stretched across his chest quite nicely. As he talked to someone in the kitchen through the window behind the bar, he rubbed a fuzzy jaw that gave him a rugged look, made him seem a bit older than the late twenties I knew him to be. Yup. Trouble.

And what was with this Rainbow Tavern business? The cheerful multicolored logo on his shirt looked like something out of a Portland Pride parade, a big change from the traditional ship's anchor logo that the last tavern had used for decades. Folks around here relied on the tavern for a greasy burger, cheap beer, and its reas-suringly familiar facade. And from what I'd heard, Mason's re-do offered none of those things—all organic meat this and local lettuce that and microbrews with whimsical names and brand-new decor that seemed intent on proclaiming exactly how "welcoming" the place was.

Which was all well and good, and, unlike some in the town, I didn't have a bone to pick with his "gay tourism" agenda except for the part where it made getting my dinner-break burger a mite more...uncomfortable than it had been previously. That was all. I didn't much care for feeling exposed as I waited for the food, all eyes on me, people *wondering*. I'd gone almost forty years of working my ass off to avoid that kind of wonder and speculation.

But still, the tavern was the closest eating establish-ment to the police station, and the local economy sorely needed a boost. I wasn't going to take my business to the chain fast-food joints up on 101 just because I was scared of some idle gossip. That'd be the sign of a coward, and that was the last thing I was.

A blessedly short few minutes later, Mason brought my food. The Ringer boy who was tending bar always had been a bit skittish around me, so it wasn't much of a surprise that he was making Mason wait on me. "One house burger, a salad, and I had Logan toss on a few fries, on us. I just wanted your opinion on the new sauce."

No, no I would not be giving Mason Hanks my opinion on his sauce. Ever. But my mother had raised me with manners, so I nodded. "Thanks."

"We bake the bread in-house and—"

"Are you planning on hovering my whole meal or just till I start chewing?" I couldn't resist messing with him, just a little. His cheeks colored. Yup, there came trouble, all right.

"No, of course not. But if you have any feedback —"

"Still hovering."

"Got it." He licked his lips before backing away. His full, surprisingly pink lips. His much, much too young lips. Too young. Too *Hanks*. Too out — I'd known about the Ringer kid ever since I caught him up on Mill Peak Road making out with the star running back, and he and Mason had been thick as thieves back then. I wasn't all that surprised when I heard Mason had gotten himself a fancy boyfriend up in Portland. I had been surprised that he'd come back to town — usually when people left Rainbow Cove, they left for good. And ever since the mill closed and the fishing business bottomed out, more people had been leaving than coming, that was for sure.

"Oops. Forgot your iced tea." And there he was, back again, this time with a full glass of some pale stuff that didn't look like any tea I'd seen before.

"That's tea?"

"It's an organic green blend we're trying out."

"I'll stick to water, thanks just the same."

"Darn." Mason looked like I'd kicked his raggedy dog — the one that used to follow him everywhere. "Thought people might like a change —"

"Change is hard." Didn't I know it. I put all my years into the advice I handed out, trying to remind myself that I was indeed older and wiser here. "Take it slow. Change the buns if you must, get that fancy beef, but maybe leave a man his Lipton, you know?"

"Not so much change. Got it." He nodded, and for a brief second I finally saw his younger self in his grownup visage. He'd always nodded like that while promising me he'd never speed again, only to go and do whatever fool thing he wanted next. I had a feeling this would be more of the same—no Lipton forthcoming.

Still, after he finally left me in peace to eat, I had to hand it to them—the burger really was first rate. Nice yeasty bread, grilled, with a thick patty that had a perfect sear on it. I wasn't really a picky eater, but this was top shelf. With forty approaching faster than I liked, I'd been trying to avoid fried food, but it would have been rude to not at least try the sweet potato fries. They were sinfully good, crispy and tender with the right amount of heat in the sauce.

"Dessert? Pie on the house?" Mason showed up right as I was finishing the fries. Jesus, Mary, and Joseph, the kid was so eager to please it was almost painful. A few more diners had filtered in while I ate, but the large room was barely a quarter full, if that.

"I'm good. Check, please?"

Mason looked down at the paper in his hand. "I wish you'd let me comp this."

"But I won't." I plucked it out of his fingers, ignoring the brief electric burst when our hands brushed. I was well-accustomed to ignoring this sort of attraction. Mason might be more trouble than most, but I could tamp down my rowdy body. I dug out a twenty. "Keep the change."

"So you liked it, then?"

Oh yes. Took me a second to remember that he meant

the food, not the brush of our hands. "Food wasn't bad," I allowed. "Suppose I'll live."

"Want me to set you up a tab now?"

I laughed, a rusty sound that I didn't make much anymore, not since my dad had passed, and first my mother, then Steve, moved away. "You're quite the salesman, aren't you? They teach you that at that fancy school in Portland?"

"Culinary Institute isn't *that* fancy. And it was the restaurant managing experience that came after school that taught me to always try for repeat business. And to appreciate customers who spread the word." His smile was all gleaming white teeth. Maybe the fancy Portland boyfriend had been a dentist. And it was *not* okay, the way my hands fisted at the thought of the Portland guy.

I wasn't really a "spread the word" type, but I nodded, mostly because I needed to end this conversation before trouble could give way to temptation, something I was not going to let happen.

The walkie-talkie on my hip crackled. "Chief? I've got a fender bender up at Butte and Lakeview," Marta reported. "Locklear's on a call already."

"I'm on it," I spoke into the radio. Our department was so tiny that even calling it a department was a bit of politeness. Three officers including me, a dispatcher, and some part-time office help, that was us.

Mason blanched and dug out his phone. His family lived down Butte Road, way on the outskirts of town. His face brightened as he tapped around on the gadget. "Good. It's not Jimmy."

"This time," I added, because that was the way of it.

Might not be Mason's brother tonight, but it would be some time again soon. Seemed like I couldn't go a week without a Hanks causing some kind of commotion, and I'd do well to remember that.

TWO

Mason

Flint was back. He sat at the same table—by the window and near the door. It was Tuesday, shortly before close. We had a grand total of four other people in the place. Two of them were tourists—a pair of men from Ashland doing the Highway 101 scenic coastal drive on their way to Lincoln City. Wonderfully chatty, they'd been the first to find us via one of the ads I'd taken out on LGBTQ travel sites. Go me.

Flint had been in twice over the weekend, ordering exactly the same thing each time and eating with grumpy efficiency that didn't invite small talk. Not that I was eager to talk to Flint, but Adam and Logan kept making me wait on him, and Flint had a way of acknowledging my presence the same way one might a raccoon who raided the trash cans.

"Hanks." He nodded as I came over with a menu.

"Mason." God, I hadn't even been back two months, and I was already tired of being a Hanks. I was *not* one of the Hanks boys, never had fit that mold. "Would you like to hear this week's specials?"

"The usual is fine." He leaned back in his chair, not touching the menu. I hadn't expected more from him, but I didn't need him pointing out my service shortfalls if I forgot the menu again.

"Late night for you?" I asked as I wrote the order ticket.

"You could say that. Busy week and a call right at dinner time." He made a pinched-in face, one that made me think he needed a shoulder rub or something. And that was exactly the wrong sort of impulse to be having around him.

"Well, we're happy for your business."

"Liar." His smile was unexpected and hit me like a punch. Damn. That thing was lethal. Nash Flint had dimples. Dimples on that granite face just didn't fit, and yet it completely transformed him into someone approachable—and lickable and...

No. Can't think like that.

"We are." Seriously. It had been a slow, slow opening weekend. I'd happily take whatever cash Flint wanted to throw our way.

"You're probably worried I'm gonna scare your customers away."

"You're not the health inspector." I smiled back at him. Felt weird as fuck, bantering with Flint, but it also made my chest warm.

"Now that would have broken my poor father's heart." He made a little shooing motion with his hand. "I haven't eaten since eleven. Not to be rude but—"

"Going." Duly dismissed, I scurried off to the kitchen window.

"Order," I called to Logan. "It's for Flint, so whatever you can do to hurry—"

"Tell me he didn't order his usual." Logan came over to the window. His blond hair was sweaty, not in its usual careful style, and his apron was splattered with the remnants of a full day of cooking.

"He did. What's the problem? I know we've got bread." I saw to that myself, working on the bread in the morning while Logan prepped for food. My specialty might be back-of-the-house management, but I hadn't endured the long hours of culinary school for nothing.

"Not the bread. The burger patties. Remember how Sunny Skies called and asked if they could deliver tomorrow morning instead of today? Well, I'm out of beef patties."

This was the problem with working with small, local suppliers. I'd been happy to accommodate when Zeb at Sunny Skies had said his truck was acting up, but now someone was going to have to try to coax Flint into ordering something else. As a group, we'd decided to go local as much as possible, but the responsibility of sorting out all of it fell to me. My back tightened. I couldn't shake the sense that I was letting people down—Flint, who just wanted his burger, and Logan, who deserved reliable supply deliveries.

"You want to come out, tell him about the specials? Maybe hearing it from the chef—"

"Ha. He scares me." Logan was every bit as bad as Adam.

I groaned. "You didn't even grow up around here.

And you drive like a grandma. You've got nothing to worry about."

I'd met Logan at culinary school. In the years after, he'd complained about always getting sous chef jobs and never the executive chef position he desperately wanted. I'd convinced him to go in on this place with Adam and me. With us, he had freedom to craft his own menu at last, but I knew small-town life would be an adjustment for the Portland native.

"Still. I better stay back here. You handle Flint. Tell him my chicken's top notch."

Grumbling the whole way back to Flint's table, I dreamed up a number of punishments for Logan and Adam as a distraction from the gnawing sense of guilt that the supplies weren't running as they should. But still, next family with six kids who came in was all theirs. Flint was looking at his phone when I got to his table.

"Chief?"

"Yeah?" He looked up, mouth quirking as if he already knew he wasn't going to like what I had to say.

"How do you feel about chicken?"

"Chicken?" He sounded as if I'd proposed cockroaches.

"We're out of beef patties, see, but Logan makes this amazing crispy chicken sandwich with a sun-dried tomato aioli—"

"I don't much care for chicken. Or tomatoes." Flint shook his head, and I felt his disappointment all the way to my toes. I hated not being able to deliver what he wanted. I'd never admit it, but watching Flint devour our food was a near-sensual experience for me. He never really complimented it, but he ate with such gusto that it was hard not to feel a little bit proud.

"How about pizza? We've got a few on the menu. One's a white sauce with sausage and mushrooms. You might like that."

Flint's skeptical eyes said that he doubted that very much, but he gave a heavy sigh and nodded. "Guess that'll do."

"Great." I turned to head back to the kitchen.

"And my water?" Flint called after me.

Crap. Some server I was. But I had something I thought might make up for the lack of a burger stashed away in the bar fridge. I hurried up and got him a glass and raced it back to his table in record time.

"What's this?" Flint eyed the glass with clear distrust.

"Tea. Lipton. I brewed a pitcher just in case..." *You came in* sounded a bit desperate. "Just in case," I repeated. *Lame.*

"Ah. Well...thanks." Another Flint smile, just as disarming as the first, and enough to make me want to brew gallons of tea to earn more.

Right then, the travelers from Ashland finally got up from their table, heading for the door. "Have a safe trip," I called.

"Oh, we'll try." They slowed up, the taller of the two speaking to me. "Thanks again. The burger was amazing."

Next to me, Flint's groan was almost audible. The Ashland traveler's eyes skimmed over him, going wide with obvious appreciation. "And, I must say, what a *progressive* and inclusive community you have here."

Oh, crap. I knew what the guy was assuming, and I wasn't sure how to deflect it.

"We try." A muscle worked in Flint's jaw. "You all drive safe now. Watch that light up at Lakeview and 101."

"Will do. And thank you for your service. Always a pleasure to see one of the family in blue." And with that, the couple was gone, and I was left dying on Flint's behalf.

"Tourists," Flint muttered. "What did he mean by 'family'…?"

Heck. I was absolutely not going to be the one to tell Flint that they'd misread him as gay. That would drive him away for sure.

"Tourists," I echoed lamely. "I'll have the pizza right out to you."

He nodded, effectively dismissing me. As I walked back over to the kitchen window, a little question danced in my head. *What if…*

What if the Ashland couple had been right about Flint? I'd never really stopped and thought about it before, other than my extremely guilt-ridden macking on his hotness in uniform the last few times he'd been in. But the more I thought about it, the more I wondered. He'd never once been linked to a girlfriend that I could remember—he was the consummate bachelor cop, totally married to the job. The town was liberal enough that I didn't think Flint would be fired for being gay, but his father was even more of a hardnose than Flint, so maybe that played a factor. Who knew?

On a whim, I glanced back over my shoulder, and to my surprise, Flint looked away fast. *"Maybe"* and *"what if"* joined forces to dance in my gut, but I silenced both with a heavy dose of *"oh hell no."* It didn't matter what Flint was — he wasn't for me.

Nash

I didn't like pizza. Thin crust. Thick crust. Meat-lover's. Hawaiian. None of it worked for me. Too messy, juggling crust and sauce, and it always seemed to leave me hungry again an hour later, probably because of all that work trying to not end up wearing it. But I hadn't wanted a whole *thing* with Mason, what with him reciting the menu and being helpful and me being picky. My father always made sure that I ate what was in front of me. Not that he would have been a patron of Mason's tavern or a fan of its brand of upscale bar food — or the idea of our town as "inclusive."

I'd played dumb with the tourists and Mason, but I'd known what they were implying. There were risks in patronizing this place, but truth was that Rainbow Cove needed Mason's big idea to succeed more than I needed to feel comfortable. And like Steve had always harped on, maybe I cared a mite too much what others thought or assumed. The tourists were on their way up to the more populated parts of the coast with a favorable impression of our little town. That was what mattered, or so I told myself.

By the time Mason brought my pizza, I was the only one left in the dining room, and the Ringer boy had started wiping down tables and sweeping up, all while giving me a wide berth. I sighed. I knew he still wasn't over me catching what he'd been up to in high school, but I wasn't the one who'd outed him, no matter what he might have thought. My job had been making sure him and Mason didn't break their fool necks with their pranks, nothing more than that.

Not that they were boys any longer. Ringer had had the lumberjack thing going on for several years now with a full beard that matched his red hair and bulky muscles, and Mason...well, the time past puberty had been very kind to him. He was wearing another Rainbow Tavern T-shirt and tight jeans, ones better suited to that bar in Portland I'd let myself visit last time I went up to see my mother. Lord, but that had been overwhelming, an unqualified mistake.

"Here you go." Mason set the steaming pizza on one of those little pizza-rack things, sliding an empty white plate in front of me as well. "If it's not what you had in mind, it's on us, okay?"

"It's food. It's hot. And I'm hungry enough to eat my Jeep." I grabbed a knife and fork and set to cutting up a slice.

Mason raised an eyebrow at me using silverware to eat a pizza, but I didn't much care what he thought. I had a uniform to keep neat. So I gave him a hard stare, one that sent him back to the bar area. Finally in peace, I tried the pizza and it was...

Portland folks were always using "orgasmic" to describe food or drink—something I'd never seen the logic in. But as I chewed on my first slice, I could finally see the appeal of gushing over a food product. My tongue had seldom known such rapture—the sausage was crisp and savory, the sauce creamy and well-spiced, and the cheese a snowy blanket over the pie. I ate the whole thing before I even realized what I'd done.

"Not bad, right?" Mason was back, clearly not scared away for good by my grumpiness, and why that pleased me I couldn't say.

"It hit the spot," I allowed. "You got the check? I figure Ringer's about to run me out so you can close."

Ringer regarded me from across the room with cool blue eyes, not disputing my assessment. Yup, still not over high school, that one. He said something to Mason when he went over to the bar to run my card. Whatever it was, it made Mason's cheeks pink.

Damn, but I liked a man who blushed. It was a... thing, I guess you could say. A thing I had. Steve had been a blusher, something I used to tease him about privately, and I got a major kick out of trying to make him go red. I hadn't missed Steve in ages, filing him away under "chapter closed," but longing hit me all over again right then, watching Mason.

I'd say I needed a Portland weekend, but that had been such a disaster last time. No, I was better off simply tamping down whatever strange urges Mason Hanks brought out in me.

Resolved, I headed out into the windy summer night as soon as I got my card back. I'd parked in front, coming straight from a call about a suspected vandalism over at a jewelry gallery near 101. So that meant moving my official Jeep a whole half a block down to the parking lot behind the station, which was really just a glorified annex onto City Hall.

This time of night, we kept the door locked, so I used the keypad to enter the building.

"Evening, Chief." Marta looked up from her knitting. In her late sixties, she'd been a dispatcher for my father, back before that was even a full-time position around here. She dispatched the police, fire, and rural ambulance crew, holding down the fort at a wooden desk in the station's main room. "Candace isn't in yet."

"That's fine. I'm in no hurry," I lied. Candace, my fresh-as-a-calla-lily junior officer, was always running a step or two behind. But we'd had a dickens of a time filling the third officer slot, and I wasn't about to chase her away.

"You get food?" Marta asked, not missing a stitch as her fingers flew.

"Yup. The tavern again."

"That place." She made a face. "It's never going to be the same. You need to go clear out to Rowdy's on Lakeview to get a decent hamburger now."

"Food's actually not bad." I was many things, but a liar wasn't one of them. "You should check out their house burger sometime."

"I won't be going in *there*, thank you very much." She made a *tsking* noise, and her needles clanked. "And you should be careful, too. Don't want people getting the wrong impression."

Or the right one. I rubbed my jaw as the image of the tourists from earlier popped into my head. "It's good to give them business. It's what the town needs—fresh ideas." She wasn't going to agree with me on that, but I tried, anyway. The town was half-full of aging hippies, but Marta was one of the die-hard traditionalists, upstanding singer for the First Evangelical choir, and loud objector to the whole gay tourism plan.

She shook her head. "We'll just have to agree to disagree. And to think it's one of those Hanks boys to boot. That whole family never amounted to a hill of beans." On that last bit, we were in agreement, but I kept my mouth shut, same as I always did when she got to gossiping. "Surprised he even serves you, after you went and locked away Freddy."

"He got a fair trial." I shrugged because who knew? Maybe Ringer wasn't the only one with a grudge against me. Mason seemed hungry enough for business that he might not care that I'd been instrumental in convicting his fool of an older brother for felony criminal mischief. Regardless, it was another reminder of why I couldn't go getting too friendly with him. He might not spit in my food or turn down my cash, but the whole damn Hanks family had swung far away from me the day Freddy got sent away. We were never going to be friends.

THREE

Mason

Adam came into the kitchen where I was helping Logan plate a big order. He had a shit-eating grin on his face, which immediately put me on edge. We finally had a decent dinner rush, and it had me and the two teenagers we'd hired as weekend waitstaff hopping. Thank God.

We had a grant that had covered the renovation and that would, in theory, get us through the lean early months, but we did need to start showing profit at some point. We'd each invested a huge chunk of savings in the endeavor, and the weight of knowing that Adam and Logan had their futures riding on this idea kept me up at night.

"Tell me nothing's wrong," I ordered Adam because I wasn't sure I could handle a screw-up on what was supposed to be a *good* night.

"Flint's got a date." Adam's grin got wider.

"He's got a what?" I almost dropped the bread I was

adding to a salad plate. Saving it, I loaded the finished plate on the tray.

"A *date*. Flint just walked in with Curtis Hunt. Not in uniform."

Logan looked up from the grill. "The crazy wood-carver guy with the gallery in the old gas station?"

"The crazy, *gay*, recently single woodcarver guy." Adam hopped from one foot to the other. "I better get back out there, but I put them at Flint's regular table."

Carrying the tray of salads out to the table full of couples in the center of the room, I took a long look at Flint. I wasn't sure I'd ever seen him out of uniform before. He looked good. Light tan polo shirt that made his eyes look greener than usual, dark blue jeans. The working-man kind, not the designer kind that Logan and I wore clubbing in Portland. His short brown hair looked damp—shit, if Flint had showered first, maybe this *was* a...something.

Not a date. Flint didn't date, right? But ever since the other night when the tourists had put questions in my head, I'd found myself wondering where exactly Flint went to get some. And, in a sign of the coming apoca-lypse, he was actually reading the menu. And laughing. I distributed the salads then headed over to their table.

"Evening, Chief. Curtis." I nodded at his dining companion. A couple of years older than Flint, Curtis Hunt hadn't changed much since I'd been gone. Same wild brown hair, same rippling sleeve tats, same bulging biceps on an otherwise slim frame. Even if Flint was into dudes, I couldn't see him being into Curtis's escaped-from-a-biker-gang vibe.

"Mason Hanks. You got big." Curtis gave me a smile,

one with far more appreciation than I'd ever gotten from Flint. I owned a mirror. I knew that I looked nothing like the photos of my teen self that I'd begged my mom to burn. And I'd used that distinction to my advantage to sow some seriously overdue oats in Portland, but Curtis's frank appreciation still made me a bit...squirmy.

"Iced tea for you, Chief?" I directed my attention toward Flint instead.

"I'm not on duty for the first time in a blue moon. I've got Holmes and Locklear holding down the fort. You got Bud on tap?"

My face screwed up before I could stop it. "We've got a selection of local ales and lagers—"

Flint's ton-of-bricks sigh cut me off. "You've got meat in tonight, right?"

I bristled at that. "Of course."

"We'll both have the Lighthouse ale." Curtis's voice reminded me that it wasn't just me and Flint that night. "Try something different, Nash. You might surprise yourself." He winked and I wasn't sure which of us it was for. "And is your vegan burger soy-free?"

Flint made a snorting sound. "Don't think you can call it a burger if it never mooed."

Was this seriously a date? They certainly bickered like a couple. "The black-bean burger is soy-free and vegan. I've got a sourdough roll for it to go on and almond cheese as well." Almost a decade working food in Portland had taught me how to speak alternative diets fluently.

"Nut cheese?" Flint shook his head. "My usual please. With the real stuff."

I've got all the real stuff you can handle right here. I didn't know where that flirty retort had come from, and I bit it back. "Got it. I'll have the beers right out."

The dinner crowd kept me busy. I got Flint and Curtis their beers but didn't have time to linger—or listen in. In the kitchen, Logan was cursing up a blue streak and attacking ingredients with a vengeance. Adam was busy making drinks and running relief for the waitstaff, and it was all glorious. This was what I'd envisioned back when we first heard the old tavern was on the market. Adam had come to Portland for a weekend, and we'd done some brainstorming. My friend Brock had suggested we apply for a state grant targeting rural businesses to help purchase the place. It had been a late night with lots of drinking and dreaming, but I'd seen *this* and been powerless to deny the appeal.

I whistled to myself as I brought out entrees and didn't complain when Adam sent me to the storeroom for another case of the local ale that was selling well that night. The storeroom was down a long, narrow hallway at the back of the building, right beyond the two restrooms.

Thump. The door to the men's room opened right as I was passing, and Flint crashed into me. Luckily, I didn't have the beer yet because I almost certainly would have dropped it under the shock of having Flint's bigger body pressing against me before he righted himself.

"Sorry." He took a step back but didn't rush away. His eyes had flared darker and his mouth quirked. Was he as rattled as I was? I hated that I couldn't tell.

"It's okay." My voice sounded deeper than usual. "Everything good tonight?"

Flint shrugged. "Your guy can cook. Beer's okay. Still

think you should have Bud on tap for the local drinking crowd. Not everyone wants to spend six dollars a bottle on the fancy stuff."

"Noted." God, he was close. I wasn't going to be the one to move away first. "Flint...I mean Chief. What are you doing tonight?"

"Tonight?" One of Flint's eyebrows flew up. "I'm having dinner."

"With Curtis?" I prompted. I wasn't ever going to get another chance like this, so I took a deep breath. "You on a date?"

"You taking up gossip as a new hobby now that you're back in town?" His voice was just as deadly as his sneer, but there was something else in his expression, a flicker of something I couldn't name in his eyes.

"No. Just curious, that's all. You're both more than welcome—"

"It's not a date," Flint gritted out.

"You sure? Does *he* know that?" I prodded, driven by reckless impulse.

"I'm sure." Flint took a step forward, crowding me against the wall. His voice was low and hot as sin. "Trust me, if I was on a date, he'd know."

"Yeah." I didn't even know what I was agreeing to, only that I didn't want Flint to move.

"Curtis is an old friend. Troy and I went to school together, and after he died last year, I've been worried about Curtis keeping too much to himself. I asked him to get some food, and he chose here. No big drama." He still didn't step away.

It was hard to breathe, hard to think. "So he's not

your type, you're saying?" I was lucky that the words didn't squeak out.

"He's not my type," Flint growled and leaned in and —

"Oops!" A female tourist wearing a shirt advertising a town in California bumped into Flint's back. I'd served her a second daiquiri not long before, and she had a tipsy laugh. "Sorry."

"No problem." Flint stepped back, and I felt the loss of his warmth immediately. "I better get back out there."

Flint didn't look back as he strode down the hallway, leaving me reeling. Fuck. What had almost happened there? Had Nash Flint seriously been about to kiss me?

Nash

It wasn't often that I was an idiot. I'd been raised to use my common sense, restrain any wild urges, and rely on logic and planning for my actions. I was a lawman, and I took that role very seriously. I didn't lose my cool. Ever.

Except, apparently, around Mason Hanks, where not only had I lost my cool, but I'd gone full-on insane to boot. I made my way back to the table where Curtis was waiting, calling myself every name in the book. Had I seriously been about to kiss that smirk off Mason's face? I didn't know, and the not knowing chased away my previously good mood.

"I like what they've done with the place." Curtis gestured, indicating the colorful room. For the first time since I'd been at the Rainbow Tavern, there were people on the dancefloor and a pleasant din of happy chatter and clinking glasses in the main dining area.

"It's all right. They need Bud or PBR or something cheap on tap," I groused.

"Tightwad." Curtis should know, seeing as how I'd only gotten him to come out with the promise that the meal would be my treat. Otherwise, Curtis would be eating whatever rations of sprouts and potatoes he culled from the garden out behind his place. Curtis didn't spend any money he wasn't forced to.

"You should get out more, then. Come give them some weeknight business." Why I'd suddenly become free advertising for Mason, I couldn't say. First Marta, now Curtis. Mason should be paying me for the word of mouth. Of course, thinking about Mason and mouth in the same sentence was *not* a good idea.

"I just might." It wasn't hard to follow Curtis's eyes as he watched Mason's trek across the room with a loaded tray. "That Hanks boy...sure grew up fine, didn't he?"

"Didn't think you'd be wanting to fish in those waters," I said, barely restraining a growl.

"I'm grieving, not dead. And we both know even Troy would have noticed that ass." Curtis gave me a sly smile. "And you did, too. Don't deny it."

Curtis and Troy had been among the very few in town to know the truth about me, part of it at least. "Too young." Maybe if I repeated it enough, I'd start to actually believe it. "And a troublemaker."

"You need more trouble in your life." Curtis laughed as the Ringer kid, not Mason, slid steaming plates in front of us. I refused to feel a pang of...anything about that, except maybe guilt if I'd chased Mason off, acting like a trapped bear in the hallway.

"You guys need ketchup?" Ringer spoke to Curtis, not me. "Second round of drinks?"

"We're good, thanks." Curtis gave him what would be a winning smile on other people, but it made Curtis look that much more feral.

A thought occurred to me as Ringer hurried away. "Please tell me you and Troy never fished there."

"Adam?" Curtis made a clucking noise. "Never. Too toppy for Troy, too emotional for me. It'd be like taking a teddy bear to bed. Too damn cuddly."

Thank God for small mercies. I nodded even though I was going to need brain bleach to get the image out of a cuddly Adam Ringer out of my head.

"Mason, though…he'd be fire in the sack."

A low growling sound escaped my throat before I could call it back. Curtis grinned at me. "Yup, you've noticed, too."

"He's a Hanks. And too young. And I'm not interested in anything local. You know that."

Curtis sighed. This was an old argument between us. "No one would care if you were…more open. Really."

"*I* care." I dug into my burger with an emphatic bite.

"Your father's dead, Nash." Curtis shook his head as he took a bite of his food. "Time to move on."

That wasn't ever happening, but I didn't want to fight, so I focused on my food for the next while. And tried hard not to track Mason as he made his way around the room, serving the various tables. It didn't matter what had almost happened in the hall—he'd be a flame to the carefully guarded kindling that was my life. Didn't matter how much Curtis prodded, I wasn't going there.

Mason was the one to bring us the check. "Any dessert? I'm trying out a key-lime cheesecake on the specials board, if you're interested."

"Oh, we're interested." Curtis was going to sprain something, what with those winks and grins of his. "Nash?"

"None for me." I slid Mason my credit card. Our eyes met and he looked away fast. Definitely none for me. I'd probably scared him in the hall, going all caveman like that. I should apologize, but fuck if I knew the right words for that, and certainly not in front of Curtis.

Later, after I'd dropped Curtis at the converted gas station he both lived and worked out of, I headed home. My house was not that far from the square, one of the small streets that dead-ended at the bluffs that led to the ocean below town. We didn't have an ocean view—Dad was one to value square footage, proximity to the station, and garden space over fanciful things, and our neighbors were lifers, unlike the folks who owned vacation cottages closer to the state park and beaches.

It wasn't often that I had a Friday night to myself like this, and I searched for some purpose to keep the aimless feeling at bay. House was quiet as I let myself in. Too quiet. I'd never lived anywhere else—I'd been born here, right in the back bedroom, grew up here when it was noisy and full of Trisha and Easton and me. Stayed on to help Mom when Dad first got sick. It had been noisy then, too, with the hours and hours of TV news he insisted on watching. I'd remained when Mom moved to

Portland to be close to my sister Trisha and my aunts after Dad died.

Now it was just me and an empty house, too big for me, really, but I'd been unable to even think of getting something new. Still restless, I headed straight for my vice—the thing I knew could chase Mason Hanks from my head. Got the metal box out of the garage, picked my favorite chair in the living room to get comfortable in, and set to freeing my mind.

I sorted the lures first, going over my collection, deciding what I'd make that night and wondering if I could sneak in some early morning fishing before I had to be back on duty. Duty. That was what I had to focus on. Duty to the town, first and foremost. I couldn't let Mason Hanks distract from that.

FOUR

Mason

Red lights flashed in my rearview mirror—never a good thing.

Not in any hurry, I'd driven the long way around town—taking Montana Street from the tavern up to Lakeview, grabbing a moment to admire Moosehead Lake on this clear Monday afternoon. The bulk of the town was squashed between the lake to the north and the bay to the south, with the best houses having a view of one or the other. It went without saying that the Hanks family wasn't among those vying for prime real estate. We lived to the east of town, out in the dusty sticks down Butte Road.

Just as I exited the Butte and Lakeview intersection, I noticed the red flashing lights. I pulled in to Ralph's Bait Shack's parking lot, not wanting Flint to get side-swiped on Lakeview.

And it was Flint—I'd recognized his Jeep.

In the mirror, I watched his large frame stride toward

my car. When he stopped, his voice—deep and cop-cool —invaded my open window. "Do you know—" He blinked, lowering his mirrored sunglasses. "Hanks?" And *damn*. I'd never been one for the whole hot-for-cop thing, but the shades and the glower and the authoritative stance were a sight to see.

"Mason," I corrected him yet again.

"You know why I pulled you over, *Mason*?" Flint's deliberate emphasis on my name made my stomach do a weird flip.

"Honestly, no." I hadn't been speeding, that much I knew. I was never in a hurry to get to my dad's place.

"Your right brake light's out."

"Oh, f—*thanks*." I tried to remember if that was something they wrote tickets for. Jimmy and Freddy had had just about every ticky-tacky traffic violation there ever was, but I hadn't had so much as a speeding ticket since leaving Rainbow Cove behind. "Am I getting a fine?"

"Not this time." A muscle worked in Flint's jaw. A very sexy muscle that reminded me of a highly inappropriate dream I'd had the other night starring Flint's mouth. And I could not be thinking about that dream with Flint still leaning on my door frame. "You got a registration for this rust bucket or this one of your brother's specials?"

"In the glove box. I sold my Maxima to get more money for the restaurant, but I don't trust Jimmy's cars. This one's all mine."

"Smart boy. Those heaps your brother passes off as working automobiles are a menace."

"Not a boy," I muttered. It was stupid, arguing with

Flint when he'd said he was letting me off, but I was still wincing from Friday night and that encounter in the hallway. I wasn't going to let Flint get away with acting like I was fifteen again. I was all man, and we both knew it.

"No, no, you're not." Flint regarded me coolly over the rim of his sunglasses, making me feel just as crowded as if he were pressing me against that wall. "Which is why you'll be smart."

I wasn't sure what he meant by that. Smart would be staying far away from Flint, that was for sure. "I'll have Jimmy fix the light before I come back down tonight. And double check the work myself."

"Back down?" He frowned. "You're not staying with your family?"

"F—no." I'd tried that when I'd first come back and almost lost my mind dealing with Dad and Jimmy's drama. Not that I was going to share any of those ongoing conflicts with Flint.

"You can curse around me, Mason." Another rare Flint smile. "Promise I'm not gonna tattle."

"I think I'd kill my dad or Jimmy if I stayed there." The confession slipped out, but then I remembered who I was talking to and quickly backtracked. "Not *kill*. Or fight. Just…"

"I get it." A different muscle worked in Flint's jaw, this one making it seem like he was having a hard time not laughing. That was okay. I wanted to laugh at me, too.

"Anyway, I'm renting the old Ransom place. Block from your parents' place." Why I was making small talk with Nash Flint, I had no clue. It was this way when he came to the tavern as well—as if I'd do anything to prolong the contact.

"I didn't see a moving truck." Nash frowned like it was a personal affront that something had happened in town that he hadn't noticed.

"Didn't need one. I travel light." That was an understatement. I'd been so fired up to get out from under Dad and Jimmy's thumb that I'd packed everything I needed in a single car trip. "Your mom still there?"

"She went on up to Portland after Dad died. I'm still there, though, so don't go egging the house." Flint's frown slid into a rather disarming wink. "You gonna get Flora Ransom to sell you that pile of boards?"

"She was a friend of Mom's." Mom and Flora had both been waitresses at the old tavern way back when, and Flora'd always had a soft spot for me. "Not Flora's fault the place fell into disrepair."

Flint's face softened. "Your mother was a good woman. I should have offered my condolences sooner."

Good was stretching it a bit, but she'd tried hard, loved fiercely, and was missed every damn day by me. I nodded.

Flint's radio crackled. "I better let you get on, then," he said to me, moving away from the window. "Drive safe."

"Always do."

He chuckled at that as he walked away, but it was true—I'd left my reckless years behind long ago, even though Flint and my feverish dreams about him certainly threatened to bring that streak back to life.

I tried not to think about Flint or my dreams as I made my way back up Butte to my family's place. On the outskirts of incorporated Rainbow Cove, the family seat was a messy sprawl of acres of junk with a few trailers tossed in. My uncle Gunnar had my grandparents' old house by the road, then a long dirt drive led to my dad's house, and beyond that was Jimmy's trailer.

A dilapidated sign near the turn-off read "Hanks Scrap Metal." Nominally, there was a rusty gate, but most of the time they were too lazy to bother with it. I pulled in front of Dad's place and grabbed the two bulging sacks I'd filled with leftovers from the weekend that wouldn't keep. Back in Portland, we'd donated our excess to charities. Here we had the Hanks.

Feeling guilty, I'd had Adam take some cheesecake to his mom's. Dad needed to lay off the sugar, anyway. He came to the door, leaning on his cane, pair of beagles preceding him.

"You're later than you said you'd be." He wasn't mean about it, more resigned, as if he hadn't expected better from me.

"Sorry. Got pulled over by Flint for a busted brake light." I made my way into the house, which as always smelled of cigarillos, dust, and dog. I'd largely outgrown my asthma or at least learned to manage it, but it was a wonder that my lungs didn't seize up every time I came here.

"Flint. That son of a bitch." Jimmy sneered from the old brown couch near the one working TV. It was stacked on top of two that didn't turn on anymore.

"Hey, I was grateful for the heads-up. Can you fix it for me?"

"Yeah, yeah." Jimmy made a dismissive gesture that

meant I'd have to prod him a good four more times before he actually did it.

"You watch yourself, Mason," Dad added. "First it's a light. Then it's five miles over. Next he's harping on your license renewal. Always something."

And never your fault. I sighed. Same as always around here.

"Uncle Mason!" The real reason I'd come and the reason I even worried about food for this place came barreling in from the kitchen and dining area.

"Hi, Peanut." I swept Lilac up into a hug. My niece was seven and the spitting image of my mother—fine, blond hair, green eyes, and delicate features.

"Did you bring bread?" Her voice was all hopeful. "We're out."

"Of course." I rubbed her head. "You got peanut butter?"

"Of course," Jimmy imitated my smoother speech.

Lilac usually stayed with her mom, but Francine was off dancing in Coos Bay again. She'd turn back up eventually, but without my mom here I worried about Lilac being fed and getting to the last week of school. And, unfortunately, if her teachers got concerned about her, it wouldn't be the first time Jimmy and Francine had landed on the radar of child protective services. Thus far, they'd managed to scrape by with warnings, promising to work out their domestic squabbles peacefully and to stay clean and sober, but my heart beat faster at the thought of the state getting involved with our family again. We'd had cousins in and out of foster care, and it wasn't a fate I wanted for my Lilac.

"You do your homework?" I ignored Jimmy and spoke directly to her.

"Yeah." She shrugged, miniature version of Jimmy when he put on a world-weary attitude. "Math is hard."

"You can skip it." Jimmy's tone said he was already bored by my presence.

"No, you can't. I'll help." I glared at Jimmy. "I'll do a load of laundry for you while I'm here if you round up your school clothes."

"You're a good wife." Jimmy's tone was teasing, but there was a bite there.

"Watch it," Dad said before I could. "Your brother helps out, which is more than I can say for your lazy ass."

"Little ears." I gestured at Lilac, but it was a losing battle, getting Jimmy or my dad to clean up their language.

"I'll put the food away." Jimmy grabbed the bags from me and headed to the kitchen.

Dad settled back into his recliner with a groan. He was the other reason I kept coming around—he might be cranky, but he was the only parent I had left. Mom's unexpected death had hit me hard, underscored all the times I could have eased her burdens but hadn't, too wrapped up in my Portland life. I was determined not to repeat the same mistake with Dad, even if he lacked her quiet gratitude.

"Leg acting up?" I asked.

"Just the weather." He'd never admit to diabetic circulation issues. Mom would have pressed him into going to the doctor, but I didn't have her sort of leverage.

"And, son, you really do have to keep an eye on Flint. He's got it out for us."

Not again with the conspiracy theories. "He gives me business at the tavern. That's all I care about."

Dad shook his head. "I don't trust him one lick. Not since Freddy."

"Freddy was fool enough to listen to his friends and vandalize a police car. Burning it up wasn't Flint's doing."

Dad shrugged. I wasn't winning this one. "He didn't have to throw the book at him. That's all I'm saying."

"Uh-huh." I busied myself picking up the toys from the living room floor. This was just another reminder of why I couldn't go lusting after Flint. Dad might have grudgingly accepted me being gay—a shocker for sure and at least partly Mom's doing—but he'd never tolerate Flint.

Nash

I worried about Mason getting rear-ended the whole way back to town—he might think I was being picky, but a broken brake light was no joke. I also didn't like the little electric jolt that had gone through my body when I'd seen it was him. Annoyance, for sure, but there was something else there, almost like I was happy to see him, and that just wouldn't do.

"Chief? I've got a call in about Vera Matthews." Marta's voice crackled over my car radio. "Her daughter thinks it's another heart attack. The EMTs are there and have a call into life flight. Can you secure the landing zone?"

"I'm on it."

Our rural ambulance service was good, but we didn't have an ER or hospital, just an urgent-care clinic, and we relied on the ambulance service plus life-flight helicopters for real emergencies like this. I headed to the urgent-care clinic, as that was where the helicopter usually landed. My job was to make sure that things went smoothly, no idiots getting in the way of the crew, and that the crew had everything in hand.

I checked that the lights on the landing pad were on and waited for both the chopper and the ambulance. When the ambulance arrived, I headed over. Vera was a friend of my mother's, and I figured she might take some comfort from my presence.

I greeted the two EMTs who were getting Vera ready for transfer to the chopper.

"Vera? We're going to take good care of you, hear?" After my dad's series of strokes, the docs and nurses had told us to keep talking to him. I might not be much of a praying man, but I'd never seen the harm in a positive word.

"She's stable," Derrick told me. The young EMT was married to Candace, my junior officer. They were a nice couple, one of the few new families in town the last few years. We needed more like them, young folks looking to stay around rather than move on like so many of our kids did after graduation.

The chopper arrived and the EMTs got Vera transferred without incident. Derrick and I stayed around a bit afterward, shooting the breeze about when the fishing would get good again and whether it was a decent market to buy a house. It was past dark by the time I headed back to the station, what with a quick patrol of 101 and downtown and all.

The car ahead of me was doing six miles over. And ordinarily, I'd let it slide, but it was Jimmy Hanks' beat-up Mustang, and I couldn't rule out another DUI for him. I flipped on the lights, but it took him two full blocks to decide to pull over. Typical.

I waited for him to roll down the window and then greeted him. "Evening, Hanks. You know why I pulled you over?"

Jimmy muttered something unintelligible and less than charitable sounding, but his breath didn't reek of alcohol and his speech was unslurred when he finally raised his voice. "Nope."

"You were six miles over the limit."

"That ain't nothing." He glared at me, really testing my decision to just give him a warning.

"Think you can slow down around town?"

"I guess." Another glare and some muttering. "Heard you pulled over my brother today, too. Banner day for you, riding the Hanks boys?"

I bristled at that. Jimmy Hanks had a way of pushing all my buttons, but I had long experience being calm and not letting my temper get the better of me. "You fix that brake light? We don't want him getting into an accident."

"Yeah, I fixed it." He chomped down on the wad of gum in his mouth. "You need to leave my brother alone."

For a split second I wondered if Jimmy had some sort of psychic powers to read all the inappropriate thoughts I'd been having about Mason. Then I shook my head. "As long as he keeps his head down, he'll do fine. Nice establishment he's got going. Gainful employment's a good look."

"Hey, now. I *work*." Jimmy almost spat. He bought junkers here and there, spent ages half-fixing them, and sold them on the cheap to people who always regretted it. "I've been working longer than Mason. He was always spoiled. Soft."

I could *not* get into it with Jimmy, no matter the strange urge I had to defend Mason, who honestly was the hardest working Hanks I'd met. I might be skeptical, but the kid was trying to make something of himself, which was more than I could say for most of his family. "You go on now, Jimmy. Keep it under the limit." I ground out the words, hands fisting with the desire to wring his fool neck.

There were lines I just didn't cross. And, unfortunately for me, Mason Hanks was one of those lines. I didn't need a warning from Jimmy to see that. Didn't matter how nice Mason was, how hardworking, how hot —he wasn't for me.

FIVE

Mason

I didn't know what to wear to the Chamber of Commerce meeting, but as soon I saw Nash Flint inside the Rainbow Cove visitor center, I knew I'd picked wrong. He looked me up and down like he'd never seen a dude wear peach before. It was one of the few shirts with buttons that I owned, and Felipe, my ex, had always said it made me look expensive, for whatever that was worth. I'd paired it with khakis that I'd actually ironed. I wanted to make a good impression.

Flint was, of course, wearing his uniform. *He* always commanded respect and made a great first impression, but then he'd been born a Flint, whereas the sight of a Hanks in dress clothes had to be raising more eyebrows than just Flint's.

"Since when do you come to Chamber meetings?" I grumbled at him. It was seven thirty in the morning, and I did *not* do mornings, unlike like Flint who was probably one of those guys who woke up at five just for the heck of it.

"Coffee's over there, Sunshine." Flint gestured to a table against the far wall of the visitor center where someone had mercifully set out two large urns of coffee and a generous tray of pastries from Dolly's Donuts. They got a little sign advertising their generosity. I needed to find out how the tavern could donate next month.

"Mason? Could you help me with my flip board?" Brock, my friend from Portland who'd driven down to attend the meeting, approached me. He looked at Flint with undisguised interest, while Flint's eyes narrowed. Brock had an air of "city" about him. Dress shirt that probably cost more than my monthly rent to Flora, haircut that required careful application of product, hipster glasses, and skinny pants that showed off his Pilates-and-paleo slim frame.

"Sure." Even though I was desperate for the coffee, I followed Brock out to his car—a foreign make that Jimmy would undoubtedly salivate over, but all I knew was that it was so shiny it made me nervous to ride in it.

By the time I helped him lug in his stuff, Flint had already grabbed himself a coffee and a seat near the front. The coffee was undoubtedly black—the man didn't seem to have a single sweet tooth. For all the times I'd served him at the tavern, it was odd how little I knew about his partialities, other than a preference for red meat. I tried to tell myself that it was just my restaurateur's soul that had me wondering how to wow Flint—and not the libido I kept trying to tamp down.

"That Sheriff Sexy?" Brock asked in a low whisper.

I groaned, keeping it soft. "Adam told you that ridiculous nickname?"

"That he did." Brock sighed dramatically. "Forget my Bonobos shirt fetish. Next time I'm here I'm wearing my 'I'd bottom you so hard' T-shirt."

"He's...straight."

"There was a pause there, Mason." Brock's eyes sparkled.

"That was not a pause."

"I distinctly heard a promising pause—"

"Can we all come together? Get your coffee and get a seat." Everleigh Atkins, who ran the visitor center and the Chamber, clapped her hands once as she strode to the front of the room. "Mr. Whatley-Lewis, you can come up here."

Brock followed her, tossing a look over his shoulder that said we weren't done talking about Flint. But we totally were. I was *not* going to encourage this crush of Brock's, nor was I owning up to any such thing of my own, no matter how much I wished I could fill in that "promising pause" with some concrete information. My hallway encounter with Flint had done nothing but confuse me for over a week now. He'd been in for food since then, always polite but distant, and I didn't think I was imagining the relief in his eyes when someone else had to wait on him.

I grabbed a coffee and doctored it to my preferred light tan and highly sweetened consistency. I took a plain donut to be nice, but I was already dreaming up what baked goods we could bring to one of these meetings. I'd never been much of a line cook, but I did love to bake, and doing the breads and dessert specials for the tavern was a point of pride for me.

Everleigh handed around the minutes. Like Flint, she had to be a morning person, scheduling these things so darn early and looking all put-together in a sweater set embroidered with seashells and matching skirt. She'd gone to school with my mother, but they hadn't been friends—my mom dropped out to have Freddy while Everleigh snagged a business degree and an insurance-salesman husband who ensured that she lived in the newer part of town with an ocean view and beach access. She hadn't been into the tavern and had been more than a little skeptical of our plans in our prior meetings, but I wasn't giving up hope for her backing quite yet. We'd gotten the state grant, which had been step one in our plan, and we'd been at prior Chamber meetings, trying to drum up support for the next stage of our goals.

She went over the old business first, of which the only interesting item was the ongoing discussion of whether Rainbow Cove needed a festival.

"Other local towns do hugely popular festivals. There's the cranberry fest, the softshell crab fest, and ones devoted to sandcastles and kite flying and local beers." Everleigh's blond bob swayed as she gestured with her hands. "It's time for us to get on the map."

I raised my hand.

"Yes, Mason?" Her tone was the same as every teacher's I'd had in the Rainbow Cove school system—she'd already decided she wouldn't like what I had to say.

"Coos Bay did a Pride Fest last year, and further north, Lincoln City does one, too. We could—"

"We'll get to your ideas for us later, m'kay?" She made a dismissive wave of her hand. "But first, I wanted to brainstorm. What are we famous for?"

"The smell coming off Moosehead Lake." Ralph, who owned the Bait Shack, cackled.

"The old haunted mill?" Adam's mother, Patsy, spoke up. "My guests always like that story." Frankly, Patsy's guests at the B&B liked whatever stories Patsy told—her chatty nature was as much a reason why people returned as her breakfast quiches.

"See?" Everleigh beamed. "That's the kind of thing we could use. A spooky fall festival, anyone? And be thinking about ideas for later in the year, too!"

The next twenty minutes were spent reviewing other festival options and going over other old business like the scholarship fund and a shoe drive for foster kids. All good works, but I was eager to get to our part of the agenda. Flint, of course, had plenty to say about the policing of said festivals which got the issue tabled until the next meeting. *Officer Buzzkill. That's what we're famous for.*

Finally, Everleigh made her way down the bulleted list to Brock's name. God, I hoped this worked and people listened. The dream that four of us had hatched together in his Pearl-district loft had been so perfect a year ago. But now, even with the grant and the business launching, long-term success seemed more tenuous than ever.

"Sorry I'm late!" Curtis came rushing in, sawdust raining down from his hair as he took the empty seat next to Flint. "Lost track of time, but I didn't want to miss the grand 'Make Rainbow Cove Gay-er' plan. That is still on the agenda, right?"

I glared at him. He of all people should be taking this seriously. "LGBTQ tourism is huge money," I piped up. "And tourists love to spend cash on unique art." *Including the overpriced tree stumps you sell.*

"Well, by all means, bring on the gay money." Curtis made a go-ahead gesture to Brock.

As Everleigh introduced Brock and gave background to the agenda item for those who hadn't been at prior meetings, Brock set up his large flip board on the easel he'd brought with him.

He smiled, adjusted his glasses, and began talking. "Now, as some of you know, the Rainbow Tavern received a grant through the state. Part of why I'm here today is to discuss more businesses applying for funds. My development group is particularly interested in seeing more remodeling and new businesses opening or expanding, particularly if we can do it in a unified fashion."

"Can you break that down into something I might have a chance of catching on to?" Ralph asked, leaning forward.

"If the town embraces the rainbow theme, and the Chamber of Commerce and businesses go in together on ads in some of the largest gay publications, that would be a big positive for my group to make a substantial investment in the area." Brock continued in MBA-speak, albeit slower now.

"He means they're thinking about buying the old Sandview Resort," I explained for him, referencing the beachfront hotel that had gone bankrupt a decade ago, taking a lot of jobs and tourists with it. The news sent an excited murmur through the group of business owners, exactly the way I'd hoped it would. He unveiled a series of drawings showing a renovated Sandview, complete with pastel colors and depictions of happy tourists. The Chamber of Commerce's support was integral to Brock's investors committing to the project, but the city council and other permitting agencies would also need to be involved going forward.

"And we're investigating whether the area could sustain a golf course. And a spa." Another set of drawings, this time accompanied by tourism stats, some of which looked dire when compared to other areas on the coast. But where I saw economic flat-lining, Brock saw opportunity.

Curtis made a scoffing noise that ended abruptly. Flint must have kicked him or something because he didn't pipe up again. I sent Flint a grateful look, but he didn't meet my eyes.

"I do like the sound of a spa," Patsy chimed in, obviously well-prepped by Adam to be onboard with all this. "That could mean guests who linger in town a bit longer. Spread their cash around."

"And fish." Ralph tugged at his ball cap. I'd lived in Rainbow Cove most of my life and had never seen the man without a cap advertising his business. "Do golfers fish?"

"I'm sure they do." Brock smiled broadly. "Now, the next step is going back to my investment group with support from local organizations for the purchase, the Chamber included. Can I get a vote on that?"

The motion of support carried easily as Brock had

predicted. Few business owners would vote against the resort being profitable again. But the next part was likely to be more controversial.

"The investors would love to see a united front. The Rainbow Tavern is going to sponsor ads in a number of gay-friendly publications, and if you're interested in being listed in the ads with them, I have a form for you." Brock gave the room a winning smile before sending a clipboard around. "If you'd like a rainbow decal to put on your store door or window, I have some of those as well. And local services can put up the rainbow or a pink triangle. Like here at the visitor center or at City Hall, even."

I wasn't surprised to see Flint send the clipboard and sticker pack right on by, but I was a bit...disappointed maybe.

"I'll take one." Ralph looked up as the clipboard reached him. He was seriously one of the last allies I would have expected. "All money's green to me."

"That's the spirit." Patsy signed her name with a flourish. The B&B was already planning some package deals with us for a room and dinner.

"Participation is, of course, optional." Should have known that Everleigh would have to get another word in. She sighed before making a motion to get an update on progress with the resort and the ad campaign at the next meeting, which I supposed was the best we could hope for.

"I know we're running behind schedule"—she fixed a glare right at me—"but Chief Flint has been nice enough to come talk to us about the recent rise in vandalism."

"That's right." Flint stood. I knew firsthand how his

voice could go hard and cold. But his usual speaking voice was just right for reassuring people—all deep and soothing. "There's nothing to get alarmed about. We have noticed the rise in graffiti and property damage, but we're doing increased patrols of our businesses." He went on to explain about some of the specific cases, and I started squirming in my seat. I swore I could *feel* Everleigh's eyes on me. And she wasn't the only one zeroing in on my space. When Flint said that he didn't have a particular suspect, two shop owners actually swiveled their heads so they could look at me, like they had to verify that, yes, there was a Hanks in their midst.

And I knew everyone was thinking about Freddy and his friends and their penchant for marking shit up in their teens. They'd done worse as adults—they'd had the bright idea of trying to steal the logbook from the front seat of one of the police cruisers, thinking they could "erase" a bust for one of Freddy's buddies. Somehow their prank had gone sideways and the car ended up on fire. Freddy got a fast conviction and a trip to the pen for his stupidity, my family got another reason to hate Flint and the police department, and the town got more fuel to stoke their mistrust of the Hanks family.

"When did all the vandalism start?" The jewelry store owner—couldn't remember his name—spoke up. "How do we know this isn't someone upset at the direction the town is taking? New businesses and such?" He ended with a pointed look at me.

"There's no evidence of that." Flint's voice was calming, but my back muscles still tensed. "It's probably some bored kids. School's out and there aren't enough jobs. We'll keep an eye out."

"We all will," Everleigh added. "It's important to report any suspicious activity right away."

I nodded along with everyone else. It felt weird to agree to neighborhood-watch type activities. I could almost hear my dad's scorn and skepticism, knew how he'd roll his eyes at the caution being taken and say that Flint and the business owners were making a big deal out of nothing.

By the time the meeting adjourned, I was still off-kilter, torn between the voices of my past and the pressures of my present. I had a hard time returning Brock's smile.

"That went well." He gathered up his materials. "We're still on for you coming up to Portland end of next month to help me with the next round of convincing the investors about the resort, right? I think you'll add the right dash of local color."

"We're on," I said even though I didn't necessarily agree that I was the best one to represent the town. Everleigh had far more experience, Patsy far more charm, and anyone else far more credibility.

"Do you need a ride back to the tavern or your place?" Brock asked as we lugged his stuff to his car. He'd spent the night, so we'd ridden to the meeting together. "I'm behind schedule for making it back to Portland in time for my afternoon meeting."

Typical Brock. He had a five-hour drive ahead of him, and of course, he had something vital waiting for him at the other end. He'd probably be on business calls on his hands-free device the whole way home, too.

"I'm good. I can walk back." The visitor center was at the far southern edge of town, right off of Highway 101 and next to the town sign—a giant wood monstrosity carved by Curtis with a rainbow and leaping fish and ocean waves all competing for real estate. It'd be a bit of a hike, but I didn't need to slow Brock down.

"It's going to rain." Flint's voice startled me. I hadn't realized he'd approached us. His frown was as dour as the skies above us. "I'll give you a ride."

"Perfect," Brock said before I could reply. "I'll just be on my way." He leaned in to give me a hug that lingered a bit too long—entirely for Flint's benefit, I was sure.

"You don't need to give me a ride," I said to Flint after Brock got in his car and started the engine. "I don't mind a little rain."

"Come on." Flint jerked his thumb in the direction of his Jeep. Bossy, bossy man. I opened my mouth to protest again, but then Flint smiled, eyes crinkling, and I was a goner. "I won't even make you ride in the back. This time."

SIX

Nash

I wasn't sure why I'd offered Mason a ride. Being neighborly wasn't exactly my strong suit—I just liked to do the right thing. And I guessed that not making him walk in the rain counted as the right thing. But my motives weren't entirely heroic. I hadn't enjoyed seeing Mason with that city boy with the double last name and designer duds. Their hugs and touches and little teases all said there was a history between them. And I hated that it made my fists clench and back tighten—jealousy had never been part of my personality, not even with Steve. And I had no claim on Mason Hanks, none at all.

Still, my tone was sharper than it needed to be as I unlocked the Jeep. "Your friend in town long?"

"Brock? I'm surprised you didn't note the strange car in town and his exact arrival time." Mason laughed as he settled his long legs in my seldom-used passenger seat. "He came down last night. Too busy for a long visit, and I think one night on my couch is his maximum."

"Book him at Patsy's next time." The leap in my pulse and new lightness to my voice was purely coincidental. I was *not* relieved to learn that Mason had slept alone.

"I thought about that, but we wanted to catch up."

"You guys know each a long time, then?"

Mason chuckled like he'd figured me out. "Are you asking if we dated? Suddenly curious about my love life?"

I reminded myself that I'd known Mason long before he had any business having a love life. The first few fat raindrops hit my windshield before I got my voice level enough to answer. "Nope."

"I think you're lying. And Brock and I tried it on like forever ago, but we're too…similar in some ways to work as a couple. Better off friends. That's how we started, anyway—he was friends with my ex. Ex moved on, Brock stuck around."

"You have a lot of these exes?" I asked before I could stop myself.

"Ha. I knew you were curious. And nope. Felipe was the main guy. Dated some others but nothing lasted. How about you?"

"How about me, what?" I bristled. Had he discovered some rumor about Steve? And if not, why on earth did my lips feel loose, like I was dying to tell *someone* about how it felt, him leaving.

"Exes? Why haven't I heard about you hooking up with someone?"

"I'm too old for hookups, and my job comes first." I'd given the answer before, but it sounded awfully hollow right then. The rain picked up, and I flipped on the wipers, heart beating too fast, Mason's questions slicing too deep.

"You haven't always been older than dirt. Come on. What about when you were younger? Have a girlfriend? Boyfriend?"

I thumped my hand against the steering wheel, suddenly noticing that traffic on 101 was barely crawling. I welcomed the distraction and hit my radio button. "Marta? What the heck is with traffic on the highway? We're practically at a standstill."

"Yes, sir, Chief. I was just about to message you." Marta's voice crackled over the speaker. "There's a hay truck that's lost part of its load about three miles out of town. Sheriff's office and the highway patrol are on it, but it may be a while before things get moving again."

Jurisdiction was a pain in my backside, but however much I wanted to go investigate, I knew when to hang back and let the county sheriff and highway patrol handle things. "You let them know that we're ready and willing to help if needed. It may be a few before I get back into the office, though."

"That's fine. Over and out." Marta signed off, leaving me alone with Mason and his pesky questions and a line of cars that wasn't moving.

"Did I piss you off?" Mason leaned forward in his seat. "I didn't mean to. It's just…I saw how you looked at me that night at the tavern. That night when you came in with Curtis—"

"I know what night you meant," I ground out. "And my personal life is just that. Personal. No one in town wants the police chief to air his private business, and I'm not about to start just because you want to go on a fishing expedition."

"I'm not the gossiping type." Mason sounded wounded. "And I'm not asking you to take out advertising with the tavern or anything. Just asking you as a man—one *you* pushed into a wall—whether you're into guys. Because as much as I don't want to upset you, I want to know. For me. Not the world."

"For you, huh?" Warmth crept up the back of my neck. I wasn't supposed to like hearing that, not one bit. And yet my body felt strangely overheated at his confession.

"For me," Mason said softly, and a tendril of longing licked up my spine. Lord, but I'd been right. He was trouble. So much trouble.

"It's irrelevant," I said firmly. "That night was a mistake. I was out of line."

"Oh, I think it's highly relevant." Mason's laugh was warm and filled my drafty Jeep. However, his next words chilled me but good. "You know we're having Pride Night on Saturday?"

"You're what?" I tried to will the cars in front of us to move.

"Pride Night. We're going to do it once a month or maybe bi-weekly depending on turnout. We're gay-friendly all the time, but for Pride Night, there will be special music and an emphasis on meeting new people."

"You're turning into a hookup joint?" I wrapped my sarcasm around me as tight as an undersized sweater.

"A gathering spot for the local queer community. You should come. Dip your toes in the water—"

"I'm not dipping anything in anything." My voice

was far too loud for the enclosed space. "And this is what I mean by not relevant. It doesn't matter what I'm into—I can't be seen at any bar's happy hour. Not yours, not Rowdy's, not anywhere. No one in town wants to see their police chief out for a good time."

"You're wrong." Mason's voice was low and gentle to my loud. "People really wouldn't care, Flint. And you're not your dad. You don't need to keep to a 1950s ideal of policing. You're a real guy, not some...mythic fantasy figure."

Curtis had said similar to me, a hundred times at least, and so had Steve, and I was sick of it. "You don't know what it's like to be me, okay? So don't go telling me about how easy things are."

"Tell me." Mason didn't back down in the face of my anger, instead leaning forward more, voice insistent. "Tell me what it's like to be you."

Tiring. So very goddamn tiring. No one, not even Curtis, had asked me that before. "You want to know what it's like to be me on any given Saturday night? Okay, I'll tell you. Two years ago when the Jensen teens wrapped their car around a tree on Mill Peak Road, I was the one who had to tell Mrs. Jensen that her kids would never come home. There's not a day goes by that I don't remember the look in her eyes. Another week some out-of-town teenagers have a party at their folks vacation place and I've fifteen drunken kids and their angry folks to deal with. Some summer weeks it seems we can't have Saturday without someone blowing some body part off with fireworks on the beach. And we can't have a weekend without at least one domestic dispute call. Every single Saturday night, that's what I'm thinking—

how can I keep my town safe? Not how can I get lucky. I want to know how I can do my job better so I never have to knock on another door like that again."

"That's hard." Mason reached over, patted my leg. It was a friendly gesture, but one people almost never tried with me. I felt the warmth of his palm clear through to the bone. "Sounds pretty damn lonely, actually."

"It's not lonely. I'm never truly alone." I had no idea why this was spewing out after years of keeping it all in. "I wake up and I start going through the list of who needs me, who needs taking care of. I worry about Vera Matthews' daughter, all alone while Vera's recovering in Eugene. I worry about that stoplight up at Lakeview that always wants to go out. I worry about Dolly's son going off the wagon again. I'm never alone, not with worries like those."

"That's not the same as having *friends*. People who care about you. People who can ease that burden of being you."

"It's not a burden. It's a privilege." That was something my dad had always said, and I believed it with every fiber of my being. "It's a privilege to serve my community. And an obligation. I'm not trying to hold myself up as some kind of hero. I'm just trying to hold it together, period."

"But what if you didn't have to?" Mason pressed. "Not every minute. What if you got to take a load off, let go of the ridiculous standards you seem to have for yourself. You could come to Pride Night, prove to yourself that the sky won't fall if you let yourself enjoy something."

I want to enjoy you. The thought was there before I

could call it back. I hadn't sparred with someone like this since God knew when. Nor could I remember the last time I'd vomited words like that.

Finally, *mercifully,* traffic started moving again, and we came to the turn-off for First Street that would let me bypass the mess on 101.

"Am I dropping you at the tavern or your place?"

Mason sighed, and I didn't think I was imagining the disappointment there. "Tavern. We've got to get ready for lunch. You coming in later to eat?"

"That's probably not a good idea," I admitted as I turned onto Montana, heading past the square and City Hall. Further down the block was the tavern, and I pulled into their lot. It wasn't right to get a small thrill at the idea of seeing Mason again later, wasn't right how much I'd already come to enjoy the meals he served me.

"You have to eat sometime. And okay, so you won't tell me about your personal life, but tell me this. If you could add one item to our menu, what would it be?"

"Oh, I don't know. I eat what's in front of me."

Mason made a frustrated noise. "Consider this a request for help. You were right about the plain iced tea. What else would customers such as you like to eat?"

"It's the wrong time of year, but you can't go wrong with a good beef stew. That'd go nice with that bread of yours," I allowed. "Or maybe do a pie as a special one day—strawberries and rhubarb are in season now. My mom always used to make that in June. Folks raved about it."

Mason smiled like I'd handed him the biggest trout out of the river. "Come to lunch tomorrow. Maybe I'll surprise you."

Of that I had no doubt, but I wasn't sure that was a good thing. But before I could tell him no, he was out of the car, giving me a little wave. "Thanks for the ride, Chief."

Nash, call me Nash. The offer was on my tongue, but he was already out of earshot, which was for the best. Other than Curtis and a couple other folks who had known me as kid, I was Chief Flint around here now, and that was the way it was supposed to be, no idiotic mooning over what my name would sound like on Mason Hanks's lips.

SEVEN

Mason

"Tell me again why we're making beef stew in June?" Logan looked up from the carrots he was dicing. It was the day after the Chamber of Commerce meeting, and we were gathered for the morning prep work in the tavern's kitchen.

"I told you. We had a request."

"Yeah, and every time you mention it, your neck turns red." Logan's white chef's jacket contrasted with his designer jeans and shoes, a reminder that he'd always been more in step with Brock's crowd than mine.

"It's Sheriff Sexy." Adam was supposed to be peeling potatoes, but judging by the band-aids on his knuckles, this wasn't a task that Patsy had made him do often. "Come on, admit it. *Flint* made the barest mention of stew, and now you've got us browning meat and boiling potatoes."

"It's not like that." I slapped the rye dough I was kneading harder. Little rye rolls shaped like knots would

63

be perfect with the stew. "We just haven't done a soup as the special yet."

"Uh-huh." Adam didn't even pretend to believe me. Life-long best friend and he couldn't give me the dignity of pretending I wasn't out to impress Flint. Luckily, Adam didn't have access to my phone—where I'd stored a good two dozen strawberry-rhubarb recipes for consideration—or I'd never hear the end of it.

"And you're sure I can't play with the seasonings? Chipotle and cheddar? Or maybe cranberry and beer?" Logan had moved on to celery, lightning-fast flashes of knife work.

"Beer is cool." I had to give Logan something to work with. "But just keep it classic. You can do a twist on the sandwich for the other side of the specials board."

"If you'll have extra rye, I'm thinking an updated Reuben with roasted beets."

"You've been awfully into vegetarian options lately," Adam observed.

Logan shrugged. "The vegan woodcarver guy is just as bad as Flint—always the exact same order. Maybe I want more choices for the vegetarian crowd—"

"Or maybe you've suddenly developed a taste for eccentric?" Adam shook his head. "Trust Mason and me here—Curtis Hunt is nuts. Like carves-outside-shirtless-in-January nuts."

"There's a rumor he recycles his piss to water his plants," I shared because I was totally on board with anything that distracted from Flint and my motives for making stew.

"He once hacked up this big eagle he carved because one feather was off." And with that, Adam was off to the races with Curtis stories to try to shock Logan, who'd never known that chainsaw carving was a thing until he came here.

By lunchtime, I was confident that they'd forgotten about Flint, even if I hadn't and kept stealing glances at the front door. But the lunch rush came and went, and no Flint. I was feeling ridiculous about the whole stew thing when the door chimed at almost three and in walked Flint, heading right to his usual table.

His broad shoulders slumped as he sat, and he rubbed at his temples once he removed his sunglasses. I could practically feel the weariness rolling off him, so I grabbed an iced tea on my way to his table. Our conversation yesterday had changed how I saw him—made him more human, more of a man and less of an authority figure who quite frankly had scared me more than a little for years. I'd never thought of the burdens he must carry, but the anguish in his voice had been unmistakable. Nash Flint needed a friend in the worst way. I was probably the least suitable person in the world for the role, but I couldn't deny how much he'd been on my mind. I wanted to see more of the human, humble Flint I'd glimpsed yesterday.

"Long morning?" I set the tea in front of him.

"You could say that." Flint took a long swig of his tea. "Saw your specials board on my way in. It's June."

"The stew sold surprisingly well with the lunch crowd." My voice was just a tad more defensive than it needed to be.

"I guess I better see for myself." He gave me a tired smile that made my stomach do a weird little wobble.

"Extra bread, if you've got it. And I'll skip the salad today."

"I'm on it."

"And Mason…" He rubbed his face again. "Thanks."

That thank you warmed me as thoroughly as a bowl of Logan's stew, and I took more care than I needed to dishing up Flint's lunch, giving him two rolls, plenty of butter, and a nice garnish on the stew.

"You've got it bad." Logan heckled me from across the kitchen where he was cleaning the grill.

"Shut up." Laughing, I shook my fist at him before taking the tray out to Flint.

"Here you go." Wanting to see his reaction to the bread and stew, I hung back after sliding the plate and bowl in front of him.

"You going to hover like that, you might as well take a seat." Flint gestured at the empty chair in front of him. "You eat yet yourself?"

"You implying I'm too skinny?" I had to work hard to keep the muscle on, but I was a far cry from the scrawny kid I used to be. After some dithering, I went ahead and slid into the chair. Flint was the only customer in the joint, and Adam was back having his food in the kitchen, so it wasn't like he could tease me.

"Didn't say that." Heat flared in the appraising look Flint gave me. He might not have admitted it in so many words, but Nash Flint was *not* straight. And I could tell myself all week that I didn't care one way or another, but I couldn't stop the little thrill at his purposeful glance.

"Just…" He sighed, and it hit me how often Flint must eat alone — he lived alone in that big house, ate alone here, and I couldn't see him socializing much over meals with his junior officers and employees.

"I'm going to grab a soda." I rushed to the bar, made myself the fastest root beer ever, and was back in the chair before Flint could change his mind about inviting me to sit. "So…your morning?"

"Tell me what's in the bread. It's not white flour, is it?" Flint asked like he really wanted to know, not simply like he was dodging my question. So I told him all about my sourdough starter and the rye flour I sourced from a northwest mill. He asked good follow-up questions, and some of the tension in his shoulders and neck seemed to bleed away.

"Soup's good. Your guy's got a good eye for seasoning, I'll give him that."

"He's not my guy." I laughed, but I wasn't sure how much more obvious I could get—I'd been pretty shameless in telling him that Brock had slept on the couch. I was *not* supposed to care so much that Flint knew I was single. "Logan's a great chef. I've known him since culinary school."

"Why'd you end up in culinary school, anyway?" Having demolished one roll, Flint started in on the second.

"Because of my asthma, I couldn't go for sports like my brothers, and I was limited in how much I could go running after them on our property. So I spent a lot of time with my mom in the kitchen."

"My father never would have stood for that." Flint shook his head. "Probably why I can barely boil water now."

"My mom always said hungry people have to eat, and

if you don't cook, you have to help clean. I'd much rather cook than clean. I left dish duty to the others." Not that Freddy and Jimmy had done a ton of dishes, but Mom had tried to instill some basic self-sufficiency in all of us. It was sad that Flint's dad hadn't seen a need for that.

"Smart woman." Flint took a big bite of stew. "And a damn fine waitress, too—food in the old tavern wasn't anything like this, but the service was always top notch."

"Thanks," I said, both to the compliment on our food and the nice memory of Mom. She had worked hard for the old owners when she wasn't working equally hard at home. "And after school, I'd hang out here when she had a shift and no one to babysit me. The old cook used to let me come watch some."

"I remember Clinker MacMahon well. He was a character." Flint laughed. Man, I liked hearing him laugh, seeing him unwind even a small amount.

"But really, I owe a lot to Mrs. Mueller at the high school—shop class was full my junior year, and they stuck me in home ec. She talked me into taking my love of food and trying for a scholarship. Way out of this town." I remembered who I was talking to and added, "No offense. Obviously I love it here. But when you're eighteen, you just want...something different, you know? Didn't you ever want to explore?"

Flint shrugged. "Not sure. Dad always painted the future as either the military or law enforcement. Easton picked the marines. He always was gung-ho on getting to see the world. Me, I was happy to do my four years in Eugene, get my degree in criminal justice, and come on back home."

Flint's older brother who'd died in Iraq was a hazy

memory in my childhood. He'd gotten some big medal, and his funeral had been a huge deal in town. "My mom cried when your brother died," I offered. There might be no love lost between my family and the Flints, but from all accounts, Easton had been a stand-up man.

"Me too." Flint's gaze got far away and his mouth narrowed. Damn. I hadn't meant to wander into unhappy territory.

I toyed with the table-top flyer for Pride Night that I'd put by the condiments on each table. "They say you only live once…"

"*Mason.*" Flint shook his head at me, but he smiled, which was exactly what I'd been after. "Quit trying to drum up business for your deal. And just so you know, I texted Curtis. Told him he should come out. Socialize."

"Come with him," I urged.

The door jangled before Flint could reply, and I hopped up to greet the trio of customers who came in. "I'll be back," I said to Flint.

"See to your business." He waved me away. "And thanks for the company."

His words pleased me, far more than they should have. It made my shoulders lift to know I'd been a good distraction for whatever bad morning Flint had had, even temporarily. I liked being a refuge of sorts for such a stoic man, but pride was a dangerous, dangerous emotion, every bit as stupid as the notion that Flint needed a friend. Even so, I couldn't stop myself from hoping he'd be back for more.

Nash

I didn't tell Mason, but I had Saturday night off—Candace Holmes had the shift with Locklear backing her up if need be. I went home when Holmes came on duty and showered like I always did after a long shift, then I went to stand in front of my closet.

Like an idiot.

Say I did want to go to this...*thing* of Mason's? What the hell would I wear? On my disastrous last trip to Portland, I'd worn my usual off-duty wardrobe of a polo and Wranglers. The first guy I'd worked up the nerve enough to approach had called me grandpa and laughed. Apparently, I was officially near death by gay standards and no longer prime hookup material.

I'd lied, of course, when I told Mason that I didn't hook up. Over the years, I had very sporadically. Here and there, always away from Rainbow Cove. Even Coos Bay was a bit too close to home. Eugene was bigger, farther away, and the college town had a surprising quantity of guys okay with discreet encounters. But I hadn't been lying about being too old for all that now.

Mason had sat with me again yesterday when I'd had a late lunch, bringing out his own sandwich, and seemed happy enough to tell me about his cheesecake recipe and share stories of him and his chef at culinary school. But that friendliness didn't mean he wanted to knock boots with me.

Not that I wanted to knock anything with him, either.

Mason was still trouble. But that didn't explain why I was standing with my closet door cracked, wondering about buttons versus a pullover.

My phone rang. I grabbed it off the bed, not sure whether I wanted it to be the station needing me or not. It was my mother, who lived up in Portland with my sister. In my dithering about whether to go to the tavern, I'd forgotten our weekly call.

"Hey, Mom." I tugged my towel tighter around my waist.

"Sweetheart, I'm so glad I caught you." She'd never have gotten away with the pet name when Dad had been alive—he'd always been quick to criticize her for making us soft. But Portland living agreed with her, had buffed off some of the hard edges created by years of living with Dad. "Off-duty tonight?"

"Yup."

"You eating? I worry about you. Heard the Dairy Queen went out of business again."

I hadn't frequented that place since my early twenties, but I made a sympathetic noise. "Yeah, sad to see another business close. I eat. Been going to the new tavern—they reopened under new management."

"I *heard*."

I sighed. "You've been talking to Marta."

"I have. Someone had to tell me Vera Matthews was in the hospital."

Oops. I'd been so busy that I'd neglected to make that call. Or maybe I'd known we might end up on this topic, and I'd delayed it, which wasn't like me. Then again, I was acting in all sorts of out-of-character ways lately. "I'm sorry. I should have called. She's due back home any day now."

"And Marta had to be the one to tell me about the

tavern. That's why I asked about you eating. You can't be getting good food there."

"Actually, it's decent stuff. Nice portion sizes, tasty flavors. Bit pricier than Rowdy's, but nothing like what you pay in Portland."

"Oh, do *not* get me started on prices around here." She made a clucking noise. "Or portions. I'll never get paying for a 'taste.' Ridiculous. I'll send you some vouchers for the sub place on 101. At least they're healthy—"

"Mom. I make decent money. I don't need vouchers."

"Well, I don't like you eating at *that* place. What would your father say?"

Wasn't that the ten million dollar question? I was almost forty, had been on my own in this house for years now, and still his ghost dogged me everywhere I went. Even knowing how silly it was to care, I couldn't shake the image of his disapproving face. "He might be happy about increased business for the area. Times have been tough, tougher even than when he was around. Something's got to change—"

"But not our core values." My mother was a good woman, always quick with a casserole or a kind word for ailing neighbors and a loving mother who had comfort to spare, but my father's hard-line traditionalism had rubbed off on her in ways that made me grab the back of my neck and suppress another sigh.

"It's a restaurant, not a strip club. I don't think their sweet-potato fries are going to corrupt anyone."

"Don't you be flip with me." My mother could still do stern when she wanted to. "Nash, you have to think of your image. I know…your personal life is one thing, but just think of your reputation. That's all I'm saying."

Ah. Now we were getting to the heart of the matter. And it wasn't anything that I hadn't been telling myself for weeks now, yet it still stung. My father had never known—or at least not so as we ever talked on it—but Mom had figured out me and Steve years ago. We'd had an argument, and she wasn't the type to disown me over it. However, she never missed a chance to remind me about my professional image. "I know," I said wearily.

"I love you, Nash. You know that. I'm just concerned for you."

That concern felt like a wet wool blanket pressing down on any lightness I'd managed to gather over the last few weeks. "Love you, too. How's Trisha and the kids?"

Conversation shifted to the grandkids, as I'd hoped it would, and I wandered back across the room. I shut the closet door firmly, closing off my earlier foolishness. I didn't know what I'd been thinking, acting like I could actually go out tonight. I hung up with another round of "I love you" and headed downstairs to search for a dinner that wouldn't be half as good as what Mason served.

EIGHT

"If you keep watching the door so closely, you're going to need Lasik by Christmas," Adam joked as I brought a tray of empties to the bar.

"Not watching anything," I protested. "Just wish our turnout had been better."

Our first Pride Night wasn't a bust, exactly, but turnout was far below the last few Fridays, and by ten o'clock, we were down to a few stragglers and not heating up as I'd hoped. An older, more mature crowd had come for Logan's amazing food, but we'd yet to get much of a weekend drinks-and-dancing crowd, tonight included. Still, though, it had been nice to see so many same-sex couples there—including the local librarian and her partner. Never guessed about those two growing up. A few couples had even driven up from Gold Beach and Brookings, which was nice.

"You and me both. But, honestly, I'm okay with it being not too busy." Adam's hand shook as he poured a rum and coke. Fine lines radiated from his eyes and his shoulders were tense.

"Headache?" I knew all his warning signs. Adam might look like an indestructible lumberjack, but he'd struggled with migraines even as a kid. We'd bonded over missing lots of school, and, even now, the urge to protect him was strong.

"Yeah. Not terrible—"

"Yet. Listen, it's getting quieter. I can mix drinks and handle the close."

"You sure?" Adam had to be really hurting to not fight me on leaving. "I'll see who needs a refill and then if it's still bad—"

"You'll go home regardless. Need me to call Ramona for a ride for you?" I asked. Adam lived with his sister, a few doors down from his mom's bed and breakfast.

"Nah. I can still drive." Adam rubbed at the bridge of his nose. "No need to bring her and Teddy out."

Logan came out of the kitchen. "I can drive," he said. "I'll just toss my bike in the back of your truck." We closed for food at ten, but there hadn't been a food order in the last hour. Eventually, we'd try to keep the kitchen open until midnight for appetizers and bar food, but so far, there just wasn't a demand for it. "I'm almost done cleaning the kitchen."

Logan rented an apartment over Adam's mom's garage. She'd branched out her business interests beyond the B&B and had invested in several rental properties. She owned a large chunk of her block now, all properties with a view of the lake.

Logan's shaggy blond hair was artfully styled, even after a full day in front of the hot grill. His teen-idol looks were more suited for one of Brock's hipster Portland haunts than our small-town kitchen. His eyes swept over the sparse crowd.

"You're just as bad as Mason." Adam shook his head and winced. "Curtis Hunt wouldn't come out for something as tame as Pride Night. We start offering alligator wrestling or a leather night, then maybe he'll be interested."

"I'm okay with offering a leather night later in the summer." Logan shrugged. "Wouldn't mind seeing who turned out for that. And I don't have a thing for the woodcarver guy. Not remotely interested. I was just looking to see if there was any reason to...socialize."

"Hey," I protested. "I thought we agreed no picking up customers."

Adam snorted. "You didn't really expect that to hold, did you?"

"This is *not* a hookup joint, not for us, anyway. We need to be professionals." I took the bar towel from Adam, started wiping down the glossy surface. Before we'd opened, we'd talked about this—we didn't want a reputation for hitting on customers, and I'd worked at enough places to know that the line between friendly and uncomfortable could get blurry in a hurry.

"Says the guy who keeps taking his breaks with Sheriff Sexy—"

"You're lucky you're sick." I waved the towel at him. "And stop calling Flint that."

"Okay, enough already." Logan got between us, his tolerance for our brotherly bickering low as always. "You ready, Adam?"

The two of them helped me get the last of the glassware through the dishwasher, and then they were gone, leaving me to open a few more beers for the stragglers and start the process of wiping down the tables and chairs. By midnight, when I flipped the sign to closed, we'd been empty awhile.

I made fast work of the remaining cleaning, and then took the trash out to the dumpster behind the building. The sound of footsteps cut across the still June evening, and my spine went rigid.

"Big night?" Turning at the sound of Flint's voice, my arm jerked, and I whopped myself in the face with an armful of cardboard.

"What the heck are you doing?" I asked.

An ancient truck was parked next to my car. Should have noticed that sooner—my lack of attention had me frustrated at myself and shoving the cardboard into the dumpster with jerky movements.

"Sorry." He stepped closer. "Didn't mean to scare you. I just happened to be in the area, saw that you were the only car in the lot, and wanted to make sure there wasn't any...hassle over your night."

"Didn't scare me," I lied. "And happened to be in the area?" I looked him over—jeans, long-sleeved polo shirt, no uniform, and no official car.

"Remembered that I needed gas in the truck." He nodded like that wasn't the thinnest excuse in the world.

"You weren't on duty tonight, were you?"

He shook his head. It might have been a trick of the dim lighting, but I swore I saw shadows of regret in his eyes.

"You were going to come. I'd put money on it. You actually thought about it."

Flint leaned against my car. "I think about all sorts of bad ideas. Did it go well?"

"Okay crowd. Very little dancing or mingling between groups. But don't try to change the subject. You were going to come, but you chickened out, and I want to know why."

"I don't chicken out of crap." Flint drew himself up to his full height and loomed over me.

I, however, refused to be cowed and poked at his chest. "You did this time. Did you even eat? I can rustle you up something."

"I ate." Flint's shifty look said it had been something microwaved and barely worth the price of its plastic container. "Probably shouldn't come in so much, anyway. People are going to start talking—"

"And why do you give a fuck? You're chief of police —small-minded gossip isn't supposed to faze a man like you."

"Man like me." Flint shook his head. "Why is the world always trying to tell me what sort of man to be? That was always my dad's thing—'a man does this' and 'a real man does that' all day. He thought it was his job to teach us how to be like him—better, even."

The more I learned, the more I was starting to hate Flint's father. "You can be a man and be gay or bisexual or pan or anything else. You know that, right? The 'real man' stuff is nonsense. You're one of the most masculine guys I've ever met. You could wear a pink Pride T-shirt everyday, and nothing would change that."

Flint shook his head. "You know what happens when you're a guy like me and you come out? You become an oddity, a footnote, and people can't talk about you without the label. You think I haven't watched what's happened with the out mayors in the state? 'The first openly gay...' Never hear them say the mayor or representative's name without also mentioning that they're gay or bisexual or trans—*that* label gets all the headlines. I'd forever be 'the gay police chief' and I don't want that."

"But you've thought about doing it? Coming out, I mean."

"Hell, yes. You think..." Flint made a frustrated noise. "Fuck. I have no idea why I'm telling you all this. You're—"

"You say a Hanks and I'll deck you, officer of the law or not."

"Trouble. I was going to say trouble." Flint took a step forward, backing me against the wall. His movements were deliberate, giving me plenty of time to push him away as he slowly lowered his head.

But I wasn't going anywhere, my hands fisting in the cotton of his shirt as he crowded into me. Proving Flint's point about being trouble, I ran headlong toward his kiss, meeting him eagerly when our mouths finally connected.

He kissed like he ate—a starving man who didn't know when he'd next get hot food or a chance to enjoy a meal. There was a fair bit of wonder and surprise in our connection, too—as if he hadn't expected to enjoy it so much, like he was surprised to find himself devouring what was in front of him. And he absolutely made a buffet out of my mouth, nibbling and teasing until I opened up, allowing him to feast in earnest.

I wasn't usually a passive kisser, but with Flint I found myself hanging on for dear life and letting him have his way. I wanted to see where he'd go with the freedom. He growled, pushing me more firmly against the building, but he didn't break the kiss. His chest was firm against mine, a solid wall of muscle trapping my hands between us, and his groin pressed against my aching dick. Not rocking, not grinding, just *there*, and fuck, I needed more of it.

"*Flint,*" I sighed against his mouth as he pulled back slightly. "More."

"Nash," he corrected me. "This is insanity."

"But it feels so good." I yanked him closer for another kiss. *Nash*. It suited him more than Flint in this moment —Flint was hard, unemotional, and buttoned up tight. Nash was a powder keg waiting to go off. Nash had soft lips and hard muscles and possessive little growls that made my insides quake and my dick throb. Freeing my hands from between us, I pulled his shirt loose and snaked one hand up to stroke his back. He responded like I'd hoped, nipping at my mouth before deepening the kiss, tongue thrusting against mine in an insistent rhythm.

Gravel skittered as a car pulled out down the alley, but it was enough to make Flint—*Nash*—step back, breathing hard.

"Come home with me," I said before he could say anything. "Let me lock up, and then come home with me."

"Can't." He wiped his mouth with the back of his hand.

"You live a block away. Park at home if you're worried about gossips. But come over."

"This...*that*..." He waved his hand in the general

direction of my mouth. "Can't happen. Ever. That was a mistake. An accident."

"What? Like we tripped and ended up with your tongue halfway down my throat? That kind of accident?"

"I didn't mean to…" Nash sighed then straightened. "You're right. I need to own my actions—it wasn't an accident, but it can't happen again."

"Why not? We're both consenting adults. I'm not asking you to fly a Pride flag at City Hall. This would be just for tonight." I had as many reasons as he did to not want a relationship or something serious, but my body wasn't shy about letting me know how much it craved Nash Flint. I needed more of those kisses in the worst way.

"I'm not sure once would be enough." Nash's bit of honesty made me laugh, made me like him that much more, damn it.

"I'm willing to try." I grinned at him.

Gravel crunched under tires again, closer this time, and Flint shook his head. "Early morning tomorrow, anyway. You take care getting home, you hear?"

"Nash," I called after him as walked toward his truck. He didn't turn. "*Flint*. You can't just pretend that didn't just happen."

He didn't answer. Fucker probably planned to do exactly that—pretend. Pissed, I kicked at the dumpster, which made a satisfying loud rattle as Nash—*Flint*—pulled away. He might be able to act like nothing had happened, but I sure as hell wasn't forgetting what he'd felt like pressed up against me anytime soon.

NINE

Nash

Sunday evening I was on call, restless as hell, distracted, and hungry as I rode around town. A spectacular sunset was threatening over the coast as I drove the shoreline roads, checking for unauthorized fires and double-parked cars by the beach access trails. Down at the rocky coast, families were catching the last of the sun, laying out dinner picnics while the ocean lapped at the giant boulders that littered the shore. My stomach rumbled at the sight of the food. Microwave meals just didn't cut it for me, and I was out of food in any case, the contents of my fridge little more than tumbleweeds. I needed—

Mason.

Okay, okay, I lied. Hunger took a back seat to distraction and the memory of that searing kiss. I wanted the tavern's food, yes, but I wanted to see Mason more, and that... Well, I was Nash Flint. I didn't get scared or spooked. Didn't do rattled or unsure. And yet, I was all those things. Which meant that I was torn between avoiding discomfort, pretending I wasn't still reeling from Mason's kiss, and marching into the tavern, facing the issue head-on, same as I did everything else.

I turned back from the coast, heading through downtown, which of course took me right by the tavern, temptation beckoning just as surely as their neon open sign. I drove on by, reminding myself that they closed earlier on Sundays. Only another couple of hours to outrun the temptation that was Mason.

What had I been thinking with that kiss? And it had absolutely been on me—he was right that it was no accident and I couldn't claim that he'd made the first move. No, I'd lost my freaking head and pushed him up against that wall because one second I'd been so damn angry at my father, at the world, and the next I'd had to kiss Mason or fall into a pit of that anger.

But now I had to rejoin the real world, the one where I couldn't keep kissing Mason and had to stop fantasizing about what would have happened had I taken him up on his offer to go home with him. And, in the real world, I had to eat. Food would help. I headed up Lakeview. Marta was right—Rowdy's did a decent burger, and I hadn't given them business in far too long.

With lower prices on food and plentiful drink specials, Rowdy's catered to a rougher, more local crowd than the tavern. The parking lot was full for a Sunday, and I had to park the Jeep on the far edge of the gravel lot. As I walked toward the door, a group of young men came barreling out of the place, pushing and shoving.

Slowing my steps, I hung back, waiting to see what they were about.

"Motherfucker! You lost the bet. Pay up." Jimmy Hanks poked at the shoulder of Chester Fremont—those two had been trouble together since their teens. Supposedly friends, but you'd never know it from how often they tangled.

"That wasn't a clean throw. You can't play darts to save your ass, Hanks." Chester gave a hard shove in return. "You're as big a pansy as that brother of yours."

"I've had about enough of your mouth." Jimmy's arm drew back, and I was more than half tempted to let him cold-cock Chester for daring to drag Mason into their fight.

But I was an officer of the law, not Mason's personal champion, so I did the right thing and strode over to them. "What's going on here?"

"Ain't none of your business, Flint." Chester sneered.

"Oh? You boys aren't thinking of fighting in this parking lot?"

"You've got it all wrong." Jimmy dropped his hand. "Chester and me were just talking, that's all."

"And if I walk on by, no one's going to end up bloody?" I let my skepticism come out in my tone.

"Nope. We're all friends here." Jimmy glared at me.

"Good. Speaking of friends, I've been meaning to talk to you two. You wouldn't happen to know anything about the recent vandalism we've had downtown, would you? Got any friends I should be talking to?"

"You think I'm your personal snitch now?" Jimmy looked me up and down, shaking his head. "Get real."

"You trying to imply something?" Chester stepped forward, and now, instead of fighting each other, the two were united in their ire towards me. "I don't know nothing. And even if I'd heard, not like I'd share."

"I'm just keeping an eye out," I said mildly. "But it's getting expensive for the businesses in question. Hate to see more jobs leave town."

Chester spat on the ground. "Fuck, a few pranks aren't what's scaring away jobs, Flint. You ain't that stupid, man. The jobs are gone for good."

"Maybe not." Couldn't help but think about the ideas Mason and his buddies had for attracting new business to town. It surprised me how much stock I was beginning to put into the concept. But, man, it would be nice to have resort jobs for guys like Chester again, keep him out of trouble.

"You're as delusional as my brother," Jimmy scoffed at me. "This town's always been a shit hole. A bunch of rainbow flags ain't gonna change crap around here."

"Wouldn't be surprised if that's what's got people pranking." Chester shrugged, voicing the same worry that I'd had since the Chamber of Commerce meeting. A prickle raced up my back.

"Well, you hear anything, you let me know." I gave them both stern looks. Way I figured it, the culprits were probably bored teens, but that didn't mean that these two overgrown lug nuts and their posse didn't know something. "And I mean it on no fighting."

They both mumbled something uncharitable under their breath, and then they meandered toward their cars. I glanced at the front door of Rowdy's. My desire to go in there had fled. I didn't belong here, out with the Hanks and Fremonts and the rough-housing, dart-throwing, fight-starting crowd. Waiting for Jimmy and Chester to pull out, I walked slowly back to my Jeep.

On my way back to town, I pulled into Hauser's, our local grocery store. No chains in Rainbow Cove, not yet, anyway.

"Evening, Chief." Old Melvin had worked at Hauser's long as I'd been alive. "We got in some more of those meals you like," he said. "The new ones with higher fiber. They're back in the freezer section."

Yes, sir, I surely did love living in this town where everyone knew my business, right down to the fact that I was dining alone again on a meal targeted to weight-conscious older women. Mason might want to tell me how nothing would change if I came out, but it was a lie. God, just the thought of everyone all up in my personal life gave me goosebumps.

I grabbed my frozen meals and some bottled iced tea and headed back to the station, planning to restock the ancient freezer in the rear of the office and tackle some paperwork waiting to keep me and my nuked meal company. As I passed the tavern, I tried not to slow down, but my car had other ideas. Mason was out front, washing off the specials board, biceps rippling as he worked. It would be so easy to turn into the tavern's lot, let him feed me. Heck, we'd be doing each other favors — business was probably slow again, and he was far better company than a stack of traffic reports. But then I remembered Jimmy's bullishness and Melvin's nosiness and who exactly I was and what I couldn't have. I drove on, hating the way my chest went tight and my hands clenched around the steering wheel.

Mason

Wednesday lunch rush came and went without Flint stopping by, which meant it had been four days since our kiss and four days since he'd done more than drive by our place. And, oh yes, I had most certainly noticed the drive-bys. I never would have thought of Nash Flint as a coward, but here we were.

"So, I just had a weird phone call." Adam walked into the kitchen where I was helping Logan with dishes. "Sheriff Sexy wants to know if we can do takeout. Says the old tavern used to run him food when he couldn't leave the office."

Yup, just as I'd figured. A huge coward. But I wasn't fessing up to the kiss with Adam and Logan, so I just nodded. "You told him yes?"

"Knew you'd do it." Adam rolled his eyes at me. "Yeah, I told him not to spread it around, but I said we'd get something over to him."

"His usual?" Logan was already at the grill, grabbing meat patties.

"Yeah. I told him I'd run it over since we're slow, but something tells me I'm gonna be staying right here."

"You figured right," I gritted out. Flint was too much of a coward to come see me? I sure as hell wasn't going to make this easy on him. It was a kiss, not a broken engagement. Flint needed a swift dose of reality.

"I am *so* glad that man isn't my type." Adam leaned

against the metal worktable. "Sexy as hell, but he's going to make you go gray, Mase."

"I'm not hung up on him," I lied, busying myself by readying a to-go container for Flint's usual side salad.

"Dude. If you were a deer, you'd be up on a roof rack, shit out of luck. That kind of hung up."

"You guys are going to make me burn the burger." Logan waved a spatula at us.

"He started it," Adam and I both said at the same time then burst out laughing. Even with two decades of friendship, some things never changed. Still laughing, I put together the rest of Flint's order while Logan finished the burger then packed everything up. The sun was shining with a nice breeze off the coast, so I walked the half a block or so to City Hall.

The police station was an annex off the back of the building, but, during the business day, they shared a receptionist with City Hall, a fresh-faced young woman named Tammy who did everything from collecting water bills and parking fines to sign-ups for the city rec soccer league. And apparently one of her jobs involved banging on the wall behind her desk to let Flint know he was needed at the front.

"Sorry. Phone's out again." She gave me an apologetic look, but this had been the system long as I could remember. "Chief! Your lunch is here!"

Flint—I refused to let myself think of him as Nash, not with the way he'd ghosted me all week—finally came striding out. "Ring—*Mason*." A-ha. He had been expecting, probably *hoping* for, Adam.

"Your order." I held out the brown paper sack.

"Thanks." We stood there in front of Tammy like a pair of idiots, staring at each other.

You're a coward, Nash Flint, I told him with my eyes while my mouth said, "You haven't been in this week. You eating?"

"I manage," he said. *Not a coward. Just busy,* his eyes flashed back.

"Well, don't be a stranger." *Come back again? Or are you too afraid you might kiss me again? Accidentally, of course.*

"I won't." Flint's eyes sparked, and I wasn't sure which question he was answering.

"Smells great," Tammy butted in, effectively ending whatever non-conversation we were having.

"Come on in sometime," I said to her. "Wave at me when you do, and dessert's on me." I had to drum up business somehow. Things were better, but we needed more consistent local traffic to survive—fretting over our bottom line was keeping me up every bit as much as obsessing over Flint.

"It's good food," Flint said, already backing out of the room. "You take care now."

Dismissed yet again, I headed back to the tavern. Rather than face Adam and Logan's ribbing in the kitchen, I started wiping down tables and straightening chairs.

The door jangled, and I looked up to find Jimmy and Lilac standing in the doorway. "Hey, Peanut!" I forced a big smile for her. "You hungry?"

"Oh, yeah. Do you have peanut butter sandwiches?"

"You need more than peanut butter in your day. I'll have Logan do a small burger for you, okay? And some fries?" I kept ignoring Jimmy as I focused on Lilac. He'd tell me soon enough why he'd shown up, and it sure as heck wasn't for food.

Sure enough, Jimmy coughed. "Nice of you to feed her. Appreciate it." Oh, fuck no. Jimmy being all polite could only mean he needed something big. And of course, he had a pleading smile for me. "Think she could stay here for a bit? I've got some things to take care of. Chester's got a lead on a car we might get."

I groaned. Chester always had a lead on a piece-of-shit car. "Where's Dad?"

"Out with Uncle Gunnar. He felt good enough to go on a run with him." Dad and Uncle Gunnar were as bad as Jimmy and Chester, always chasing shittyleads on new sources of scrap metal when the two them felt up to work.

"I can't be your babysitter, Jimmy. This is my job, not a daycare."

"It's just the one time. And she'll be good, promise. She's not a baby anymore. You won't even know she's here."

I highly doubted that. But I didn't want to argue with Jimmy and hurt Lilac's feelings. "*One* time, and you come back as soon as you can. It'd be great if she could be picked up before our dinner rush."

"I'll be quick." Jimmy didn't promise a return time, which was typical for him, and he hurried out the door before I could change my mind.

I put the order in for Lilac's food and got her situated at a table in the very back. I had to blink hard against the memory of being her age, maybe a bit older, and waiting for my mom to finish her shift. Clinker, the cook, used to fix me a big plate of hash browns, and Mom would have a bag of books from the library for me to read. God, I missed her. My eyes burned thinking that Lilac might not even remember her in a few more years.

"You got a phone, Uncle Mason?" Lilac made a hopeful face as I brought her a coloring page that we kept for customers with kids.

"Yeah I got..." I trailed off as I thought about the things on my phone that I didn't need her seeing. I wasn't prepared for childcare duties.

"Hey, Miss Lilac." Adam came over, holding out his phone. "I got you covered. I've got all Teddy's favorite apps on here."

"Teddy? He's a *baby.*" Lilac took the phone. Adam's nephew was in kindergarten, and apparently that was a whole different world from second grade.

"Say thank you," I prompted.

"Thank you." She grinned as she opened up some number-counting game.

"Jimmy can't make a habit of doing this," Adam told me in a low whisper. He was one of the few friends to know about Jimmy and Francine's missteps and the way CPS had gotten involved in the past. It wasn't just local gossip at stake here if word got out that Francine had run off and left Lilac with Jimmy. And if he wasn't doing a good job at parenting... Well, things could get ugly in a hurry, and I sure as hell didn't want that.

"I know." We'd stepped away from Lilac's table, but I kept my voice down. "I'm happy to get a good meal into her. Lord knows that neither Jimmy or Dad can cook."

"How'd Sheriff—"

"*Sssh.*"

"Fine. *Flint.* How'd he like his food?"

"Okay, I guess. We didn't really talk." I didn't mention the conversation we'd had with our eyes. I needed to keep Flint out of my head, focus on Lilac, hold my crazy family together, and not piss off Adam and Logan. Those were the important things, not all the unsaid words with Flint.

TEN

Nash

I was being a big chicken, avoiding Mason. A big *hungry* chicken. So on Friday, I went to the tavern for a late lunch before I had to head out on patrol. I rehearsed in my head what I should say to Mason—I probably owed him some sort of apology.

As I'd expected, the place was all but empty, and I headed to my regular table.

"Chief." Mason was in front of me before I'd even finished sitting down. "Your usual?" His eyes were wary, and he sounded remote. Distant. I craved his typical easy good humor far more than I would have thought possible.

"Yeah, that's fine. Listen, Mason—"

"I'll get that order in and get your tea." Mason was gone before I could launch into my rehearsed speech.

He returned with my tea but disappeared again quickly. Had I really spooked him so badly? Fuck it. Maybe kissing had been a mistake, but I missed the

93

tentative friendship we'd been growing the past few weeks, missed our easy banter. When he returned with my burger and salad, I wasn't going to let him get away so fast.

"Sit," I ordered as he set the food down. "Join me."

"I probably shouldn't…" Mason's eyes darted around again, and I followed his gaze to a table in the dining area's back corner. A pillar partially concealed the table, but I was able to see a small blond girl perched on the edge of the booth's seat. A pink paperback book and a plate of fries were occupying her attention.

"That Jimmy's kid?" I asked, even though Mason's guilty look told me everything I needed to know. I'd heard that Francine, Jimmy's on-again-off-again girlfriend, had run off probably on another bender. "Everything okay at home?"

"Yeah." Mason glanced back at her.

"Francine split town?" I pitched my voice so it wouldn't carry back to the kid. Francine and Jimmy had a long history of piss-poor parenting choices, and I wouldn't put it past Jimmy to push the kid off on Mason. And if Francine was having trouble with sobriety again, that didn't bode well for anyone. "If Jimmy's not up—"

"He manages." Mason's shoulders were stiff, and I had the strangest urge to rub them. I was not a touchy-feely guy, and offering sympathy over the fucked-up situation that was Mason's family was an entirely new impulse for me, but there I was, wishing he'd sit, wishing he wouldn't keep looking at me like I was an enemy who wanted to disrupt his family. But instead, he kept his stony expression. "*We* manage."

"They can't let it all fall on you," I said reasonably.

There had been a world-weariness to that *we* that told me that a lot was indeed falling to him, and he'd never admit to it. I'd seen his car headed up Butte more than a few times in the past few weeks, and I'd overheard Ringer mentioning that they had leftovers for Mason's family. I knew the Hanks clan—they'd be leaning hard on Mason now that he was back and with a source of income to boot.

"Is there a city code I'm breaking? Having her here? My mom used to keep me back at that same table, and your dad—the one you get all those rules from—never said a word."

"Good Lord, Mason. I don't want to haul you in." I managed to keep my voice low, but just barely. "I just feel bad for you. That's allowed, isn't it?"

Mason shrugged. "I don't want your pity."

"No one said anything about pity. How about some good old-fashioned neighborly compassion?"

Mason leaned in, voice the barest of whispers. "We both know there's nothing *neighborly* between us, Flint. But thanks."

"There could be." I met him whisper for whisper, glare for glare, not wanting to acknowledge the memory of the kiss flashing in his eyes, trying to tell him with my return gaze that friendly was all this could ever be.

"F—*heck.*" Mason scrubbed at his short hair. "Sorry. It's not you. It's just...everything." His shoulders slumped. The urge to wrap him up in my arms was both startling and overwhelming. Mason was having a bad day and I wanted to make it better.

"Sit," I offered again, gentler this time.

"I—"

"Uncle Mason?" The girl's young voice sang out across the room.

"I've got to go." Mason's eyes lingered on the empty chair as he backed away to tend to his niece and probably pacify Ringer while he was at it. Mason had a huge load on his strong shoulders, and I found myself wishing I could lighten that load, even if it was just for a little while. Make it easier for him.

It was another new feeling for me. Even with Steve, he'd had his life and I'd had mine and keeping our friendship as uncomplicated as possible had been my priority. I hadn't had much opportunity—or inclination, if I was being totally honest—to turn a bad day around for him. But I had that desire with Mason.

Only problem was that I had no idea what I could do. I knew next to nothing about kids, There was only so much extra money I could leave as a tip before Mason's pride would protest. I stewed on this while I ate and still hadn't figured it out when he cleared my plate and ran my card, head still down and shoulders still stooped, not inviting conversation.

I fiddled with the pen for long moments. Then I did something I'd probably regret and dashed off my cell number at the bottom the receipt. *If you need anything, call. ~N.*

I left before I could second-guess myself, watching through the window to make sure that it was him and not Ringer who collected the receipt. He wouldn't call, of course, and it was beyond stupid to give out a number that I worked very hard to keep private, but somehow not doing anything felt worse.

Mason

I didn't call Flint. Nash. Whoever the hell he was when he was nice to me. I didn't call him because I couldn't break family loyalty and vent about the Lilac situation to him, couldn't share how Jimmy's repeated requests for childcare help, not to mention cash and food, were straining things with Logan and Adam, and I sure as heck couldn't shoot the breeze with Flint when small talk was the last thing I wanted from him.

No, I wanted to lose myself in his embrace, grant myself a few mindless hours away from all the worries churning in my brain, but he'd made it clear that wasn't on the table. Instead, I had a stack of bills for the tavern to work my way through, limited cash to pay them, a prescription for Dad to fetch later on in the day because Jimmy couldn't come up with the funds, and a half-empty dining room saying that all those financial pressures weren't going to get any easier.

Back in Portland, I'd have gone to the gym, lost myself in a good workout, maybe hit a bar after with friends. I wasn't one to need a huge crowd or big party, but I'd had a routine in Portland, and I hadn't anticipated how moving back, even with my best friend right here, would be so lonely and isolating. And I was still readjusting to the small-town fishbowl of everyone knowing my business.

"No kid today?" Logan asked when I came into the kitchen to get a slice of cheesecake for some of our last customers on a sleepy Tuesday night. "Surprised Jimmy didn't show up again."

"Look, I know it's been stressful having her here. I'll talk to Jimmy."

"You need to do that, Mase. It's not right how they take advantage of you." Logan was a mild-mannered guy most of the time, but he could be plenty stern when he wanted to be.

"They don't," I protested even though it was true. I'd taken more food out to the house yesterday, done laundry and cleaned the kitchen while I was there. Nothing was going to bring my mother back, nothing was going to make up for all the years I'd spent away, but somehow doing what I knew she'd want made me feel calmer. I'd opened my mouth to try to explain this to Logan, when, from outside the kitchen door, there was a loud crash and the sound of shattering glass.

We ran into the dining area. The front window was cracked, a huge hole in the bottom half. Glass shards littered the front tables, which thankfully had been empty. A large rock sat on the floor in the middle of the worst of the glass pieces.

"What the fuck?" I wasn't sure which of the three of us spoke. Adam, Logan, and I all rushed to the busted window.

"I called 911," one of the customers yelled, breaking me out of my stupor. I glanced around to make sure everyone was okay, literally shuddering with relief when folks assured me nobody had been hurt. Adam and Logan stood slack-jawed next to me, and the few remaining customers beginning to cluster behind them.

"I'll get a broom," Adam said.

"No." Logan put a hand on his arm. "We need to let the police get a look at everything first."

Fuck. I did *not* want to have to deal with Flint on top of this mess, but at least at this time of night it was likely to be one of the other officers. I'd have a better chance of hiding how much this was freaking me out with one of them. Because I *was* freaking even as I tried to project calm. I kept scanning the crowd, sure we'd missed an injury, heart beating faster every time my gaze landed on the gaping hole in the window. Fuck. The tavern was supposed to be a safe place for people, and now that illusion was shattered just as surely as the glass.

My luck was shit, and Flint came tearing into the lot minutes later, lights on the Jeep flashing as he pulled parallel to the building. His long strides had him inside the tavern quickly, and he surveyed the scene with obvious authority, filling the doorway with his broad frame. I hated myself for the frisson of relief that coursed through me at the sight of him.

"Anyone hurt?" he called.

"No." My eyes flittered around the space for the thousandth time.

"Our insurance is going to go through the roof," Logan moaned.

"And we'll have to put up some ugly-ass plywood for God knows how long." Adam's face flamed red like he needed someone to pound. I shared that impulse.

Crouching low, Flint examined the area in front of the window, shining his flashlight over the debris. "No note," he said. "I'll check outside for any additional evidence. No one touch anything." He was all business, which was good, I guessed. It was stupid of me to yearn for a hug right then—Flint wasn't the type, and I was a grown man, not some little kid.

By the time he made it back inside, large plastic bag in one gloved hand, I'd pulled myself together with some of the deep-breathing exercises I used to stave off asthma attacks. Excitement over, the customers had filtered out until it was just the three of us and Flint in the tavern.

"Find any clues?" Logan asked. "This is a hate crime, right?"

"Slow down." Flint carefully bagged the rock. "I can't say one way or the other on the type of crime. We've had a lot of vandalism around here lately, and most of it has targeted long-standing businesses."

"You wouldn't take it seriously if someone did have it out for us." Adam stared down Flint, apparently having decided he was an appropriate recipient of his anger.

Flint raised his eyebrows at Adam but kept his tone as calm and collected as ever. "If there's evidence of a hate crime, then I'll be all for charging it that way, but I'm not going to leap to conclusions here. There will be a thorough investigation, I promise."

"I'm going to make some calls," Adam said. "See who might know something—"

"You're going to do no such thing." Flint's voice was stern. "No vigilante justice. You think of suspects or people I need to talk to, you call the station." His eyes landed on me. "And that goes for family members, too. No letting Jimmy go off half-cocked about this, okay?"

Flint thinking I had that kind of control over Jimmy deserved a laugh. And Jimmy was far from my protector —hell, chances were equally high that one of his so-called friends was behind this, another bored evening gone out of control.

"Fine." Adam didn't sound too convinced.

"Now what?" Logan asked.

"Well, first step is to clean this up best we can for tonight. Any of you got a source of plywood or plexiglass you can use on the hole?" Flint was, as always, a man with a plan.

"There's got to be something at my mom's," Adam said. "She's always doing renovations. She'll have something we can use."

"I'll go with you," Logan offered. "Help you gather supplies."

"I'll sweep up here and let Flint finish his investigation," I said. One of us was going to have to stay behind, and I'd just as soon not deal with Adam and his fuming. It had nothing to do with wanting to be alone with Flint, or so I told myself.

Adam and Logan headed out, and I fetched the broom and dustpan while Flint poked around some more. He took pictures from different angles with a small pocket camera. Following his lead, I did the same with my phone in case we needed pictures for the insurance company.

"Careful now. Don't cut yourself." Flint straightened as I started sweeping.

"I can handle it." I managed a bitter laugh. "Jimmy and Freddy broke enough windows playing ball as kids. I've got glass cleanup down."

"Easton and I busted a few in our time." Flint nodded. "He had a hell of an arm."

"I bet. Word is that you were something on the baseball field back in high school, too."

"I was all right." Flint shrugged, smile tugging at his mouth. Deep lines bracketed his eyes, and I finally escaped my own concerns enough to notice how exhausted the man seemed.

"What are you doing out tonight, anyway?"

"Holmes was working a traffic accident. Nasty one. I was backing her up by re-routing cars when the call came in about your place. I checked to be sure that she had everything handled then headed here." He rubbed the back of his neck. "Long damn day."

"Did you eat yet?" I tried to make quick work of the sweeping. "I can cook you something. Logan's not the only one who can cook a burger."

"I'll be okay." Stooping down, he steadied the dustpan for me. "I better get back to the station, be there in case Holmes needs to debrief about the accident."

Who will be there when you need to talk? I wanted to ask but didn't. The urge to be that person for him ate at me, made me want to rub his tense neck, get him to talk. But close on the heels of that urge was one to kiss him senseless, take solace in each other, and that wasn't happening. "Coffee for the road?" I said instead.

He nodded. "I'd be obliged. You going to be okay on your own until the guys get back?"

I bristled at the notion that I might need taking care of, even if part of me wanted him to stick around. "I'll be fine. I'll finish cleaning up before they get back."

I abandoned my sweeping to pour him coffee from the carafe Adam had behind the bar. It wasn't the freshest this time of night, but it was the best I could do. An espresso machine was on our wishlist. That might have to wait depending on what the insurance said about the window.

"Okay. You call if you need anything—even if you

hear a strange noise or something. Don't take chances."

"I won't," I assured him as I passed him a to-go cup. A jolt of electricity zoomed up my arm as our fingers brushed. Nope. Definitely not calling Flint. I refused to need this man in spite of my body clamoring for him.

Flint headed out, and I cleaned until Adam and Logan came back. The three of us patched up the window as best as we could. Adam was right. It did look like ass, but at least it was secure. Adam had to be talked out of going all mountain man and sleeping at the tavern in case the vandals came back.

"Flint would have a fit if you use your hunting rifle for anything other than going after Bambi in season," I warned him.

"God forbid we do something Flint doesn't like." Adam rolled his eyes.

"Go home, Adam. Get some rest. Tomorrow I'll handle all the insurance stuff." I ushered him out to his truck, Logan following along behind us.

"You take care of you, too," Logan said as he swung into the passenger seat.

I wasn't sure how to do that—I was too keyed up to relax by the time I got home. I lifted my free weights until my arms burned, took a shower, and pulled on a pair of shorts before heading to the kitchen. I was contemplating food when there was a knock at the door.

Fuck. If it was Logan come to tell me that Adam had done something stupid...

But it wasn't Logan. Or a family emergency. It was Flint, standing on my porch, not in uniform, no truck or Jeep in sight. Every denial I'd been making about not needing this man went up in smoke as I opened the door.

ELEVEN

Nash

I had no clue what I was doing on Mason's front porch. His lights had been on when I'd headed home after talking with Candace, who had, indeed, needed to debrief. The traffic accident she'd handled had necessitated a call to life-flight. But seeing Mason's lights on wasn't the same as an invitation to intrude, and I'd pulled into my own driveway, forced myself to go inside and change and shower.

I hadn't been able to get him off my mind. The broken window had obviously rattled him. And he wasn't angry like Ringer or quietly stoic like his chef friend. No, as always, Mason wore his worries on his sleeve, putting his business, customers, and friends before himself. But his jerky movements and need to be useful said he was struggling inside. Hell if I knew how to make it better for him.

I didn't want to make it worse, so I hadn't let myself

add to his to-do list and had turned down his offer of food. Staring at the contents of my freezer, I was struck again with wondering if he was okay. Going to the window, I glanced down the street. The house Mason was renting was the smallest on the block, set farther back from the road with a scraggly lawn and wide, welcoming porch. His lights were still on. And before I knew what I was about, I pulled on shoes and headed down the block. The fact that I hadn't driven made it hard to pretend this was official business, but I tried to cling to that illusion as I waited for him to open the door.

"Something new wrong at the tavern?" Mason's raised eyebrows said that he knew there wasn't, but he'd let me have that pretense as he held the door open, ushered me into the house.

"No, everything's fine. I drove by there on my way home. I just wanted to see how you were doing." I played it casual, like checking on him in the middle of the night was something I did all the time. The small entrance hall opened up into a living room that was almost bare—only a single couch and an end table with a lamp. No art or pictures on the wall. I'd been in his parents' place before, and cluttered didn't even begin to describe their property. I guessed that minimalism might be Mason's grand rebellion.

"I'm good." Mason looked me up and down. "You still haven't eaten yet, have you?"

"I'm okay," I lied, willing my stomach not to growl. The rest of me was close to growling for a whole different reason—Mason was shirtless. The only thing he had on was a pair of stretchy shorts. Damp hair said that he too had recently showered. But it was his chest that mesmerized me—far fuzzier than I would have expected and as muscular as those biceps of his. His nipples were a deep tan color and pebbled from the night air.

"No, you're not." Mason jerked his thumb for me to follow him to the kitchen. "I was just about to make myself something anyway. You good with an omelet?"

"Could be." I didn't want to sound too eager for him to feed me. The kitchen was a narrow, L-shaped room with an eating nook on one end and what looked like the original 1950s cabinets. The stove was probably about that old, too, but Mason slapped a space-age looking stainless steel pan on the burner and set to collecting ingredients from a fridge that didn't match the other appliances.

He tossed me a plastic bag that held the same bread he served at the restaurant. "Can I trust you with the toaster?"

"You can trust me." I hoped I wasn't lying. I owned three toasters because I kept buying new ones, hoping something different would stop me from burning things. Then Mom had gifted me a toaster oven that required an engineering degree to operate but looked nice enough on my counter. I glanced around Mason's kitchen and had to stifle a groan.

Sure enough, he owned the same MIT-level toaster oven, just waiting to confound me. He must have sensed my apprehension because he turned from cracking eggs. "Here. I'll do it. It's...tricky."

Smiling slyly, he made it appear like no such thing, getting the toast arranged just so and the toaster counting down like a rocket launch, all while he kept whisking the eggs with his other hand.

"You have plates? I can manage setting the table."

"Cabinet over here." Mason pointed to the corner cabinet next to where he stood at the stove.

Heck. Now if I wanted to be helpful, I was going to have to get all up in his personal space, which was…

Exactly what you came over for.

No. I'd come over to check on him. And yeah, on my walk over, I might have entertained the idea of him greeting me wordlessly with another of those soul-melting kisses and nature simply taking its course from there. But he hadn't gone that route, not that I was surprised.

This whole meal-sharing thing was not what I was prepared for, and since Mason wasn't acting like a guy up for kissing, I wasn't sure how to handle myself.

Coming up behind him to grab the plates, I tried hard to avoid brushing his body. But at the last second, Mason turned, and there we were, face-to-face, chest-to-chest.

"Hi." Mason grinned at me, a smile full of sin that said he knew exactly what I'd been thinking—hoping—coming here. He brushed a kiss across my cheek before returning to the eggs on the stove, normal as could be. "You're seriously cute all flustered."

Huh. Guess he *was* up for kissing. But…

"I can hear you thinking, Nash. Set the table," he ordered. I'd been right. My name did sound good on his lips, and it had been far, far too long since I'd been simply Nash, the slightly confused, more than a little turned-on man, and not Flint the figurehead.

I put the plates on the table and found silverware in

the drawer closest to the table. In surprisingly short order, Mason produced an omelet that smelled of sausage and sharp cheese, and he rescued the bread just in time, all with the effortless ease of a man at home in his kitchen. Dividing the omelet in half, he served us before taking the seat opposite me.

He took a deep breath, and I hoped like heck that he wasn't about to say grace. I hadn't had that ritual since Dad, and I didn't really want to associate Mason with *those* memories.

"Why'd you really come, Nash?" he asked instead, and for a second, I almost wished he'd gone with the prayer.

"To check on you," I answered automatically.

"Yeah...but why?"

"Because I needed to." Hell. He had me all frustrated. Man was lucky he was all the way across the table or he would have found himself thoroughly kissed.

"Do you need to...do this often, then?" His voice was too carefully pitched to be casual.

I finally got what he was after. He wanted to know if I made a habit of coming on to people. "No," I answered truthfully. "Never on duty, rarely locally, and never with someone who drives me as nuts as you do."

This seemed to please him, and he nodded, blushing.

Kryptonite, I tell you. If I hadn't already been gone on him, that blush would have done it.

"Thanks," he mumbled before tucking into his food.

The omelet was perfection—crispy sausage pieces, creamy cheese, fluffy eggs with just the right amount of seasoning. "Tell me how you did this," I asked, both to break the silence and because I **want**ed to know. Mason talking food was quietly addictive.

"You really curious or you just being polite?" He laughed as he broke off a piece of toast.

"I want to learn more. Who knows, you might inspire me to try cooking something for myself sometime."

"I'll happily give you lessons. Any time you want to figure out how to make the basics, you just give me a call. Everyone should have at least **one** go-to late-night meal that doesn't come from a box."

I coughed at that because all my late-night meals came from boxes and he knew it. The idea of coming over here more often, letting Mason show me his tricks, was more than a little seductive. "Not sure that's a good idea," I muttered.

"Sure it is." His grin was damn near lethal, the way it poked at me, made me unhinged. "Now, let's start with stocking your pantry for all the things you can do with eggs..."

As he went on about the versatility of eggs, I kept thinking of all the things I wanted to do to *him*. I had a feeling we would get there before I came to my senses and headed home, and a delicious shiver of anticipation rocketed through me. I hadn't had that in forever, the knowledge that something was going to happen, but not yet, and not knowing what or when.

"I'm going to do a strawberry-rhubarb pie this week," Mason said when he was done with his ode to eggs. "You want to come by early some day, maybe before you have to be on duty? I'll show you how easy pie crust is."

Regret coursing through me, I shook my head. It was a pretty picture, him teaching me how to do a pie, us rolling out dough together, but that was all it could be—a picture. "I'll be sure to order a piece," I said.

Mason sighed like he was disappointed for me, and I supposed I was, too.

"How bad was the accident?" he asked as he mopped up some melted cheese with his toast.

"Bad. Driver will live, but we had to get the firefighters there with the jaws of life." I had no one that I talked shop with, and discussing details with him made my chest thump. Discussing his life and food stuff was easier. "Candace—Holmes was shaken up. She was first on the scene. But we spoke, and I told her she did all the right things."

"Who do *you* share with when you've had a bad day?" His head tilted, and his voice was so full of compassion I almost couldn't stand it.

"I don't. No need to spill my guts." It wasn't exactly a lie—I kept my bad days tucked in close against me, the weight pushing down on my shoulders until I sorted myself out, but something about Mason made me wish I were wired a little differently, made me wish I was more of talker. Or that I had a listener... But that way lay madness, so I pushed the thoughts aside.

Omelet done, I took my plate to the sink without looking at him. The old-fashioned kitchen didn't have a dishwasher, so I grabbed a sponge and the soap.

Mason added his plate to the sink and grabbed a towel to dry. I'd never done something so...*domestic* before. Steve and I never had much time for shared food, and none of my other rare, brief encounters were much interested in doing the dishes.

I made quick work of the plates and silverware, and

he got them dry and back in their spots. "You're a bit of a neatnik, aren't you?" I asked.

His kitchen was almost spartan—exactly four white plates and four matching forks and a tidy row of three pans on the pot rack.

"Guilty." He shrugged. "You know my family. I swore up and down I'd live differently when I moved out of my folks' place. It used to drive Felipe nuts how I never wanted to buy anything or keep clutter. But I refuse to turn into them."

I didn't like hearing about this Felipe one bit. "You're not going to turn into your family," I said firmly. "You're already made better choices than most of them put together."

"You really think so?" His smile this time was slow and cautious.

"Yeah." I dried my hands on the towel hanging from a hook by the sink and let myself do what I'd been dying to do since I'd looked out my window and spotted his lights. I turned him to face me, hands on his broad shoulders. God, his skin was so warm and soft. Freckles dotted his shoulders and, just like his blush, the sight drove me crazy. "You're a good man, Mason Hanks."

I wasn't talented with pretty words and off-hand compliments, so that was the best I had, but apparently it was acceptable because Mason smiled wider and looped his arms around my neck. "So are you."

I might have been broader, but we were almost the same height. It was nice looking into his eyes, seeing him telegraph his intent right before he grazed his lips across mine.

That first kiss had been all me, all my pounding drive

for control and need to claim him like some crazed caveman. This kiss was the polar opposite, tender and slow and full of finesse as he led the way. He tasted salty at first, but that quickly gave way to the same addictive flavor I remembered from the first time. His lips were soft and surprisingly full, and the hitch in his breath right before he deepened the kiss nearly undid me.

Growling, I took back a little control, exploring his mouth with my tongue. He met me eagerly, joyfully even, sucking on my tongue in a way that made my dick pulse. I pressed him back against the cabinets, giving in to the need to rock against him.

"Oh, fuck yes." Mason tipped his head, giving me access to the column of his neck. His skin was slightly stubbly, and I welcomed the abrasion against my lips and tongue.

I hadn't come in my pants since I'd been a teen. I'd fooled around with Troy, long before he became hung up on Curtis, and I got hung up on...myself and all the limitations that went along with being me.

Mason revved me up far more than Troy or even Steve ever had, and climaxing just from rubbing on him was a definite possibly, especially the way he clung to me, meeting me thrust for thrust.

I discovered all the spots on his neck that made him gasp and moan, trying not to leave marks, but it was hard, much as I needed him.

"Not enough." Mason worked a hand between us, working my belt like a man who knew what he wanted, and damn if that confidence wasn't sexy enough to have me groaning. "Fuck, Nash. Should have figured you'd be packing."

I was not one to preen at dick compliments, but my shoulders lifted at that. Before I could get with the program and return the groping, Mason had my dick out and was shoving his shorts down to mid-thigh. He wrapped a hand around both our dicks and started a slow stroke. Got to love a man who wasn't afraid to go after exactly what he needed.

"Nash… God, this feels good." He was a talker, and I loved that every bit as much as his blushes and confidence. He'd gone on about me packing, but his dick was plenty meaty, a thick, uncut column pressing up against my cock, damp cockhead dragging against my own in the most blissful kind of torture.

"I wanna come," he moaned against my mouth, rucking my shirt so our bare torsos met. "Kiss me," he demanded, and his mouth met mine hungrily.

His hand sped up, but it wasn't quite enough for me —I needed to feel him. Batting his hand away, I growled, "My turn."

"Oh, fuck yes." He arched into my touch. My hand was bigger, allowing my grip to be that much tighter, and the increased friction had me moaning, too. He leaked copious amounts of precome, coating my fist, and my mouth watered with the need to taste him.

"Not gonna last," he warned. He kissed me as if I were his supply of oxygen.

"Do it," I murmured, pulling away to kiss at his jaw and neck again. "Wanna feel you go."

"Come with me. Oh, God." His voice broke. "Fuck. Gonna…"

My fist got slicker as he came in big shudders, mouth finding mine for a last desperate kiss. The kiss was what set me off. I came on a low noise, fucking into my fist, loving the way my cock slid against him, everything slippery and perfect. It felt like being tossed into the ocean from the cliffs on the southern edge of town—a long free-fall with a hard crash into a roiling ocean of sensation that knocked out my wind and rendered me stupefied.

"Oh, my God. *Nash*." Mason didn't seem to have the same trouble as me with speech. "Not sure I've ever come so hard."

I grunted my agreement, still breathing too hard to talk. Mason reached for the towel, cleaned us both off while I struggled to make sense of what had just happened.

Tossing the towel aside, he ghosted his lips across mine. "Stay. I promise my round two is a hell of a lot better than that—not that that wasn't terrific, but I've got a bed and a powerful need to get you all the way naked." He grinned at me and my chest clenched hard. God, I wanted that, but I'd given into wanting and insanity enough for one evening.

"I can't." Shaking my head, I let all my regret filter into the words. "Can't be here in the morning."

"I'll set an alarm..." Mason trailed off, obviously seeing something in my expression that inspired resignation. "Or not. This is where you get all buttoned up and distant again, right?"

I sighed, hating that he already knew me so well, hating that it had to be like this. "Yeah."

"Your loss." He adjusted his shorts and tugged down my shirt.

Yes, it truly was. Another pleading look or word from

him and I would have been a goner, following him to that bed, but Mason wasn't the begging type, and although I'd been crazy, there was a limit to my recklessness. There was only so long I could be Nash before all the weight of being Chief Flint returned, and with it, a deep sense of regret over my impulsive actions. Time to head back to the real world.

TWELVE

Mason

"No Sheriff Sexy again?" Adam asked as we went over the bar inventory together. Thursday afternoon was dead enough that we'd resorted to counting bottles.

"Probably busy." I shrugged as if I hadn't really noticed. In reality, I'd been counting the hours since Tuesday's little late-night visit. Not that I was surprised that we hadn't seen Nash.

I had been totally prepared for Nash to go all...*Flint* as soon as we both got off. In fact, the second I'd seen him on my front porch, I'd known he would bolt if I spooked him hard enough. And apparently suggesting we try that whole orgasm thing again in my bed qualified.

It had been almost surreal—one second he'd been Nash, the guy who couldn't cook and had zero flirting game and who kissed like he hadn't had it in decades. The next instant he'd been Flint again, shutting me out—

hell, Flint shut *Nash* out, too—stonewalling the parts of himself that I liked the best.

"Probably for the best. You've had enough to keep you busy what with the insurance and the window-repair people." Adam straightened a row of whiskey bottles.

"Truth." We'd had a glass-repair place come for an estimate, which, as expected, turned out to be higher than we could afford without using the insurance. Fretting over potentially higher premiums was just one more worry in a never-ending stream of concerns. What if Adam was right and we were the target of a hate crime? What if the rumors about the vandalism drove our already sparse customer base away? Could we really make a go of this business? So many people were counting on me, trusting me.

"Speaking of Flint, did you get a copy of the police report for the insurance company?"

"No, I need to do that today." I had a plan for that, actually, but I needed Adam to head out to Coos Bay to get our beer order from the brewery before I put it in action. He might be my best friend, but I didn't need him up in my love life—or lack thereof. "Speaking of to-do lists, you should probably try to beat traffic if you're going to make it to the brewery."

"Okay, okay. Wouldn't want to be pulled over for speeding." Adam dusted his hands on his jeans. Even in June he still managed to rock the plaid shirt and beard. He left for his truck, and I fished out my phone.

Sorry to bug you, but how do I go about getting a copy of our police report? ~Mason. There. No mention of Tuesday, but a bit underhanded—I knew perfectly well that I could go talk to the nice receptionist at City Hall for this business. Nash's reply was faster than I'd expected.

I'll bring one over. 20 minutes?

I smiled. I had him right where I wanted him. *I'll put in an order for your usual. Have it waiting for you. Thanks!*

I waited for him to tell me not to bother on the food, but I'd also gambled on him not having eaten and not being able to resist the offer. I fist-pumped when his reply came in. *Ok.*

It was stupid to get excited over Nash coming by and stupider still to have a plan like this. But Tuesday had only been a taste of what I wanted with him. I wanted to teach him to cook and make him laugh and get busy on an actual bed. I knew exactly how foolish anything long term between us would be, but Nash was an itch I wasn't done scratching.

I put in the order for Nash's usual burger and made the salad myself, ignoring Logan's pointed look. He wasn't as much of a teaser as Adam, thank God, and I worked fast to avoid conversation. By the time Flint strode into the still-empty dining room, I had the food waiting at his usual table.

"Your copies." He held out a manila folder.

"Thanks. That's awfully good service." I forced my voice to be teasing, not nervous.

Taking a seat, he gestured at the empty chair across from him. "Sit. We should probably talk."

I groaned even though I'd been expecting this. I flopped into the chair. "This is where you tell me what a mistake the other night was, right? And how we can't go for a repeat?"

"You're a smart man." Nash took a big bite of his burger.

Ignoring the compliment, I leaned forward. "There's no reason why we can't do that again…discreetly, of course. You can't tell me that this is out of your system already."

"Doesn't matter if it is." Nash shrugged. "It wouldn't be a good idea to start something for a whole lot of reasons."

"I'm not asking you to go steady here. But why can't we be friends? Secret friends who happen to get it on."

"I don't do friends."

"Liar." I searched my memories. Surely I'd heard of Flint having someone in town he was friendly with. His dispatcher, for certain, and he'd always been friendly enough with Everleigh and Dolly and some of the other shop owners. "You're friends with Curtis. And, hey, weren't you friends with Mr. Gabowski, the science teacher out at the high school? Thought I remembered you guys going fishing and stuff back when I was in school."

"I've known Curtis since forever." Nash gestured like that didn't really count. Then he did the most curious thing—he coughed, his neck going dusky red. "And Steve—Mr. Gabowski—was a friend, but that's long past."

I couldn't help it. My eyebrows shot up, and the words got away from me. "Oh. My. God. You were sleeping with him, weren't you? Why didn't I figure this out sooner?"

"Probably because I didn't want you to," he said levelly. "And keep your voice down, please."

"You were!" I crowed, softer now. I wasn't sure why I felt so triumphant, having uncovered this secret side to Nash. "You and Mr. Gabowski were totally a thing. What happened?"

"Steve moved to Ashland a few years back, took a better-paying job. No big drama." His flush had spread to his cheeks.

"Ha. Lying again."

Nash sighed as if he knew that I wasn't giving up until I got the whole story. Which was true. "Okay, okay. We were together a number of years. He started getting...itchy. Wanting to come out, not wanting to hide so much. I wasn't ready, wasn't going to *get* ready, so Steve left. Sent me a card last year—he's got a serious boyfriend who works at one of the theaters in Ashland. Seems happy enough, and that's all that matters, really."

"*He* might be happy, but what about you? That had to hurt, him moving on." I still remembered the pain from the time I'd seen Felipe and his new squeeze at my favorite club, not even two months after we'd broken up.

"Eh. It was what it was. No hard feelings." Nash's eyes didn't meet mine.

"Felipe and I parted amicably, but I still want his twink boyfriend to run out of hair bleach and burn every meal he tries to make. Hard feelings are inevitable."

"Which is why we can't start something, you and I. Can't have you holding a grudge against me."

"I'm not talking about years and years here. We've both been there, done that, it sounds like. I'm just talking about a casual friendship with a side of sex. No feelings involved." I wasn't entirely sure I could stick to that, but

I was sure planning to try. There was absolutely no point in getting hung up on Flint.

"Mason—"

"I'll teach you how to cook. No more microwaved meals at midnight for you." I gave him my sweetest smile.

The door jangled, and I stood.

He said, "We can't—"

"Text me," I ordered in my best facsimile of his deep, commanding voice. I walked away as if I were confident he'd do that, when in reality, I was anything but.

Nash

Text me, he said. *Just a casual friendship.* Ha, ha, ha. I wasn't some kid, falling for Mason's claims. No way was I texting him, like a teenager looking for a booty call. No, I was going to do my damn job and forget about him and appealing thoughts of repeats of Tuesday night.

I finished my food and dropped cash on the table, not wanting to give Mason another chance to make his case. As I headed out, Mason gave me a little wave from the bar area where he was getting drinks for the group that had come in.

I didn't wave back. No sense in encouraging his flirting ways, no matter how much I liked them. And I couldn't believe I'd told him about Steve—all my filters came off around Mason, and that wasn't a good thing. I spent a long afternoon doing paperwork—my least favorite part of the job, but necessary all the same.

It was just about time for a shift change when Marta called out to me. "We've got a report of some vandalism over at Dolly's Donut Shop. She's awfully distraught and asking for you. Can you go, or should I send Holmes when she gets in?"

"I'm on my way." I headed for the Jeep and sped off to the Donut Shop, which was on the other side of the square, closer to the highway. They catered to the breakfast and early lunch crowd, closing up around two. It was unusual to see a car in her lot this time of evening. The summer sun still beat down, soft light filtering across the square even though the dinner hour had passed for most of the town.

"You came. Knew I could count on you," she greeted me as I got out of the Jeep. Dolly and our family went way back. Dolly's place had been a favorite of my father's. Unlike me, he'd had a sweet tooth and favored Dolly's coffee and crullers to start his day. "Just look at what they've done. I left my checkbook here, or I might not have seen it till morning." She wrung her hands as she paced in front of the building. Despite being well into her sixties, her hair was still as blond as it had been twenty years ago, and her small frame was dwarfed by her bright pink blouse and heavy necklace.

"I see." I kept my expression neutral as I took in the huge scrawled "Cunt" on the side of the building, accompanied by some vulgar drawings. "I'm going to have to get some pictures, look for any evidence."

"Please do." She followed me back to the Jeep. "Oh, Chief, what am I going to do? People will be coming in the morning, and I don't want...they can't see that."

"Let me do my job, then we'll see about that. Power washer plus some stripper will work. Think Hal can help?"

She looked away. "He's…not well right now."

Ah. I took that to mean that her son was off the wagon again. A damn shame. I took the pictures I needed for evidence, and, as I'd expected, I didn't find anything else worth keeping—no paint cans or left-behind possessions.

"I just can't stomach this." Dolly started weeping in earnest. "Everyone will see."

"Let's get a call in to Leroy." I patted her arm as I pulled out my phone. Leroy was a general handyman and an all-around good guy who'd handled graffiti issues for some of the other businesses, but unfortunately, he didn't answer his phone.

I exhaled a silent groan. I'd suspected where this night was going the second I'd seen the graffiti. "Plan B," I said, keeping my voice light. "I've got a pressure washer in the garage. Let me finish out this shift, then I'll run home. Be back in a bit and we'll get this taken care of."

"You're a good man, Chief. Just like your father. He'd be proud." She beamed at me. That was *not* what I needed to hear right then, not when I could still hear Mason's voice offering up similar praise under far different circumstances, not when the last thing I wanted was to be like my father. I was so tired of having to live up to his image.

But it was no time for grumbling. Instead, I made sure the station was squared away, then headed home, changed to work clothes, and grabbed the power washer and some of the graffiti stripper that Dad kept for things just like this. Few hours later, the sun had set and I was a sweaty mess, but the wall was clear, probably as clean as it had been in thirty years.

Dolly offered me whatever I wanted on the house, but I'd never developed the stomach for her coffee, and I just didn't have an appetite for a dinner of sweets. So I was starving when I yet again turned onto my street. My gaze drifted to Mason's place without my permission. His car was in the driveway, and lights were on in the house. Nope, not stopping.

I headed straight for my shower instead. Images of Mason and what we'd gotten up to in his kitchen assaulted me as the hot water pelted me. Predictably, my dick hardened, but I ignored it. I wasn't opposed to jacking off, but it wasn't something I indulged in on the regular. The way I saw it, there wasn't any sense in building up an appetite for what I couldn't have.

After the shower, I padded into the kitchen. Only thing that sounded good was some eggs. I glanced at my phone on the counter. *What would it hurt?*

Before I could think the better of it, I texted Mason. Not for a hookup. Only a simple question. *How much oil do you put down for scrambled eggs?* It sure would be nice if I could do better than the sticky mess I usually made of eggs.

Mason's reply was near instantaneous. *Come over and I'll show you.*

Can't. I resisted the urge to add one of those ridiculous frowning faces to the message.

Another fast reply made my phone buzz. *I'm putting bacon on, and the side door's unlocked. I've got plenty of eggs for your lesson. Come over.*

Bacon. I'd never once cooked that without a house

full of greasy smoke and a skillet full of little black husks that might have been meat once upon a time. Man, did I love a good slice of bacon. However, I could *not* have Mason thinking that he could order me around.

One lesson, I typed out, already going for my shoes.

His reply arrived right as I locked up the house. *For now ;)*

Taking the back alley, I went to his side door, which was far less exposed than his front porch. Calling myself ten kinds of fool, I rapped on the door.

"Unlocked," Mason reminded me as he ushered me in. He was shirtless again, wearing another pair of those maddening shorts, this time in red.

"Not safe to leave things unlocked."

"I've got my own personal police protection." He grinned at me, and my brain waged a war on how I should greet him. We both knew I wasn't there only for eggs, but he flitted back to the stove before I could stop dithering about whether to kiss him or not.

"You're thinking again, Nash," he scolded, waving a spatula. "Now, get over here and learn how to do bacon."

"You better remember how bossy I'm letting you be when I'm fucking you through the mattress later."

His laugh was exactly what I needed. God, joking with him felt so right that it made my chest ache. "That a promise?" He stuck his tongue out at me, just daring me to kiss some sense into him, show him who was really in charge.

But before I could, he started in on a lecture about metal tongs and checking the bacon and medium heat and a bunch of other things that all ran together as I cataloged the freckles on his shoulders. He smelled like minty soap and had a little smear of shaving cream on his neck. I flattered myself, thinking he'd gotten ready for me.

"Nash. You're not listening." He turned, brushing his body against mine.

"Nope." I reached around him, flipped the burners off. I at least knew enough to put safety first, and I scooted the pans off the heat. The whole while I never broke eye contact with Mason, letting him know exactly what I had planned for him. He shivered as I backed him against the cabinets. God, I loved that, loved the anticipation in his eyes right before I kissed him.

He met my mouth eagerly but seemed content to let me lead, going pliant in my embrace. I kissed him like it had been years, not days, sampling his lips both like the first time and like we'd been doing this forever. I already knew what he liked—little nibbles and just enough teeth to make him shiver again—and I exploited that knowledge until he moaned against my mouth.

"Mason?"

"Yeah?" he replied dreamily.

"Show me to your bed. Now."

THIRTEEN

Mason

I did want to teach Nash how to cook. But one look at his determined expression had me grabbing his hand and pulling him to the rear of the house and into my bedroom. I kept the space as sparely furnished as the rest of the old place, finding comfort in the clean modern lines of my bed and white bedding. The only other furniture was the lone matching nightstand.

Nash didn't comment on the décor. Instead, he tugging me close for another blistering kiss.

"Did you mean your threat?" I whispered against his lips.

"I don't threaten." He ran his hands up and down my bare sides. "Only promise." He kissed me again then pulled back with a frown. "But do you have supplies? Because I really was just coming to cook—"

I snorted because that was *such* a lie. "I've got stuff." I opened the drawer of the nightstand, tossed what we'd need on the bed. I'd made a special trip to Coos Bay earlier in the week because no way in heck was I trusting Hauser's Grocery with my personal business.

"Fancy." Nash picked up the condom box, turned it around.

"Latex allergy," I explained. The detail guaranteed I'd always been damned picky about who I did this with, but the second Nash had kissed me in the alley, I'd wanted this with him.

"Anything else I should know?" The tone of his question was serious. And he was looking at the condom box like it might have snakes it.

"I'm ticklish." I tugged at his shirt. "And I hate waiting to unwrap my presents."

"I'm your present?" He sounded doubtful but let me get the shirt off him.

"Oh, yeah." I grinned at him, an obvious leer to make him smile before I went in for a kiss. Some things in life were just meant to be ogled, and Nash Flint's chest certainly qualified—strong, broad, surprisingly tan with rosy nipples, and a lot of delicious fuzz including a trail that lead straight to his zipper, which was where I was heading next.

Still kissing him, I undid his belt one-handed. I knew from the other night that we needed to seriously up his underwear game. But as long as the very basic cotton boxer briefs hit my floor in the next twenty seconds, I didn't really care.

He helped me out by kicking off his shoes as I pushed down his pants. But before I could admire Nash naked, he was shoving at my shorts, hissing when he figured out that I'd gone commando after my shower.

"Fuck. *Mason.*" Tone almost reverential, his eyes seemed to drink me in. In a single smooth move, he sank to his knees in front of me. And I could live to a hundred and three and never forget the sight of Nash Flint on his knees, rubbing his face against my cock.

He didn't give me time to adjust to this new reality where Nash-freaking-Flint was going to suck me. No. He was already licking my shaft with long, purposeful strokes. Nash didn't tease or torment, just went straight for what he wanted, all business as he swallowed me down. His strong hands gripped my hips as he started a slow, steady rhythm. I was glad for his grip—it kept me from floating to the ceiling. Gradually, one of his hands swept around to stroke up and down my crack, deliberate strokes of his broad fingers.

"*Yes.*" The combination of his hot mouth, the sight of him doing this for me, and those devilish fingers had me skating far too close to the edge far too fast. Nash didn't make it any easier when he removed his hand only to have it return with slick fingers, all while never losing his rhythm on my cock. Fingers grazing my rim, he had me panting and my balls tingling.

"Unngh. Nash. Don't wanna…"

"Then don't." He pulled back long enough to wink at me, cocky bastard. "Bed. Now. On your knees."

I wasn't usually one to take orders in bed, but something about Nash's firm voice made my cock throb and my pulse hum. I complied, tossing the comforter to the floor as I climbed onto the bed. I got on my hands and knees, and Nash was there in an instant, kissing down my spine. His fingers were back to torture me, circling my rim in a way that had me shivering all over again. He took his time before pressing inside, slippery fingers heading straight for my gland. Felt good, but I rocked impatiently.

"Just go," I urged. I'd never liked prep much—I liked the actual fucking, loved having been fucked, but the getting started business was always something I'd just as soon fast-forward through. My body didn't always cooperate, though, and I willed myself to relax as Nash took care of the condom.

Unlike a lot of my lovers, Nash seemed to get the balance I needed between hurry-up and patience, getting into position and stroking my back with his free hand. "Rock back when you're ready." The command in his tone had me going pliant in a way that my brain's commands hadn't managed.

"That's it." He praised each small movement of my hips, hand soothing my back. "So good."

His praise was a drug, making me bolder, and I took him deeper and deeper, working past the stretch to the good part where he pressed up against my gland. "Yes. That."

"Ready for more?" Nash's voice was the same blend of gentle-firm as his hand on my side.

"Yeah." I arched my back. "Need it."

I moaned as he pulled back before thrusting forward again, an unerring stroke right against all the places that felt like liquid lightning.

"Feel so good." Nash's groans mingled with my own.

"Nash. Nash," I panted, searching for something—I didn't even know what.

"I've got you." His hand found my dick, matching the insistent rhythm of his hips.

I moaned again, a low, inhuman noise.

"That's it. Let me hear you." His thrusts sped up, rewarding me for each gasp and whimper. I didn't even recognize the noises coming from my mouth. The hand on my dick was sure and strong and made my hips buck, chasing more sensation. "Can you come this way?" His tone said he already knew the answer but wanted to hear me say it.

"Yes. Oh, fuck." My eyes squished shut. That wasn't always the case for me, but with Nash's unerring skills, it was more a question of holding off long enough for him to get there, too.

"Tell me what you need," he ordered.

"Harder. God. Please go harder." This needy, begging thing totally wasn't me, either, but Nash turned me inside out, made me not recognize myself. Keeping my eyes shut, I gave in to the fuck. My head fell forward, but Nash kept me from collapsing entirely. "Need you."

"That's it." His thrusts sped up, hand on my hips tilting me to the perfect angle.

"Want to come." The tingle was back in my balls and my ass tightened as everything went white hot.

"Do it." Oh, thank *fuck*. Nash didn't torture me and make me wait. His hand on my cock added a little twist on the upstroke that had my moans turning into whines.

"Nash." My whole body trembled, right there on the edge.

"Come on, Mason." The way he growled my name, forceful and plaintive at the same time, did me in. Body clenching hard, I came, wave after wave of intense pleasure that wrung me out. My rubbery limbs gave way, and I was vaguely aware of Nash's thrusts getting erratic. He wasn't loud like me, but his satisfied groan as he collapsed on me made me shudder all over again.

"Fuck. I'm squashing you." Nash pulled out gently, but I still winced. "Sorry."

He tugged me out of the damp spot I'd landed in, gathering me up in a clumsy embrace, pressing kisses to the back of my neck.

It was almost *too* sweet, so I cracked an eye open and looked over my shoulder. "My mattress appears to be in one piece. I'm disappointed."

Nash's laugh was a deep rumble that rolled through me. "Smart ass. We'll shoot for bed breaking next time."

Next time. I liked the sound of that far more than I should, which was dangerous.

"And, hey, you promised me food. I'm the one who should be pouting." Nash shoved at my side which only made me burrow into him more.

"I'll feed you, but I really need a quick shower first. I'm pretty sure that I don't trust you with my kitchen while I get clean, so you better come, too." I smiled at him like my command had nothing to do with worry that he'd bolt. No, nothing like that at all.

"Shower? Together?" He gave me a bemused smile.

"New concept for you?" I sat slowly, loving the delicious ache when I moved, but what I really wanted to do was sleep for a week with Nash surrounding me. That wasn't happening, though, and it was time to rejoin reality.

Nash finally gave a nod, eyes looking reluctant. "You've probably got more wild stories than me."

"It's a shower, Nash. Not an orgy." I held out a hand

to help him up then led him to the little bathroom. Nash's discomfort only seemed to grow once we were in the small space. Spa-like, it was decidedly not. Similar to the kitchen, the only renovation it had seen had been decades ago and piecemeal at best. I wished I had Felipe's Rose Quarter condo's huge bath with the walk-in shower. That might distract Nash from whatever was going on in his head.

I couldn't worry too much about that—I really did need a shower because sticky with lube was *not* my favorite sensation. Leaving Nash to wrestle with himself, I cranked the shower on and climbed in the tub, leaving the curtain open.

"Those are ducks." Nash finally said, gesturing at my cheerful yellow and blue curtain with a rubber duck motif.

"I let Lilac pick it out when I took her to the Walmart in Coos Bay." I shrugged and grabbed the soap. "I'm not really much on decor."

"I noticed." A little smile teased at the corner of Nash's mouth. Seeming to come to some sort of decision, Nash stepped in behind me. However, any fantasies I had about leisurely kissing under the water were lost to the realities of two men—one of whom seemed bound and determined not to touch—in a tiny space.

Sighing, I finished my washing, rinsed the soap, and passed it to Nash. I hopped out to give him more access to the water. Maybe someday I could introduce him to the pleasures of shower sex.

Someday. There I went again with the dangerous thinking.

"I'm putting the bacon back on," I said as I toweled off. "Take your time. I'll show you how to do the eggs when you get in there."

I pulled on a fresh pair of shorts because I somehow knew that Nash wouldn't be down with naked cooking. I put the bacon on the heat and whisked the eggs before he wandered in, back in his jeans, but no shirt. Now that was a nice surprise, even if his chest was a distraction from the task at hand.

"Sorry." He rubbed his face. "Didn't mean to get weird on you."

"You didn't." I brushed a kiss across his mouth. "Although I totally want to show you how fun a shower can be sometime." I said it casually, like we'd already agreed to a repeat. I'd known once was not going to be enough with Nash Flint, no matter how stupid doing this on the regular was.

Nash made a noncommittal noise that I decided to take as a maybe since it wasn't an outright shutdown of the idea. "Did the bacon get ruined?" he asked, peering over my shoulder.

"Nope." I launched back into the cooking lesson, trying not to enjoy the brush of his bare skin against mine too much. It was the best kind of strange, cooking together after the bed-shaking (if not bed-*breaking*) sex, feeling little twinges in my muscles to remind me of how hard we'd gone. Other than the quasi-freakout over sharing the shower, Nash seemed calmer now, and it was easy to delude myself into thinking that things could always be this natural.

"Here, you try." I handed him the spatula as the eggs started to come together in the skillet. His whisking was adorably tentative. We worked together to serve up the bacon and eggs and then ate again at my little table. I could get used to this way too easily, shirtless Nash across from me, memories of the sex dancing in my head, simple food that tasted better because it was shared.

"I should let you sleep," Nash said as we finished the dishes. "I don't want to overstay my welcome."

"You're not." I captured his mouth for a kiss that told him in no uncertain terms that I could be up for another round. But right when I felt his muscles go pliant, felt him waver about leaving, my phone rang over on the counter.

Frowning, Nash released me. I scooped up the phone, because this time of night it had to be an emergency. The screen flashed with a familiar number, and my stomach sank all the way down to the scarred linoleum. *Jimmy.*

"What?" I barked into the phone. Nash was already out of the kitchen, most likely headed in search of his shirt and shoes. *Bolting.* Just like I'd known he would.

"Sorry for how late it is."

"No, you're not." I groaned and leaned back against the counter. "What do you need?"

"I forgot that Dad has a doctor's appointment tomorrow in Coos Bay. Chester needs me —"

"Jimmy, I am not your daycare." A rustling sound alerted me to a frowning Nash heading for my side door. I couldn't stop him without alerting Jimmy that I had company. *Fuck.*

Jimmy went on about how this was a one-shot thing, the last time he'd need me, he promised, but my attention was more on Nash, who mouthed, "Text me if you need me," before slipping out the door.

If you need me... Nope. I couldn't afford to need Nash Flint, much as my body liked his. Jimmy was just one more reminder of that.

FOURTEEN

Nash

"So glad you could make it, Chief." Everleigh greeted me near the door of the visitor center. I was there for another early morning Chamber of Commerce meeting, a command appearance sparked by the latest round of vandalism. But it wasn't Everleigh's sunny smile that held my attention.

Over by the far wall, Mason was setting up a display of breads and muffins and a little sign that advertised the tavern. He wore dress clothes again, and I wasn't sure what it was, but him in a pressed shirt did something weird to my insides. Maybe it was how it made him look older, more worldly, but it could also be that it was just plain hot. The peek of skin where he'd left the collar of the blue shirt unbuttoned, the muscled forearms poking out of rolled-back sleeves, the ass—which I now knew was more muscular than it looked—defined by the khaki pants.

As if he sensed me checking him out, he turned,

giving me and Everleigh a smile. No winks. No slyness. Only his usual friendliness, suitable for casual acquaintanceship, but it still jangled me all up. The other night his smiles had been more intimate, meant for me alone, and hell if the memory of the impromptu cooking lesson wasn't equally as seductive as the memory of fucking him. I hadn't been a coward after this latest bout of insanity—I'd gone to the tavern for lunch yesterday, but Mason had been out, which left me to Ringer's brisk service.

And okay, I'd been a *bit* of a coward, leaving while Mason was on the phone, but I couldn't take the risk of that brother of his coming over. Honestly, that should have been the wet blanket on any remaining lust I had for Mason, but one sight of him standing there in those clothes with a grin that was nothing but friendly, and I was back being a prisoner to my desire for him.

Everleigh clapped her hands and called everyone to order. Mason took a seat on the opposite side of the room, and I refused to feel even one iota disappointed that he wasn't closer to me. I couldn't go thinking like that.

"As all of you know, the Fourth of July is coming. We've advertised in several regional publications this year, and we're hopeful for a big turnout." The Fourth was always a huge tourism weekend all along the coast, and while I appreciated patriotism as much as anyone else, it was one of my least favorite weeks of the year— marked increase in drunk driving, bar fights, parking violations, illegal beach bonfires, and general mayhem that had the whole department pulling long hours.

Everleigh asked for my input on our policing plans,

especially for the town fireworks celebration over at Lake Moosehead that the Chamber sponsored, and that drew my attention away from Mason. My gaze did return to him, though, when the topic changed to the vandalism spree, and I had to mention the broken window at the tavern. People were understandably nervous, and I hated that I didn't have more answers for them. For Mason whose tight eyes and furrowed brow said the matter was still weighing him down. I wanted to ease those worries in the worst way, but I managed to keep my head professional the rest of the meeting, even when Mason gave an update on the LGBTQ tourism initiative. And if I was relieved that his slick Portland friend wasn't there, well, that was simply wanting a shorter meeting, nothing to do with misplaced jealousy.

As the meeting wound up, I hung back for reasons I refused to examine, drifting closer to where Mason was packing up the leftover baked goods.

"You walk?" I asked, casually as I could muster.

"Nope. Had to drive all this stuff over." The smile he flashed me had a fair amount of regret in it, as if he knew I'd been about to offer a ride.

"That's good." Fuck. Now I didn't know what to say or do.

Mason didn't seem to suffer any such indecision. He said, "I've got a marionberry pie on the menu today. That was really popular the last time I offered it. Stop by for lunch?"

"Maybe," I hedged, keeping a professional distance between us. "You need a hand carrying this out?"

"Sure." He handed me one of two boxes. "Actually,

would you like that box for the station? I kind of over-baked for the meeting."

Marta was sure to give me heck, but I nodded. "That would be nice. I'm sure the department will appreciate it."

"Good." He paused by the door. "See you around, Flint."

Something about the way he said my name rankled—I missed being Nash, being the name he moaned in the still of the night, being the guy he teased while sitting at that little table of his. I carried my bad mood all the way back to the station, and I was about to climb out of the Jeep when my phone beeped with a message.

Enjoy the food. You off this evening? I'm off early-ish, around 8, and I've got a huge craving for pasta. Really tired of burgers and sandwiches. Come over, and I'll teach you a basic white sauce. No tomatoes.

I smiled to myself, despite all my reservations. I wasn't on duty that night, but I still had no business taking Mason up on the offer. We couldn't make a regular thing of this, even if my pasta-cooking attempts had always produced gluey lumps, even if I craved him more than any dish he might tempt me with.

I shouldn't, I typed back.

His reply was quick, and from my spot in the City Hall parking lot, I could see him lounging against his car down at the tavern. *Yes, you should, if only to reward me for behaving at the meeting. I want a medal for playing it cool.*

Like a fool, I laughed aloud at that. *A reward, huh? I think I can do better than a medal,* I replied before I could stop myself from flirting.

Prove it. See you about 8:30. Down the block, Mason

pocketed his phone and headed into the tavern, a little spring in his step, as if he knew he'd won again. Damn it.

Mason

For once I had on real clothes when I opened the door to let Nash into my house. He hadn't replied to my text, but I'd known he'd be here, eight thirty sharp, even if part of him resisted my invitation. Sure enough, he'd shown up looking freshly showered in jeans and a polo, not the uniform he'd been in earlier in the day.

"Did you bring my medal?" I asked as I opened the side door.

"You're a brat." He let the door close completely before he drew me close. His eyes showed a moment of indecision, but I wasn't having any of that and kissed him lightly before he could overthink it to death.

"Guilty." I grinned at him as I pulled him over to the stove. "I've laid out everything we'll need."

Nash rubbed his jaw as he took in my counter full of ingredients. "Ah. For cooking."

"Yes, for cooking, Nash." I kissed him again because I simply couldn't resist. "Why'd you think I invited you over?"

Nash made a sound like his lungs wanted to laugh but the rest of his body wasn't on board. "You're trouble."

"Yup." I loved teasing him like this, loved knowing that he was eager for the other part of the evening, even if he didn't want to show it. "But I'm trouble with an amazing white-pasta-sauce recipe."

Nash's eyes narrowed. "Am I going to need to take notes?"

"Nope." I handed him an onion. "Can you chop this while I do the sausage?"

Nash nodded. He chopped like a nervous surgical resident—slow and careful with measured movements, wincing when he didn't meet whatever standards he was holding himself to.

"It's all going to cook down," I reassured him. "It's okay if they're not uniform."

"Yeah." Nash didn't stop his painstaking cuts. "It's the noodles I'm worried most about. Mine always turn into lumps."

"Lumps?" Making sure not to laugh, I chattered about salting the boiling water and cooking times as I made fast work of the meat, basil, and garlic, all local from the farm stand on the edge of town. Nash took directions surprisingly well, getting the onions sautéing in the pot with the sausage before I added the garlic and measured out the cream and already grated cheese.

"Now what?" Nash asked as I added the penne to the boiling water and turned the sauce down to the barest of simmers.

Before I answered, I set a timer for the pasta. "Now we have precisely eleven minutes to burn." I looped my arms around his neck. "Any suggestions?"

"Eleven minutes isn't even a start," Nash growled before nipping at my ear.

"Wanna bet?" It might not be enough time for the sort of epic fucking Nash had delivered last encounter, but it was plenty for what I had in mind.

"Not sure I want to win that bet." Nash groaned as my fingers found his belt. "Should make you wait—"

"But you won't." I pushed him against the counter opposite the stove before sinking to my knees in front of him. I'd been dying to get my mouth on him, doubly so since he'd sucked me last time we'd been together. He'd been damn good, and I was determined to show him that I was, too.

"Ah…you don't have to…" Nash sputtered as I undid his fly.

"I'm already here." Winking at him, I drew out his cock. Heavy and thick with long veins wrapping around the shaft, he smelled like woodsy soap and musk, and I couldn't wait any longer for a taste, tongue swiping at his tip, chasing his unique flavor.

"Don't tease," Nash ordered, voice deeper and gruffer now.

"But it's fun." I flicked my tongue along the underside of his cock, learning all the places that made him curse and shudder.

"Come on now." Nash wrapped a fist around the base of his cock, rubbing the cockhead across my eager lips. Oh, yes, I liked him all bossy and seizing control. I sucked the head in, still teasing with my tongue, starting a shallow rhythm as he jacked the base of his cock. His other hand landed on the back of my head, gently guiding me to the deeper strokes he wanted.

"That's it," he groaned. "So good."

I was fast becoming addicted to his praise, and I redoubled my efforts, using my tongue to milk the shaft on the upstroke.

"Can you take more?" His hand left his cock, coming down to rub my shoulder.

"Yeah." I pulled back long enough to answer him. "Fuck my mouth."

He moaned and his grip tightened as he drew my head closer. I didn't trust many guys with this level of control, but Nash wasn't going to choke me, wasn't going to push me further than I wanted to go. And I desperately wanted to get him off before the timer dinged, wanted to earn more of that husky praise.

Relaxing my throat, I let him ease forward, sucking hard as he withdrew and welcoming his return.

"Mason," he growled, holding my head almost tenderly as he thrust. "So fucking good."

"Faster," I urged as he pulled back. "I can take it."

"Yeah, you can." His head fell back, eyes closing. "So beautiful."

He went a bit deeper, skirting that edge between too much and perfect. I moaned around his shaft, my hands coming to rest on his hips, following his strokes, hanging on with the last of my sanity as he took over, a fast, deep rhythm.

He'd been stoic when we'd fucked, but he was more verbal tonight, a near constant stream of muttered praise and strangled moans, and I knew he was close as his hands tightened and his sounds became more broken.

"Mason. *Fuck.* You want my come?"

I moaned my agreement, sucking harder. Yes, yes, I wanted that desperately. My own cock throbbed in my pants, but I ignored it, totally focused on getting Nash off.

"That's it. That's it," Nash chanted as the first salty

taste hit my tongue. He pushed deeper, deep enough that I had no choice but to take it, nothing to do but let him fuck, welcoming his climax as if it were my own.

Ding. Ding. Ding. The timer went off right as I pulled back to wipe my mouth.

"I win." I grinned at him before accepting the hand up he offered.

"Fuck. That darn near killed me." He shook his head. "You're something else."

"Good." Ignoring my raging hard-on, I drained the pasta and tossed it with the sauce.

"You didn't…" Nash must have noticed my predicament. "Do you want… I can…"

"Thinking too hard again, Nash." I laughed and carried the food to the table. "Not everything has to be quid pro quo. If you're up for it, though, I'm sure some…*dessert* can be arranged."

"Oh, I'll be up for it," Nash said darkly. "Not sure how wise any of this is, but I can't seem to get enough of you."

"Likewise." I leaned across the table for a fast kiss, rewarding his honesty. "Let's not over-analyze this. You're having fun. I'm having fun. Let's have fun together a little longer. Some cooking lessons. Some easy sex. Think of it as some summer fun."

Nash was quiet so long that I'd given up hope of a reply when he murmured, "I'm going to regret this."

I beamed. It wasn't exactly a yes, but it was good enough for me, good enough for right then. More evenings like this were exactly what we both needed, regrets be damned.

FIFTEEN

Nash

By ten p.m. on Sunday, July sixth, I was as tired as I'd ever been.

"Quiet?" Candace Holmes asked as she came into the station. "Finally?"

"Finally," I agreed. "There's still people at the beach, so you'll want to keep an eye on fires and fireworks there, but traffic has slowed considerably."

Sand still clung to my pants leg after a trek down to the beach to talk to some late-night revelers about fire ordinances. The weather had been perfect for the holiday weekend, and it was no wonder that people were reluctant to head back to their everyday lives. The hypnotic crash of the ocean at night and lure of a near-full moon were just too much temptation to resist.

"I'm so ready to be done with fireworks." She rolled her shoulders. "I had to give Jimmy Hanks a warning about fireworks in Rowdy's parking lot last night."

I stifled my wince at that news. Jimmy was not going

to be happy about that, which meant that Mason probably had heard an earful on the unfairness of local law enforcement. "You did the right thing there."

"Same with a noise complaint from Patsy's B&B—Adam Ringer and a bunch of his friends were doing an impromptu show for guests. I just issued a warning because I figured that was what you'd do."

"Yup." I nodded. "Lots of warnings, all weekend long. Hopefully tonight is quieter for you." *Please don't let Mason have been with them.* That was probably a futile wish, but I couldn't exactly ask Holmes for details as to who all was there, not with Marta five feet away and still up in my business over how often I ate at the tavern.

He'd been nice enough to bring in takeout from the tavern for the whole crew on the Fourth, and that was all I'd seen of him in days. Which should be a relief, frankly. Maybe even a sign that this…whatever we had going was coming to a close. We'd had that lesson on pasta, and then, later that same week, one on mashed potatoes and oven-finished steaks and another on fish. You could almost say we had a routine of cooking and fucking going before the holiday weekend blew it all to hell, and I really should have been relieved because a routine with Mason was not what I wanted.

I finished up the changeover with Holmes and headed out. Right as I pulled into my driveway, my phone chimed with a message. Lord knew I was *not* up to anything more than a hot shower and bed, but I dutifully checked just the same.

Finally home? I've got a massage with your name on it.

Now there was an offer I'd never received before. And if Mason had suggested cooking, I would have declined and not felt too guilty about it—I was simply that exhausted. But something in me hesitated about how to reply to this new offer.

Never had a massage, I finally typed. *Not sure I like them. But thanks.*

I swore I could hear him laugh from where I stood in the driveway, and sure enough, my phone dinged with a reply. *Only way to know for certain is to try one. And I'm good at it.*

His cockiness made me smile and made it harder to turn him down. Something about when he went all confident turned my crank big time. It had to be a sign of how tired I was that my resolve weakened. He was every bit as tempting for me as the beach was for those partiers, and even if like them, I'd undoubtedly have regrets come Monday morning, I was powerless to deny the pull.

Let me shower first, I quickly texted. I might not have much experience with massages, but that seemed like the polite thing to do. And no offense to Mason, but I had the far better set up at my place.

Whatever ambivalence I'd felt back at the station was quickly replaced by anticipation as I hurried to my shower. I had no idea why I let Mason wind me up like this when the only real thing I should be doing was sleeping until I had to be back on duty tomorrow. I had no business skulking down the back alley like a common criminal, yet there I was, hair still damp from the shower, shirt sticking to me from dressing hurriedly.

"You look bushed," Mason observed as he opened the door. "We were busier than we've ever been, so I knew it had to be worse for you guys."

Damn it, why did Mason have to be so nice? This

whole thing would be so much easier if he wasn't so fucking likeable. Liking someone made everything way more complicated, as I well knew from my experience with Steve, and yet I was powerless to do anything other than kiss him hello, channeling some of my frustration into pinning him against the door.

"Hey, now." Mason finally broke away. "You're going to distract me out of your massage."

"I'm good with that." I leaned back in, but he stopped me with a hand on my chest.

"Come on. I've got everything all set up in my room."

The way I saw it, massage was pretty straightforward —you rubbed around some on the other person and hoped it felt decent. But what Mason was proposing was a different beast altogether. He'd stripped the comforter off the bed and laid out some small bottles of oil and a towel next to the pillow. The lights were turned way down, and he'd lit two candles on the nightstand. Soft music played from a speaker next to the candles. It was, dare I say, romantic, and I was *not* a guy who did romance.

"I feel like I'm at that spa your friend was talking about," I grumbled to cover my discomfort.

"That's the idea. Only I'm not charging." He pushed me toward the bed. "Shirt off."

"Maybe this isn't such a good notion," I hedged.

"Nash. Just let someone do something nice for you for once, okay?" He pulled my shirt up, and I shrugged out of it on some sort of autopilot.

"Why are you being nice?" I kicked off my shoes. "I heard from Holmes that both your brother and Ringer got busted over fireworks."

149

"And what? You thought I'd be pissed about her doing her job?" Mason rolled his eyes at me. "At least Jimmy didn't get hauled in. That's all I really care about."

My stomach churned even as my neck prickled. Chances were that someday I was going to have to bring Jimmy in, and Mason wasn't going to be near this casual and sympathetic about it.

"You're doing the whole thinking thing again," Mason chided as he again shoved me toward the bed. This time I went, and I let him arrange me face down.

"Fuck." I yawned. "I might fall asleep. This was a—"

"I've already set an alarm for you, so you can sneak back before the neighborhood wakes up. Now let me work."

He really had thought of everything, and a strange kind of gratitude washed over me. I was used to being aroused around him, used to being confounded and irritated by him in turn, but being taken care of by him felt new and itchy.

Mason didn't give me much time to stew on this, though, warming up some oil in his hands and then slathering it on my back. Not able to help myself, I groaned. The oil smelled like mint and rosemary, and I knew I'd forever associate that combo with his strong hands kneading my weary muscles.

He hadn't been lying—he was damn good at this, starting with broad strokes and working up to more intense rubbing, using his thumbs to knead particularly tight knots that I hadn't even realized I had. I'd kind of expected him to rub me down fast and then get on with our usual fucking around, but Mason took his time, working my neck, my shoulder blades, even my biceps.

"How'd you get so good at this?" My voice sounded slurred.

"Dated a massage-therapy student for a while. I let him practice on me." Mason's tone was light, but I still felt the distinct prick of unwelcome jealousy.

"I can…try…" I yawned. Staying awake to return the favor was fast becoming an issue, but I never liked keeping him wanting.

"Stop it." He lightly slapped my ass. "This is a gift. Now quit worrying and just enjoy it. Going to sleep on me is totally fine."

Not wanting another slap—or worse, for him to stop —I let myself drift as Mason worked my muscles. It wasn't entirely platonic as he peppered my neck and spine with kisses every now and again, but it also lacked the urgency of most of our foreplay. It was simply…nice. More than nice, really. I couldn't remember the last time I'd felt this boneless, this at peace. My to-do list fled along with thoughts of my phone and what tomorrow might bring. All my senses zeroed in on Mason's magic hands. I was straddling that space between awake and dreaming, but I was powerless to rouse myself.

"Okay, Chief, I think you're good." Mason's hands slowed, soothing my sides before disappearing altogether. I made a grunt that might have been displeasure at the loss of his touch, and he laughed. The mattress sagged as he stretched out next to me.

"You sleeping, too?" I couldn't be bothered to open my eyes, but I did scoot over to give him room.

"Yup." He dropped another kiss on the back of my neck.

"You need..." My hand blindly fumbled for him.

"Nope. Doesn't always have to be sex." He captured my hand, wrapping my arm around him as he burrowed in against me. "But do feel free to fuck me awake when the alarm goes off."

"Will do." Yawning again, I let sleep claim me, carrying me away from thoughts of how I was in way too deep with this man, this generous man who was much more giving than I deserved.

Mason

I wasn't sure which roused me first—the buzzing clock on the nightstand or the warm arm snaking down my torso.

"Awake?" Spooning me from behind, Nash bit at my ear.

"Nope." I snuggled against him, breathing in his scent—massage oil, outdoorsy soap, and good, clean *Nash* that immediately got some blood pumping south even as my eyes stayed closed.

"You did say..." Nash's boxer-covered erection nudged against my bare ass. He'd already been most of the way to sleep when I'd stripped off my clothes and climbed in with him, and he must have lost his jeans at some point in the night.

"I did." I bumped my ass into him. "But I don't have to be awake to enjoy it."

Nash snorted. "You start snoring and I'm out of here."

"Give me a reason to wake up, then." Arching my back, I let my head fall against his shoulder.

"Anytime, sunshine." Nash's hand continued its trek down my front, palming my thickening cock. "Can I use some of your fancy oil on you?"

"Please." I reached across to the nightstand to grab the bottle. "I wanna get off just like this."

"Okay, bossy." Nash bit my neck then covered it in kisses. "Just like this, huh?"

Taking the bottle from me, he shifted around some, and when he settled back against me, he was naked with a slick dick pressing against the small of my back and a warm hand wrapping around my cock. My groan was louder than the alarm had been.

We'd fucked a number of times, enjoyed some oral, but this was something new, and in a way, it felt way more intimate than if he'd gone straight for the condoms and lube like I'd expected. Not that I was complaining—I loved the sound of his breath in my ear, the slipperiness of his grip, and the firmness of the thrusts against my back.

"Gonna have to be quick," he whispered. "You up for that?"

"Oh, yeah. Faster."

"Bossy, bossy, bossy," he chided, strokes not speeding up one iota.

"You...said...fast," I panted as he added the twist to his hand that always drove me nuts. "Please, Nash."

"Ah. There it is." He licked a tendon in my neck.

"You get off on me begging," I accused, pushing my

body tighter against him. His cock was hard and slick against my back, making my own dick throb with each movement from him.

"That I do." Nash let out a self-satisfied groan, hips speeding up even as his hand stayed maddeningly slow. "And I should make you wait. Go first then suck you off."

Much as I loved Nash's mouth, that wasn't what I wanted, and I whined my disapproval. "Want to come when you do. *Please.*"

"Mmmm." Nash made a noise like he had to think about it.

"*Nash.* Get me off. Please."

"You need me?" His free hand came around to flick at my nipple.

"Yes. God, yes. Come on me," I babbled.

"Want to hear you." Finally, *finally,* his grip tightened and quickened.

I rewarded him with a low moan, my breath coming in noisy pants. "Nash. Nash. Gonna get me off."

"Yeah, I am. That's it. So good for me. So beautiful."

His teeth grazed my shoulder, an aggressive kiss that I felt straight to my balls, and that was it for me. "Coming. Oh, God."

"Me, too." Warmth hit my back as Nash sucked harder on my shoulder. I was going to have a mark, but I couldn't give a shit. Coming felt too good. It was different than the normal stratospheric orgasms with Nash—warmer, fuzzier, like being wrapped in my favorite blanket and surrounded by all the best emotions. Emotions that I didn't want to think too much about right then—I only wanted to drift on the good feelings.

I was only marginally aware of Nash using something to rub at my back and stomach before he whispered, "Okay, I'm out of here. You need me to reset the alarm?"

Already well on my way to sleep, I grunted at him, a noise that probably sounded like no, but I was cursing a few hours later when the sun hit my eyes and I glanced over at the clock. *Late.* Logan would be pissed that I wasn't there already for the kitchen prep work.

Sure enough, he was in a mood when I got to the tavern.

"What? Was there another Chamber meeting this morning?" He gestured at my shirt.

I tried hard to hold back a blush. I'd had to go for something with a collar to hide the love bite Nash had left where my neck met my shoulder. "Laundry day," I mumbled.

"Well, whatever. I'm just glad you're here to deal with this mess. Adam's already called the police station, and you're better than me at calming him down."

"Wait. What?" My heart galloped. Had they figured out about Nash and me?

"Didn't you get Adam's text messages? Some idiot spray-painted the side of the building. The dispatcher said Nash would be over as soon as possible."

Fuck. I hurried outside where Adam was pacing in front of the far side of the building. "Fag" was painted in a giant scrawl along with some rather graphic drawings. My stomach heaved, and I was glad that I hadn't had time for even coffee before rushing out, because I was perilously close to hurling. *Not again.* This was our dream, our safe place for the LGBTQ community, and fucking criminals kept threatening that vision. Business had been so good over the holiday weekend, too—we were *so* close to turning that corner as far as viability, and now it was threatened anew.

"This. *This* is a hate crime," Adam sputtered. "And Flint better take this one seriously."

"He will," I soothed, hoping I wasn't wrong. And for once, I agreed with Adam. This sure as fuck felt like hate, like dark nastiness dripping down on all our hopes and goals for this place.

Right as I was searching for better words to calm Adam, not to mention myself, Nash's Jeep came barreling into the parking lot, pulling up parallel to where we stood.

"Morning," Nash called as he strode over. *Flint. Flint. Flint.* Not Nash, not the guy who had breathed his passion in my ear, not the guy who'd snuggled up beside me most of the night, not the exhausted man I'd been so moved to help feel better. Flint. The police chief. Nothing more. Time to keep it professional.

"Why can't you catch these vandals?" Adam demanded before I could return Flint's greeting.

"We're a three-person department, and there's around a hundred teenagers on break from school right now, along with all the older kids already out of school. We're working as fast as we can." Even after last night, Flint still looked weary, and it was hard, wanting to rub his back again, wanting to reassure him that he was doing all he could. But I couldn't do those things.

"Similar crime happened to Dolly's Donuts the other week," he continued. "You can call Leroy Atkins for help removing it after I get my pictures, or I've got a power washer in the garage you boys can borrow and do the work yourselves."

The *boys* part rankled. I didn't feel that much younger than Nash, not when we were alone together, and I didn't like him using the word for distance now. But I couldn't call him on it, not with Adam right there, glowering like he'd be only too happy to light into Nash. "That'd be helpful. Thanks."

"Not a problem." Nash took pictures and asked questions of Adam and Logan about the state of the parking lot and tavern when they'd arrived that morning. It was all very professional, which brought back my weird feelings—it was strange as hell to be maintaining this secret arrangement with Nash. In Portland, everyone I'd dated had been out. I'd met family members, partied with friends, and known co-workers, even for short-lived relationships. This piece-on-the-side business was harder than I'd thought, and when I'd told him that this could be some down-low summer fun, I hadn't really realized how difficult managing the two sides of our relationship—private and public—would be.

What was worse was how I'd thought fucking a few times with Nash would get him out of my system, but instead, he kept burrowing deeper under my skin, making me crave more and more, making me want impossible things.

"Well, that should do it." Nash pocketed his camera. His eyes drifted over me, landing on my neck. He had to be remembering, too. His eyes flared—a quick flicker that stole some of that weariness. No, he wasn't immune. The heat we'd shared earlier was still burning for him, too. My roiling gut settled a bit. "I'll be back in a bit to drop off the power washer and some stripper. You be sure to call if there's further trouble."

I nodded along with the others, but my brain was spinning. I was still trying to deal with the realization that some asshole had it in for my business, was threatening my friends and customers, and jeopardizing our dreams. The powerlessness of knowing I couldn't protect them made me need to lean against the building, draw strength from its old timbers. And that wasn't the only worry. My heart trembled every bit as much as my jangly nerves. Yeah, there was trouble all right, trouble with my head and my heart and all my conflicting emotions about this confounding man and my confusing life in this place that had never felt less like home.

SIXTEEN

Nash

"Your order." Mason's smile didn't reach his eyes as he slid my plate in front of me. As was my habit by now, I'd come for a late lunch to a deserted tavern. However, any pleasure at seeing Mason was countered by how down he seemed. He'd been acting off ever since the latest vandalism at the tavern. We'd had a few more cooking lessons and another late-night massage date, but there was a melancholy about him all the sex didn't seem able to shake loose.

"Sit," I commanded. Ringer was off somewhere, and the cook was in the back. I enjoyed these moments when Mason could join me more than just about any other part of my day. Maybe if I said the right thing or made him laugh, I could turn his smile real again.

But Mason shook his head. "Can't. I've got to run some food out to my dad's before I need to be back for the dinner shift."

Even more than the tavern, that family of Mason's

was going to run him ragged. Last time I'd been in for lunch, he'd had Lilac here again. I knew better than to say anything to him about it, though. By unspoken agreement, his family was completely off limits as a conversational topic, despite all the time we'd spent together. I picked up on enough—Francine was still gone, Jimmy was barely holding it together for the kid, and Mason was stretched thin, both financially and emotionally. I wished there was something I could do for him.

I lacked his skill at massage, cooking for him was out of the question—even if I'd moved past burning everything in sight, it would still be like doing a painting as a present for Picasso—and earth-shattering sex didn't seem to be working to take the gloom out of his moods. Still, there had to be *something* I could do.

What about my own favorite way of resetting? There was a good chance he'd think it was stupid, but before I could talk myself out of it, I found myself asking, "What's your next morning off?"

"We're still rotating time off. Thursday I don't have to be in until around three, but I could probably switch with Adam for a different day. Why?"

I smiled at him. "I'm working the whole weekend myself because it's Holmes's anniversary. Just so happens that Thursday's my day off, too. I'll pick you up at four thirty."

"Wait. You'll what? Four as in a.m., the middle of the night?" He gaped at me, and I laughed. This was going to be fun.

"It'll be worth it." *I hope.* "You'll see. Wear old clothes you don't mind getting muddy."

"Muddy. We're going outdoors? Together?" Mason's head cocked to one side, giving him a puppy dog cuteness that my insides couldn't help but warm to. When he was adorable like this, my arms literally ached from wanting to hold him and keep him near me, keep that cuteness all for myself.

"Yup."

"You better be bringing the coffee." He opened his mouth as if to say more then closed it when the cook stuck his head out from the kitchen.

"Mason? The meat delivery's here."

"Coming." Mason's voice was as weary as I'd ever heard it. Man, between the tavern and his family, the guy was in sore need of a break. I just hoped my little plan worked and didn't make anything worse.

Mason

It was a sign of how far gone I was over Nash that I set my alarm for four-freaking-a.m. And for something outdoorsy, no less. Crawling out of bed, I pulled on old jeans and sneakers. I didn't have hiking boots or anything like that. Adam was the outdoorsy one, not me, a holdover from my childhood allergies and asthma. Speaking of, I took an allergy pill and pocketed my inhaler just to be safe—didn't need to start wheezing on Nash.

Despite it being July, the morning air had a definite bite to it, and I threw a flannel shirt over my grungy tee. There. I at least *looked* ready for whatever Nash had planned. Precisely at four thirty Nash's old truck rolled up, and I hurried out to meet him.

"Your coffee, Sunshine." He passed me a large thermos as I got in. "I doctored it up best I could for you —I know you like it sweet."

"I do." The street was deserted and still dark, so I risked a fast kiss. It wasn't just the coffee that was sweet. Nash Flint was a far nicer person than most people gave him credit for. "So where are we headed?"

"If you're still sleepy, you might hold off on the coffee. We're driving about an hour to catch the Rogue River—little offshoot on an old school friend's property. My favorite fishing spot in the world."

"In the world, huh?" I smiled at him, despite myself. "You're taking me to your secret place?"

"Guess you could say that." Nash looked away. "Haven't had a fishing buddy since…a long time."

"I've never been fishing," I admitted, trying to figure out a way to tell him how pleased I was that he was letting me in on this part of himself. Maybe this was a sign there were a few cracks forming in the hardened "chief of police" wall he'd built around his personal life.

"Not once?" Nash's eyebrows went up as he turned onto the highway out of town. "Well, I brought spare waders and a pole for you. Did some lures for you last night, too."

"You make your own lures?" I laughed. I was going to be such a disappointment for him.

"It's relaxing." His skin stayed pink, and I had a feeling that few people knew about this hobby.

"Oh. Like baking is for me." I reached for the bag I'd grabbed on my way out of the house. "Speaking of, I brought some brioche buns and honey butter we had left over."

"I packed some sandwiches, but I have a feeling your stuff is going to be more tasty."

"You made me food?" My chest went all warm. He'd brewed my coffee the way I liked it, crafted me custom lures, and even thought to feed me. God, I hoped my clumsiness didn't ruin the morning for Nash.

"Doesn't take a degree to put ham and mustard on bread." Nash gave my knee a fast pat. "It's okay if you want to doze until we get there. I know I rolled you out way earlier than you're used to. There's my old stadium blanket down at your feet if you need it."

Wow. He really had thought of everything. I wrapped the wool blanket around me, but it was Nash's consideration that warmed me, made me feel safer and more secure than I had in weeks. Nash turned on a classic country station, volume low, and I drifted off to crooning about some man Patsy Cline couldn't have.

"Okay, Mase, ready to walk?" Nash's hand on my shoulder was gentle. I stretched and took in the canopy of trees surrounding the truck as Nash pulled to a stop. We were truly in the middle of nowhere. I'd been vaguely aware of us leaving the main road, bouncing down a gravel path to this small clearing. All around us, hills full of green trees welcomed the first tendrils of dawn.

I listened to Nash's instructions for putting on the hip waders, which were more like rubber overalls only without much bib, and helped him cart the tackle boxes, poles, and food down a short path to the creek bank. The Rogue River proper was wide and deep, carving a path throughout southern Oregon. It was known for its rapids and whitewater, but this little offshoot was shallower and calmer, curving around an inlet of land lined with scrubby trees and bushes on both sides.

We set the tackle and food on a rocky outcropping along the bank. Nash had already picked the right rod and reel for me, and he proceeded to fiddle around with it, talking about tippets and leaders.

"Is this how it feels when I talk sautéing and chiffonade cuts?" I laughed, probably too heartily. I was never going to remember all the pointers he was giving me.

"Yup." Nash didn't seem to notice my worries about making a fool of myself, continuing to set up the rods. "Now, you always want your flies to match the hatch — you want ones that look like the bugs or baitfish around here. I've been coming to this spot for years, so I've got a good feel for what works. I like a nice streamer like this." He indicated the teeny tiny thing bobbing at the end of the line. I had no idea how his vision and hand-eye coordination were talented enough to craft that.

"I like streamers, too." I waggled my eyebrows at him.

"Behave," Nash said sternly. Evidently, he took his fishing *very* seriously. "We're going to practice a basic cast here on the land before we get you into the water."

"How's the city's health insurance?" I figured the chances of me accidentally beaning him with the rod were rather high.

"Worst that can happen is you get all tangled up. Lord knows I did as a kid. Now, watch me a few times."

I stepped back to give him plenty of room.

"Your dad taught you how to fish?" "Granddad actually. Dad was never one for taking days off. But Granddad had a few spots outside town he loved, and he'd take me and Easton with him. Easton never had the patience for fish, but me, I really took to it."

"I can tell. So the whole idea is to flick the line over the water?"

Nash gave me an arch look. "Bit more complicated than that, but yeah, that's the gist of dry fly fishing. I also nymph—go in deep to get them where they feed."

"There's a joke there…"

"Should have known you'd like me going in deep." He winked at me, and this whole enterprise got infinitely more fun with him teasing me as he demonstrated the basic cast over and over. It was weird, but I felt some of the tension of the last few weeks bleeding away—the vandalism, my family, worries about where this thing with Nash was headed. None of it mattered out here. The soft light of the dawn and the rustle of the trees, us the only humans for miles, the vast openness of the land, all chased those worries away. And other than eating at the tavern, this was the first real time we'd spent together where the prospect of sex wasn't hovering over us. I liked it far more than I would have expected.

"Okay, your turn. Take it nice and slow, but confident." He passed me my rod.

"Give me a turn, and I'll be slow, all right." I already had a strong sense that Nash wasn't exactly versatile in bed, but it was fun to tease him.

"Show me you listened," Nash ordered, a smile tugging at his mouth, almost like he couldn't help but get amused by me.

I tried to repeat his cast but fumbled it all to hell. "Fuck."

"That's all right. First time for everything." He put my rod and reel back in order, untangling what I'd done to the line. Picking up a nearby stick, he handed it to me. "Practice just the motion a few times. It's all in the wrist, but also the head. Gotta trust your senses."

I was *not* supposed to be finding Nash playing teacher so sexy. "Okay."

Finally, after a long while of stick practice and then practice with the actual rod, Nash led me into the water. "You can watch me a bit if you want. See how I read the water."

Yup. Sexy as fuck, Nash concentrating, at one with his equipment and our place on the river. He continued to keep up a low chatter about catch-and-release and watching how the fly drifted and where a fish was likely to grab hold. "There we go. That's a nice one." His quiet praise as he hauled out the first fish sparked erotic thoughts in my brain and had me looking forward to earning some praise for myself.

He showed me the wriggling fish, which looked like a good dinner to me, but Nash released it into the stream. "You're not going to let me cook lunch for you?"

"Granddad liked to keep the best catch of the day for supper, but I never had his talent for cleaning and frying them up." Nash gave me a sly smile. "And besides, I've got other plans for you before you've got to be back at work.

"Oh, you do?" I liked the sound of this. Distracted by sexy thoughts, I took a step that had my boot sliding on a rock and, *whoosh*, water gushed into my waders. "Oh fuck, oh fuck, that's cold."

"Now you're a real fisherman." Nash clapped me on the back. "Your turn to try."

"Okay." I tried to remember all the steps he'd been showing me, but I bungled my first few casts. Then, finally, one flew out over the river, just as Nash's had done. I let out a whoop. A sharp tug pulled at my line. "Oh, my God, I think I've got something!"

"Reel it in. Nice and slow. Steady now." Nash coached me through bringing the fish in. "And lookee there, you caught Walter—ornery old fish who lives off in the deep part over there. I've probably caught him a few dozen times. Big sucker, isn't he?"

"Oh, yeah." I was ridiculously proud of myself, and in that moment, I understood why Nash had brought me, why this was so important for him to share. This was the real Nash, stripped of the job and obligations and limitations he put on himself. And in a way, he was showing me the real me, too—who I could be if I let myself go and danced out over the water with nothing but air and sunshine to hold me back.

Nash released my fish for me, then he did the most unexpected thing ever and gave me a firm kiss. "Well done."

"Thanks." I bloomed under his approval, and not even the frigid water inside my boots could keep me from trying again.

"You've got the knack." Nash smiled broadly a while later as I hauled in another fish. "You like this, then?"

His tone was uncertain for the first time all day, and I

stepped close enough so that I could brush a fast kiss across his lips. "Yes. Thanks for bringing me."

"Maybe I'll take you to another of my favorite spots next time..." His words drifted, as if suddenly remembering that this thing between us was supposed to have an expiration date.

"I'd love that," I said quickly. We could discuss ending our friendship later. This was far, far too good to release quite yet.

Nash nodded. "You text me your next couple of off days. I'll be thinking of some places."

"Will do." We fished in quiet companionship for another stretch, breaking to eat our snacks.

"Probably ought to head back," Nash said at last with obvious reluctance. "Got to get you warmed up and dry before your shift."

"Oh? You going to help with that?" I followed him to the truck.

"Maybe." Nash gave me a wolfish grin.

Since I didn't fall asleep on the way back, we talked easily about fishing and music and everything other than the heavy stuff that had been weighing me down. It was nice, how he never pushed me to talk. Felipe had been a big talker, to the point where his constant questions and feedback felt like amateur therapy. Sometimes I just wanted to ignore my issues, not take them out and analyze them one by one. Nash seemed to get that, gifting me this time away from all the pressures of my life.

I was surprised when Nash turned down the alley for our street, going straight past my place to pull into the freestanding garage behind his house.

"Well, I guess I better head out…" This was the awkward sort of parting I'd hoped to avoid.

Nash raised an eyebrow. "Didn't you want to get clean and dry first? I've got something inside to show you."

"Lead the way," I said, a bit too eagerly. In all our time together, he'd always come to me. I'd never once been in his home, and it felt like a big deal that he was inviting me in. His backyard was ringed by a tall wooden fence, blocking us from the view of any neighbors, but he still glanced around as he unlocked the back door.

Yup. Still the secret friend. I tried not to sigh. I'd been the one to propose our arrangement, and now I had to live with it.

We stepped into a kitchen that I immediately noticed had been recently remodeled—new white cabinetry and a gleaming stainless-steel gas stove I bet he seldom used. He led the way into a comfortable living room with recliners and a long leather couch, and, as we entered a hallway with polished hardwood floors and walls hung with pictures of his family through the years, I had to acknowledge that his place was much cozier than mine.

"You were hot in high school," I observed, stopping in front of a picture of him in a baseball uniform.

"Hush." He laughed, cheeks going pink again before he opened a door. "This is what I wanted to show you. Did this last year, and it turned out all right, if I do say so myself."

"Oh, my God. Okay is such an understatement." I took in the bathroom, which looked like a post from an interior-decorating-porn thread on Pinterest. The space was huge—I'd put money on him having knocked out some walls to accommodate the double sink, walk-in shower, and hugest tub I'd ever seen. "You've totally been holding out on me."

"Maybe a little." Nash grinned at me and headed over to the tub. "You want me to run you a bath?"

"Nope." Grinning back, I crossed the room to loop my arms around his neck. "I want you *in* the tub with me."

SEVENTEEN

Nash

Mason was looking at my tub like it was a six-layer cake and I was the frosting. I frowned at him. "Us? Together? Oh, no. I'll just rinse off in the back—"

"You will not." Mason started in on my buttons with determined fingers. "Tub like this? It's meant to be shared."

"I just wanted something I could soak in. My bones are getting old—"

Mason cut me off with a snort. "Don't you start in with this old business. I'm on to you. You're a closet hedonist. Bet you've got nice sheets, too."

"Hedonist?" I shook my head, letting him peel my shirt off me. "This is simply a nice spot to have a beer after a long shift. And if you watch that sassy mouth of yours, I'll show you my sheets shortly." I neatly side-stepped the question of whether they were expensive. Ever since my sister gifted me some nice ones a few

Christmases back, I had actually developed a taste for finer linens, but I wasn't admitting that to Mason.

"I think you've got a better use for my mouth." He leaned in for another kiss. "Come on. First at my place and now here. What's with the reluctance to get clean with me?" His eyes narrowed. "Did something...*bad* happen to you in a shower?" His tone said he'd happily battle any demons in my past, and that was adorable enough to make me smile.

"Nothing like that." I struggled to explain. "I just... don't like being naked. Exposed." I gestured at the sunshine coming in through the frosted windows. "Hated locker rooms in school. Always tried to get in and out as fast as possible, keep my head down." I'd been so terrified of sprouting wood at the wrong moment that those locker room visits had been nothing other than fraught for me even though I'd loved playing sports.

"Well, I happen to think that you naked is one of the seven wonders of the world." He went for my pants next, undoing my fly and taking the time to tease my not-uninterested cock. "And as fun as you are in a bedroom, there's plenty of trouble we can get up to in other places."

"Oh, I'm sure." I bent to take off my boots. He was winning, of course. There wasn't much I'd deny this man, not that he needed to know that. He started the tub filling, cranking up the hot water exactly how I liked it.

"There's no one here but us." Mason made quick work of his own clothes. "It's okay to enjoy yourself, Nash. Really."

I made a noncommittal noise, trying not to shift from foot to foot and reveal my discomfort with being naked.

"Come on. In the tub with you." Mason pointed to the steaming, half-full bath.

"Okay. Okay." I dumped in some body wash I kept on the side of the tub. Maybe I'd feel less bare in the sudsy water. Climbing in, I sat against the far side of the bath, groaning at the combo of the cool porcelain at my back and the hot water loosening my tired muscles.

"My turn now." Mason didn't give me a ton of warning before he stepped into the tub, and instead of sitting opposite me like I'd expected, he settled himself with his back to my front. The tub was wide and deep enough that the position was technically possible, but I hadn't been ready for it.

"Oof." I tried to arrange myself so that my knees weren't jabbing into his back, and ended up with him more or less in my lap, my legs on either side of him, my cock trapped between us. Sighing happily, he leaned against me. "Happy now?" I asked.

"Very." He stretched out, wriggling his feet under the stream of water. "Isn't this nice?"

"Everything's nicer with you," I said without thinking. But it was true. There weren't many scenarios where a lap full of Mason wasn't a treat, and the hot, sudsy water was melting my reservations about this whole enterprise. My arms came around to hold him tight against me.

"Forget hedonist. You're a closet romantic." He tilted his head so that he could brush a kiss on the edge of my jaw.

"I'll leave that to you." I made a sweeping gesture indicating the tub. "You're the one with big ideas. I'm just along for the ride."

And wasn't that the truth. I couldn't seem to stop my imagination from leaping ahead—thinking of more fishing trips for us, thinking how Mason would love the rich fishing on the Elk River in the late fall, when I had no business dreaming beyond this latest encounter. He'd said it was all just a bit of summer fun, but my heart and brain refused to keep with the light-and-breezy agenda.

My hand twitched, needing a distraction from this line of thought. Grabbing a washcloth from the little basket next to the body wash, I lathered Mason's chest. Tub full now, he used his foot to turn off the taps before arching back into my touch.

Abandoning the washcloth, I rubbed circles around his nipples with my thumbs. I loved how responsive he was there, drank in his moans and gasps. "You can go harder," he whispered.

"Oh, yeah?" Pinching the little nubs, I rolled them between my fingers, making him squirm against me, delicious friction.

"More, Nash. More," Mason panted.

"I've got you." Snaking a hand lower, I grabbed his cock under the water, jacked it a few times, liking the slide of it against my palm.

"Wait. I want something for both of us."

"This is. Watching you get off is better than Christmas." I wasn't lying. Him stretched out against me like this, head on my shoulder, hot breath on my neck was my idea of perfection, reservations about sharing the bath be damned. I tweaked his nipple again for good measure, loving how it made him wriggle.

"You...can...fuck me after," Mason groaned, body

going pliant against me, giving himself over to my touches.

"Don't write checks your body can't cash." I nipped at his ear. "Quit focusing so much on when I'm going to get mine and let me make you feel good."

"And you say I'm the bossy one?" Stretching, he gave me a sloppy kiss.

"You are." I tightened my grip just to make him writhe again. Playing with him, I went hard for a brief spell, tight, fast strokes that had him moaning, before I slowed way down and went back to flicking his nipple and lazy, barely there touches on his cock.

"You're pure evil, Nash Flint." Mason's back arched, body trying to chase more of my touch, but I wasn't getting him off until I was good and ready. I waited until he was cursing and the water was starting to cool before I sped up again.

"Wanna come," he moaned.

"Nothing stopping you." I slowed my hands.

"Bastard."

"You love it." I kissed his head.

"Hate it. Please get me off."

"There's my favorite word." I jerked him with more purpose now, adding the feathery touch on the upstroke that always seemed to get him there.

"I'm gonna..." His voice broke as his whole body bowed upward, fucking my fist as he came in big shudders. The spunk was slippery on my fist before the water washed it away. But I didn't care about that—my attention was riveted on his face, how the wonder of it all hit him, how his features went slack after, how he smiled at me as he came back to earth.

175

"Now the water's all dirty." He laughed before turning so that he could kiss me.

"I don't care." Pulling him close, I kissed him slow and deep, a leisurely exploration that went on until the water cooled for real.

Mason pulled back enough to speak. "Let's rinse off and then you can show me your bed."

"We don't have to fuck." I waited for him to get out of the tub before following him to the separate shower.

"Hello. Interested again." Laughing, Mason pointed to his cock, which indeed was hard, bobbing against his stomach.

I let him wash me in the shower, and as he slowly soaped my chest and abs, some of my nerves about being exposed, about putting myself at risk, melted away. Sharing this with him was...well, fun wasn't the right word, but it was...special. And special was dangerous, but I couldn't seem to stop myself. I even laughed as he grabbed for a towel after we rinsed. "Now where's that bed?"

"This way." The master was right next door to the bath. I had changed it a bit since it had been my parents' room—new coat of gray paint, king-size bed to replace their old double, the linens my sister had picked out, and, on the wall, some paintings of the beach outside town that a friend of Curtis's had done.

"Oh, fuck. I don't have supplies." Mason flopped on the bed.

"I do. Got your fancy brand when I was in Coos Bay the other week." Even if I hadn't wanted to admit it, I'd been working toward having him over here, little by little making sense of it in my head.

"You got condoms? For me?" Mason's eyes were wide, mouth slack. He looked way too touched for a simple ten-buck purchase on my part.

"No one else I'm gonna use them with," I mumbled. We hadn't ever talked about exclusive or anything like that. Hell, Steve and I had fooled around for years and never had that conversation.

"Me, either. Not right now." Mason tugged me down onto the bed next to him. Lord, I liked knowing that. I kissed him with strange urgency, trying to put my gratitude into the kiss without crossing over to sappy places neither of us wanted to go.

Tumbling backward onto the mattress, Mason pulled me over him. "Fuck me."

Levering off him, I ordered, "Flip."

Mason frowned. "Between the bath and the fishing, my legs are jelly. Can't we do it like this? Just once?"

It was true that for all our fucking I had a bit of...a routine, I guess you could say. Mason hadn't complained before, though. I hesitated, not sure how to reply.

"Is it the exposed thing again?" he said gently. "I want to see your face when you fuck me. And we can kiss this way. If you've never done it this way, I think you might surprise yourself—"

"I've done it before." My voice was gruff. True, this position wasn't typically my first choice, but for Mason, for the soft openness in his eyes, the sweet curve of his mouth, the warmth of his touch, I'd make the effort. Hell, I'd carry him clear past the mountains if I thought it would get me another of his smiles. Reaching over to the nightstand, I grabbed the unopened box of condoms and the same brand of lube Mason kept at his place.

He grabbed the blanket I kept folded at the foot of the bed, pulling it over my shoulders. "See? Not so exposed. Kiss me again."

It felt a bit ridiculous, making out under the covers on a sunny July day, but he was right—it did help, not being so...*bare*. I claimed his mouth hungrily, letting the kiss stoke my fire again until we were bucking against each other. Getting a hand on his thigh, I hitched his leg over my waist so that my fingers could delve a bit lower. He hissed in a breath.

"Too sensitive?" I whispered. "I can go like this—"

"Stop worrying about *me*, Nash. Fuck me."

I already knew that he wasn't one for a lot of fingering, instead liking a slow and steady start, so I took care of the condom and lube, getting him slick, but not teasing. I went to my knees between his legs, blanket fluttering to the floor, but I was too far gone to care. Holding the base of my cock, I pressed against his rim, letting him rock against the pressure.

"That's it," I praised. "Let me in. Gonna make you feel so good."

"Yeah, you are," he groaned. His head fell back as I breached the tight inner ring of muscles, and I had to admit this position had certain advantages. I might not want to be watched, but doing the watching, seeing the way his face alternately tensed and went slack, made the blood in my cock throb.

"Fuck." He hissed out a breath as I thrust deeper.

"Too much?" I went as still as I could.

"Nope." He yanked me forward into a fierce kiss. He was tight and hot and I couldn't resist rocking my hips as we kissed, urging him to let me in with gentle nudges that gradually built up to full-fledged thrusts until we were fucking in earnest, and I forgot what the hell my reservation had been about this position. It was perfection—his strong arms and legs holding me close, his mouth on mine, little gasps and moans escaping even as we kissed, me able to see every flicker of emotion on his face.

"Nash." His breath came in pants against my neck. "So good."

"Yeah." It took a little calculation and adjustment, getting my angle right from this position, but I knew I'd succeeded when he shivered and moaned. "That's it. Just like that."

"That's my line." He laughed. His laughter washed over me, as welcome as the ocean on a ninety degree day. Getting off with him was fun—especially the intensity of riding the edge of a climax, pushing him over while trying not to take my own tumble over that cliff too soon. But lately I'd begun to worry about the sea of emotions churning beneath us. It was getting bigger, harder to control. Felt like someday I'd take that fall and never recover, end up swamped by feelings I had no idea what to do with.

"So beautiful." I brushed the hair off his forehead, trying to memorize the glassy haze of his eyes, his kiss-swollen mouth, the tension in his neck and jaw.

"Now you're going to turn me into the self-conscious one." He pulled me down for another deep kiss.

"You're perfect," I whispered as I came up for air, right before I claimed his mouth again. I meant it—there wasn't a thing I'd change about Mason Hanks, except for the part where he could never be for me, where I could never be everything he needed, where this thing between us was doomed to an early death, no matter how many cliffs of emotion I dived off. But right then, as our bodies surged together, I was all in, chest thumping with unfamiliar feelings, heart whispering, *"Maybe...maybe..."*

He whimpered, clutching me tighter, bucking against me. Warmth hit my belly. *Holy fuck.* "Did you just..."

"Yes. Oh, God, yes." Mason shuddered in my embrace, and in that instant, he was everything I'd ever wanted from the world—sweet and strong, fearless and trusting, giving and needing. My thrusts became more erratic, muscles tensing almost involuntarily, my attention still riveted on Mason's face.

"Come on, Nash. Come in me."

I opened my mouth to call him on being bossy again, but the quip died in a long groan as fire licked up my spine and my brain melted. I was powerless to do anything other than what this man requested, powerless to do anything other than fall off the cliff, almost joyously. Tumbling over the edge had never felt so good. Even knowing how deep and treacherous the water was, I couldn't do more than hold him tighter.

"Oh, wow." Mason brushed a kiss on my jaw. "Did that really just happen?"

"Think so." I eased out of him, hating his wince. I used one of our towels to wipe our stomachs off. "Did I go too hard?"

"Not more than I begged for." Laughing, he stretched and yawned. "I'm going to feel you *all* shift, though. I'll love it even if I am going to be tired as hell."

"You've got time for a little nap." Sex always left him sleepy, whereas it jazzed me up, made my brain churn.

"Wake me up with time to get a change of clothes at my place?"

"Will do." I let him drape himself around me, happy to be his pillow. I couldn't deny the realities of who he was, who I was. Who I *had* to be. But right then, I couldn't do anything other than watch him sleep and pretend for a few precious moments that he was mine.

EIGHTEEN

Mason

"I don't see why it's such a big deal." I flopped on the bed, wet head landing on Nash's bare stomach, but he didn't flinch, probably a testament to how wrung out he was after another epic late-night sex fest. He had barely moved when I'd headed to his shower after he was done fucking me against his big headboard—still no bed-breaking, but we'd certainly rattled the old house's walls.

"It's just not prudent." Nash reached down and ran his hand through my hair. We'd started this discussion over the pasta carbonara I'd made on his big stove. Since our fishing trip, we'd been fooling around more at Nash's place—he had the bigger kitchen, the better shower, and the secluded backyard for sneaking in and out. And sneaking was exactly what we were arguing over.

"We both need to go to Portland. It's over a five-hour drive. Why on earth should we take two cars?"

Earlier, Nash had been checking out his work

calendar to try to find a date when we could slip away for another fishing trip. I'd been looking over his shoulder and noticed he was going to Portland for his mother's birthday the same week that I'd promised Brock I'd come up and speak to the investment group. Making the trip together made sense—we'd get to spend time together, and we'd save time and energy by carpooling.

"People will notice." Nash didn't slow his scalp massage, and I had to work to not stretch like a cat and drop the topic in favor of getting more caresses.

"Look. I'll leave my car in the garage, and we can leave early in the morning, like I know you'd prefer anyway. And it's not like we have to stay together in Portland. I'll just crash at Brock's—"

Nash growled and his hand tightened in my hair. "No need for that. I usually get a room when I visit."

I liked him jealous of Brock, but my stomach churned with my own jealousy as I thought of reasons why he wouldn't stay with his mom. "You usually go...*fishing* when you're in the city?"

Nash snorted. "Not going to lie. I've tried it a time or two, but it never works out. Guess I'm too old and craggy for that kind of fun."

"You are not." I shoved at his thigh before nosing at his cock which was showing renewed interest in my attention. "And we should go out while we're there. I'll show you some of my favorite places." I tried to sound upbeat. I didn't want to think about a future where Nash and I were little more than a memory, and he could go back to quarterly cruising or whatever it was that he'd been used to.

"I can't..." Nash's body moved with a shrug. "Can't take you to the birthday party. Too many questions."

I released my breath in little huffs, trying not to give in to the heavy sigh that wanted to escape. I *knew* Nash wasn't coming out for me, but it still stung. "That's fine. I'm sure Brock will keep me busy. After all, it's mainly a business trip."

"Yeah." Nash didn't sound particularly sure, but his cock was plumping up, and I could spy a partial victory at least.

"So will you at least think about it?" I let my breath brush over his cock.

"We can ride together," he allowed, hand on my head dragging me closer to his cock. "If that makes you happy."

"It does." I rewarded him with a lick along the thick vein wrapping around his shaft.

"And you're staying with me." His voice was a possessive growl that did a lot to cut past my hurt over his reluctance.

"Bet we can find uses for a hotel room." I took another deliberate lick. I wasn't ever going to get tired of Nash's flavor, both the idea and the reality of doing this for him.

"You the whole night?" Nash propped himself up on his elbows so he could smile down at me. "I can use that."

"Me, too," I said around the lump in my throat. We hadn't ever done more than doze together, stolen naps before alarms went off, always needing to sneak out before we were discovered by nosy neighbors ready to comment on an early morning stroll. The idea of sleeping next to Nash all night long turned me on almost as much as the idea of wild, hotel-room sex, maybe even more.

I lavished attention on Nash's cock, trying to tell him what I couldn't put into words—how much doing this together meant to me, how much I wasn't ready for this thing between us to end. I'd been so brash weeks ago, telling him to think of this as a summer thing, but the longer it went on, the less I wanted to think about expiration dates. We'd been in such a good place since the fishing trip. I wasn't ready to derail that, not yet. *Just give me a little more time.* I sucked him down, letting his hand on my head guide me to his favorite rhythm. This was where I belonged, this was where everything made sense. And I wasn't giving that up, not yet.

And when Nash finally erupted down my throat, showering me with whispered praise and husky moans, I knew I wasn't going anywhere, not until forced. This was too good, too special to waste on regrets and might-have-beens. Fuck expiration dates—I was in this as long as he'd have me, even if his closet threatened to stifle us both before it was through.

Nash

"Got coffee?" It was still dark out when Mason swung himself and a duffel bag into my sedan. I usually relied on either the Jeep or my old truck, but I liked the car for longer trips.

"Yup." I gestured to the thermos and blanket waiting on the floor for him. Ignoring the coffee for the moment, he pulled the blanket around himself and snuggled up against the door. I found myself wishing for an old-fashioned bench seat so that I could be his pillow. I settled for reaching over to pat his leg before turning onto 101 to take us out of town.

The car's headlights bounced off the guard rails, and I got a little thrill looking forward to watching the sun come up over the bay in an hour or so. I always loved early morning starts because they reminded me of fishing trips with Granddad and secret adventures with Easton. We only passed a handful of other cars on our way out of town. We'd be on the two lane coastal highway past the bigger town of Coos Bay, all the way to Reedsport, where we'd catch highway 38 and take that to I-5. Way I figured it, Mason would probably sleep most of the way to I-5, maybe even to Eugene.

The plan, such as it was, involved the five a.m. start at my insistence, a stop in Eugene for breakfast, then a lunchtime arrival in Portland. And, as per the plan, Mason's car was tucked into his garage. No one knew we were traveling together, and that was how I liked it.

And if I felt guilt over that, if my chest got heavy every time I thought about the web of half-truths we were weaving, I tried to push it aside and focus on the idea of a night all alone with Mason, no prying eyes to worry about. The hotel room was a good distraction from the weight of knowing I was disappointing Mason, at least a little. He never spoke of it, but his long sighs and downturned mouth and pinched eyes let me know that the strain of being with me was starting to get to him.

If I were a kind man, I would've put a stop to our fun and games a long time ago. But I wasn't kind. I was selfishly enjoying secret fishing mornings and late-night cooking and more sex than I'd thought myself capable of. And, although I'd always considered myself a strong person, turns out I just wasn't strong enough to let Mason go, not yet at least. Eventually, he'd move on, tired of putting up with me, just like Steve had, but I wasn't going to be the one to shove Mason out the door.

South of Reedsport, Mason stretched and reached for the coffee. We rounded a corner between rocky cliffs that gave way to the sort of ocean view that even after a lifetime spent on the coast never grew old—cloudless blue skies, gleaming blue-green ocean lapping against rocky shores. But that view wasn't near as pretty as Mason gulping his coffee, full lips and long throat working, and I had to work to keep my eyes on the highway.

"You want to switch drivers after we get food in Eugene? I've got the perfect place for breakfast."

"You can choose the food. I'm not picky." I smiled indulgently at him. "But I'm good to drive."

"You don't give up control easily, do you?" Mason laughed.

I do to you. All the time. But of course, I wasn't admitting that to him, wasn't about to tell him how much I liked him leading in the kitchen or demanding that we take another bath together or coaxing me into letting him give me a massage. "Nope," I said instead. "And you like me in control."

"I do." Mason winked at me. "But I'm just saying if you ever want to change things up…"

I knew exactly what he was getting at. "Maybe," I allowed, more than half hoping that would satisfy him enough to change the subject.

"You and Steve ever go away like this?" he asked.

Okay, that wasn't really the change in topic I wanted. "We fished some. Camped a few times. Tried to not make a habit out of any of it." I glanced over at Mason as I merged onto Highway 38. His expression was guarded, eyes distant, and it was hard to say whether he was pleased by this news or not. "Too risky."

"But he wanted to?" Mason pressed.

"Yeah." I didn't like the memory of those conversations, and my voice was harder than it needed to be. "He was always on me to go away in the winter, get a little sun, but I couldn't leave the job. Plus, the more time we spent together, the more people were going to guess. My mother did. Not sure who else suspected." And that shouldn't have rankled me near as much as it did, the not knowing.

"Your mom knows?" Mason's voice was higher than usual, and even without looking, I could bet that his eyes were bugging out. "I didn't think *anyone* knew."

"I do have friends," I said, a mite too testily. "Troy learned because we were stupid kids together. And he trusted Curtis, so I did, too. He hasn't figured out about you, though."

"Oh, of course not." Mason waved my reply away, voice resigned. I had a brief pang in my gut, almost a longing. It would be nice to get Curtis and Mason in the same room, show off Mason's cooking, let Curtis rib us both. But I'd long ago learned to turn off those sorts of wishes. "But your mom guessed about you and Steve? And she was okay?"

"Okay is quite a stretch." God, I didn't want to be having this conversation. I looked out at the trees on both sides of us as the road twisted, hills alive with the colors of summer—bright greens and yellows, patchy places where there had been logging or forest fires in years past. "It…uh…only came up after Dad's death. When she wanted to move to Portland to be near Trisha and her sisters. She said it wasn't as if I was likely to give her grandkids." I forced myself to shrug as if that conversation hadn't damn near killed me. "Which she was right about. But we don't really talk about it, other than her telling me to keep my head down."

"She's wrong," Mason said firmly. "She was wrong to move away from you—"

"No, she wasn't." The trees gave way to a wide-open field, an old brown barn set back far from the road, and lazy cows and horses watching us pass. I was half tempted to hijack one of the horses to avoid Mason's questions. "She never cared as much for Rainbow Cove —she was a Portland girl Dad convinced to come back with him. She missed the big city, missed her family and sisters. And she wasn't going to let Trisha's kids grow up without her. It made sense." It didn't mean I didn't miss her like crazy, but I wasn't holding on to much resentment there.

"Well, she's still wrong to tell you to stay closeted or whatever she said." Mason leaned back in the seat, stare intense, like he was personally affronted by my mother.

"We've been through this." I let out a frustrated noise as we finally hit I-5, where we could go fast enough to maybe leave this talk behind us. "I'm not ready to be a spectacle. To have people treat me different."

"Oh, Nash. It's a dying town with aging hippies and a few rednecks. No one cares all that much about our personal business."

"Not going to be dying much longer if that friend of yours has his way." I carefully skirted his main point about no one caring and the way that Mason had lumped us together—*our* personal business, like there was an us that would deal with this together, an us that my actions affected. I really wasn't ready to confront that *us* yet. Sure, it existed in the quiet hours of the night when I watched him doze on my favorite pillow or when my heart swelled watching him laugh and flip pancakes. But that didn't make me ready for a public us, not yet.

"Speaking of friends, the breakfast place I want to hit is owned by a friend from culinary school. Not sure if she'll actually be there, but if it's too weird for you…"

"It's not." There was a bit of a challenge to his voice, but that wasn't why I gave in. Thinking about disappointing him, depriving him of a chance to say hi to a friend, made my back sweat. I hated letting him down.

Mason was quieter the rest of the way to Eugene, turning up my radio until it was time to give me directions to a little cafe in a strip mall near the college campus. It had a giant green awning and, even at eight, the outdoor tables were full. After we parked we headed toward the entrance, and I noticed a couple customers were taking pictures of their food with their phones.

"They do that at your place, too?" I asked Mason, desperate to lighten the tension between us.

"Oh, yeah. But they do it here because Cat's stuff really is that good. You'll see."

We had to wait for a table, something that almost never happened in Rainbow Cove, and I felt very… aware, standing there next to Mason. It seemed like people might be able to guess what we were to each other just by watching how Mason's eyes crinkled when I made a joke about him needing a fancy coffee and how he stood a little closer than strictly needed. Which I loved, damn it all to hell.

Right as a teal-haired server led us to a recently cleared table for two, a tall woman with an infant strapped to her front came rushing toward us. "Mason Hanks. Text a girl, why don't you?" She had a big hug for Mason and a questioning smile for me.

"This is Nash. Nash, this is Cat." Mason said with a careless gesture, not elaborating on who exactly I was. I supposed I appreciated his discretion, but my chest tightened in a strange way as I looked over at him. And I had to wonder how it might feel if he'd claimed me as someone important, as someone who was a solid part of his world.

"I'm so glad you guys stopped by. I miss seeing your face." She lightly shoved Mason's shoulder. "Last time I saw you was this little man's shower. Felipe and some of the old crowd came down for brunch the other week and to do the Saturday market. He asked about you."

"That's…uh…nice." Mason's face went pink even as he bent to make a face at the baby.

Ah. Felipe, the ex. My arms tensed, wanting to touch him, that urge to claim and be claimed growing. I didn't much like the idea of this Felipe asking after *my* guy. Except, as I continually reminded both Mason and myself, he wasn't mine.

"Don't be a stranger, Mase. You don't even update your social media anymore. What's up with you?"

Me. I'm up with him. I bit back the words and waited for Mason to answer.

"Oh, not much. Busy with the tavern. Keeping Logan and Adam in line. Learning how to fish."

I knew that last bit was just for me, and I couldn't help smiling at him.

"Fishing, huh?" Cat's knowing smile said she hadn't missed my reaction. "That's...interesting. I better get back to the kitchen, but Tara will take care of you. Biscuits just came out of the oven."

We took our seats, and Mason studied the colorful menu like it was one of the crime novels I occasionally picked up. As was typical for Eugene, there were little symbols indicating what was vegan and gluten free and which dishes were locally sourced.

"I can't decide between the pulled-pork hash and the biscuits and gravy." Mason finally looked up from the menu. "What would you say to ordering both and sharing?"

Back in Rainbow Cove I would have declined— sharing from the same plate was a little cutesy for my tastes, the type of thing that only couples would do. But here, miles from home, all I really wanted was another of his easy smiles, to make him happy with something so simple. "Sure. But I'm taking my coffee black. I'll leave the latte to you."

"No problem." Sure enough, his smile warmed me through, was worth any discomfort I felt about his friend maybe guessing that we were more than acquaintances.

And it was sort of...cozy, sharing the two heaping plates of food, him waxing on about the flavors. I wasn't ever going to be a foodie like him, but I also wasn't likely to get tired of watching how his face went slack with pleasure when he really liked something. It made me remember how he looked in my bed and caused me to shift around in my seat.

"That was nice," Mason said after a tussle for the check. I'd paid, same as I'd won the argument about who was driving the next stretch. "Wasn't it?"

The uncertainty in his voice pricked at me. He deserved better than me, deserved someone who would hold his hand on the way to the car, someone who would proudly share food with him back home, someone he could introduce to his friends with no awkwardness.

"It was." I slid into the driver's seat then surprised myself by leaning over, squeezing his leg, meeting his eyes with more than friendly intent.

He smiled slow and sly and gave me a fast kiss. And the world didn't end. No one whooped or hollered or honked. I didn't self-combust into a pile of shame and guilt. No, I...well, I *liked* it. Far more than I should have. Ready or not, I was changing thanks to Mason Hanks, and hell if I knew what to do with the person emerging.

NINETEEN

Mason

"Come on, admit it. You've missed this." Brock stretched, a subtle roll of his shoulders because even the guy's movements were classy, and gave me self-satisfied grin.

"Okay, okay," I groaned. "I've missed good sushi. Happy now?" I was in serious danger of needing to be rolled out of Yama, a restaurant near the firm Brock worked for and his downtown condo.

"And I've missed you." Brock clipped me on the shoulder right before he slipped the waitress his corporate credit card. This had ostensibly been a working dinner to celebrate the pitch to the investors going well. "It's got to be hard being all isolated down there in the middle of nowhere."

"Oh, it's not so bad." I laughed. And it was true. A year ago, I'd dreaded the idea of ever moving back, and as recently as the spring I'd worried that I might die of boredom in Rainbow Cove, but sometime in the past few months, a new peace had settled over me, even with all the worries about the business and the vandalism and my family stuff. And I knew more than a little of that was due to Nash.

"So where are we headed now?" Brock tipped an eye-popping amount before shutting the little bill folder. "Bet it's been forever since you've gotten some."

I choked on my water.

"Okay. Or not." Brock laughed and slapped me on the back. "Please tell me it's not Logan. *That* would be a disaster—"

"It's not Logan. Or Adam."

"Or some redneck." He shuddered. "I get being hard up, but flannel scares me."

"It would." I laughed, because someday Brock was going to meet his match. Probably some equally well-groomed urbanite, but I'd pay money to see someone knock him on his carefully sculpted ass.

"So can I interest you in Silverado or somewhere more refined? Or is this mystery thing something exclusive?"

"It's...complicated." I guessed we were exclusive. We hadn't revisited the subject since the first time we'd fucked at Nash's house, and we sure as hell hadn't put a label on this thing between us, but I had zero interest in fucking around. "And I'm sorry, but I've got other plans."

Brock's eyebrows shot up. "With your secret man? Can I meet him? *Please.*"

"You're a shameless gossip." I laughed as we made our way out of the sushi joint. "And no. Not ready for that."

I didn't add that I wasn't ever going to be ready for that. Or more precisely, *Nash* wasn't ever going to be up for that. There was no shiny future for us where I got to watch Nash fumble his way through an evening at one of Brock's favorite hipster restaurants, got to watch him put Brock in his place. A hidden part of me craved seeing the most important people in my life at one time. And when had that circle come to include Nash? "Include" was a mild way of putting it—Nash had become the goddamn center of my life, and hell if that didn't scare me.

"Okay." Brock sighed. "Be that way. At least the meeting went well."

"It did, didn't it?" I grinned, trying to defuse some of his disappointment at me calling it an early night. The investors had listened closely to Brock's pitch for renovating the resort and had good questions for me about how our advertising efforts were paying off. For the first time, I was truly hopeful that our big plans might actually come to fruition.

"I can't wait to call you with good news in the next few weeks." Brock gave me a fast hug. "But now we better not have you late for your date with Mr. Mystery. You sure I can't walk you—"

"*Positive.*" I resisted the urge to dig out my phone, see if I was running behind for meeting up with Nash at a bar I'd picked near our hotel. After saying goodbye to Brock, I hurried through the downtown blocks, dodging the evening foot traffic. All the towering buildings and wide sidewalks full of people weirded me out after a summer spent on the coast, in a town with mostly single-story buildings and a sparse population. Funny how fast the city had left me.

Nash had spent the afternoon and dinner with his family. We'd agreed to meet afterward at a low-key place I thought he'd enjoy. And I wanted a damn medal for not jumping him the second we'd checked in to our hotel room earlier. I'd been good and had changed into my business clothes for the meeting, settling for some intense kissing before we'd gone our separate ways.

I wasn't sure I liked being desperate to reconnect, not when things were still so tenuous between us. This trip together was kind of a big deal in some ways—it had a "real couple" feel to it that I knew made him nervous. Still, it was hard to control the bounce in my step as I approached the bar, the grin that spread over my face when I saw him there, waiting near the entrance, the speeding of my pulse when his eyes lit up at my approach.

"Hey, you." I grinned, unsure how to greet him. Two guys holding hands stepped around us to enter the bar, and my stomach clenched, wanting that easy affection with Nash, settling for his return smile. This place had an older crowd than the nearby dance clubs that Brock and I usually frequented. I thought Nash would appreciate that, not that I was letting him get away with his whole "I'm too old" routine.

"Missed you." Damn, his sincerity felt nice. His eyes swept over me. "Not sure what it is about you all dressed up, but I like it."

I'd had a tie on for the meeting, but it was in my pocket now, leaving me in my best button-down shirt, one that Felipe had picked out, and a pair of gray dress pants.

"I like you out of uniform, too," I said as I followed

197

him into the bar. Nash was in a variation of his usual off-work clothes—a green polo that looked almost new and khaki pants in place of his usual jeans. "How did it go with your family?"

"It went." He shrugged. "Kids were loud, Mom's apartment was too small, and Trisha cooked enough food for triple the people."

"Aww. Poor Uncle Nash. Drinks on me." I worked my way to the bar. Nash got Jack on the rocks and I got a vodka soda because Brock had foisted sake on me earlier and I needed something to sip slowly. We took our drinks to one of the booths. Small lamps at the center of each table made the dark wood-paneled walls glow, and I hoped the soothing ambiance would relax Nash.

Still, though, his eyes widened when I squeezed in next to him on the U-shaped bench seat instead of sitting across from him. "Better people watching this way," I lied.

Nash said nothing, just took a long pull of his drink. "You come here often?" he said at last. "Doesn't seem like your sort of crowd."

"I'm not some party guy. I'm not much of a dancer, and I figured you weren't, either."

"That I'm not." Nash laughed self-consciously. "I about tripped over a bachelorette party last time I tried that place down the street."

I let out a Nash-worthy growl. I didn't like the sound of Nash hitting the well-known meat market one bit. "Yeah? Well, just so you know, you've got a sure thing tonight."

"That so?" Under the table, his hand found my knee

and squeezed. Oh, I liked this. I scooted a little closer, testing his comfort level.

Nash glanced around but didn't move away from me. This was a very couple-centric place, lots of hand-holding and snuggling and not as many single guys, although Nash did draw his share of appreciative looks from men waiting at the bar. It was a shame that he simply couldn't see how hot he was. Or, actually, maybe that was a good thing, as it meant more hotness for me.

"You play pool?" I asked, gesturing to the back of the bar. The tables were taken, but I figured we could get in line if he wanted.

"Some. I'd rather just enjoy my drink with you, though." Nash's smile was so sweet that I almost went into sugar shock. I had a feeling his response had more to do with the fact that playing pool would involve being center stage among the bar patrons who were playing back there. I still liked sitting like this, especially when his arm snaked around my waist. He held me where people couldn't see, but it was as close as Nash had ever come to PDA and my heart stuttered. For an instant, I let myself want, let myself believe in a future where it wasn't only my plans for Rainbow Cove coming to fruition, but also my most secret hopes for the two of us.

TWENTY

Nash

Mason was happy, and God, it felt so good to see. His face was soft with more than just drink loosening his muscles. I tightened my hand on his waist, pulling him close. I had visited gay bars before, but this was the first time I'd gone with someone. Not being on the prowl or worried someone would recognize me was novel and surprisingly freeing.

Here, I could be with Mason, really *with* him, and I didn't want the feeling to end. I sipped my drink slowly, letting the background music of the bar wash over me as the Jack created a familiar burn in my chest. It was Mason's kind of music—freewheeling and popular—but the wood decor and soft lighting went a long way to calming me down, allowing me to enjoy this moment with my guy. Tomorrow we'd have to return to our real lives, but we could have tonight.

I pressed a quick kiss to Mason's temple. It was the barest of contact, but it still felt like a personal rebellion.

His smile made it more than worth whatever effort it cost me.

"I think I like you out of Rainbow Cove." His eyes studied my mouth like he was contemplating how soon until he got to kiss me again. I liked that thought.

I like me out of town, too. Like me with you. And I like you far more than I should. I didn't let myself say that, of course. I just wrapped my arm around him tighter. I tried to imagine doing this back home. Off duty, but out somewhere. An arm around him as we walked to Dolly's. Maybe a fast kiss when he brought me lunch. No sneaking around. Could that really be my future?

"Hold on a sec." Mason dug out his phone which was buzzing. Moving away from my embrace, he answered the call. "Jimmy? This better be good."

The sound of his brother's name added a new image to the scenes I'd been imagining. And it wasn't a pretty one. If Mason took up with me in a public way, the grief he'd get from his brother, his father, his old friends would be considerable. And I knew I wouldn't be worth the aggravation for him. My job would always have to come first, just as Mason's family would have to come first for him.

Mason finished a fast conversation that had been mainly hissed replies on his end. "He in trouble?" I asked, trying to keep my voice even.

"No. Just needed a reminder that I'm not his freaking daycare. Don't worry. I didn't tell him I'm in Portland."

"Thanks." I felt far more relief that our secret was safe than I should have. "Sorry he's giving you grief—"

"It's fine." Mason gave me a hard stare that reminded

me why his family was always off-limits. "You want another drink?"

"Nah." I'd lost my appetite for the drink and for being out with him. My feelings for him were so damn complicated. Even with the reminder about his family, the idea of not ending things, of letting the months drift out into something more permanent, was more tempting than any alcohol. That was where I needed to be careful, and not just with my reputation—my heart was on the line here, too.

We walked back to the hotel in silence, not holding hands or touching, and Mason's shoulders turned inward, like he was hunkering down inside himself, steeling himself for my rejection. Opening the door to the room, I let him enter first.

"I...uh..." Mason glanced at the big bed in the center of the room. "You sure you don't want me to crash at Brock's?"

"I'm sure," I growled, pulling him to me even though the sane thing would be to let him go, protect us both from the pain we'd suffer when this thing finally ended. But hell if I could bring myself to push him away. "Didn't you promise me I was getting lucky?"

"I did." He gave me tentative smile. "Sorry that Jimmy kinda ruined our night out."

"He didn't." It wasn't a total lie. Most of the fizzle was my fault, my reservations and fears ruining what had been working up to a pretty nice moment. To make up for it, I did the one thing that made sense and kissed him. He kissed me back the way he always did, eagerly, greedily even, but there was a sadness there that hadn't been present when we'd kissed a few hours ago.

"I don't want to need you," Mason whispered against my jaw.

"I know. Me, too. I didn't expect this. Not even a little." I pushed his hair back with my hand, liking the crunchy feel of whatever he'd tamed it with before his meeting. And I did know exactly what he meant. That was the real reason I'd frozen up back at the bar—not Jimmy, not the worries about what others would think, it was this thing between us, bigger than either of us could control. Our hearts had gone and gotten tangled while we were supposed to be having careless fun, and now I had no clue what came next.

"Nash…" Mason's exhale was shaky as I rubbed my hands up and down his back, holding him to me. "What the hell are we going to do?"

"I don't know," I admitted, my three least favorite words. "I'm a selfish bastard and not ready to let you go."

"Then don't." His mouth was urgent against mine, and my tongue found his, teasing until he was panting against my lips. Maybe I couldn't give him everything, but I could give him this.

"Fuck." Mason pushed me against the closet door— and Lord, there was a metaphor there, one that made me release an unsteady laugh.

"What?" He nipped at my neck before tugging my shirt free.

"Nothing. Just laughing at my stupid self."

"Quit being so hard on yourself, Nash. I mean it. There isn't anyone who judges you harder than you, and that's sad." He punctuated his words with a soft kiss on my bare chest before he started to sink lower.

I halted him with a hand on his shoulder. "Bed. Not sure my old knees—"

"Stop it with the old business. Is that what's really holding you back? The age difference?" He shoved me in the direction of the bed, kicking off his shoes as we went.

"No." I sighed. "Or at least not just that. You deserve someone closer to your age, though. Someone young and fun—"

"I've had that. And I've never had anything like I've had with you, so how about you let me decide what too old is, okay?"

It was a testament to how much I wanted him—all of him—that I nodded. I wasn't convinced, but I didn't want to argue anymore, didn't want to spoil this evening any further, wanted to savor his admission that this was something new for him. Stripping off his clothes, Mason studied me with feral intent.

"You're the sexiest man I've ever had, and you don't even know it."

I laughed at that. I had no idea what he saw, but he himself was as fine a specimen as I'd ever seen—all lean muscles and freckled shoulders and hard cock jutting from his body. "You're the sexy one. How about you come over here so I can show you?"

"I'm here." He kissed my jaw. "I'm in this thing, Nash."

"Me, too." I kissed him again, both reveling in and hating the emotions swamping me. His hand found my belt buckle, and for once, I didn't feel my age. I felt seventeen again and perilously close to coming in my pants, from nothing more than kisses and the brush of his fingers.

He resumed his earlier determined path down my chest, laving a trail down my stomach to tease the waistband of my boxers before he shoved them and my pants down together. Urging me to sit on the edge of the bed, he sank to his knees in front of me.

"God, I love tasting you." He ran his tongue all over my shaft but didn't suck me in.

"No teasing," I ordered, but he just laughed.

"But it's so much fun." Abandoning my cock, he nuzzled lower, showering my balls with attention.

"Ah…you don't…" My word died as he sucked one into the wet heat of his mouth, fingers stroking the other. His touch was gentle, but it still sent sparks up my spine and down my legs.

"Mmmm." He made happy noises as he switched sides, licking and sucking and teasing and generally driving me insane. Then he blew what was left of my brain cells when he lifted my balls and licked behind them.

"Fuck." I needed to tell him to stop, but words were failing me, and when he urged me farther back on the bed, lifting my legs, I was powerless to do more than gasp. His mouth returned to that delicate skin behind my balls, flicking his tongue all over, lighting up some place deep inside me with the pressure of his mouth.

"Like that?" He grinned up at me right before he returned to his mission. His devious tongue kept going lower and lower.

I pushed at his shoulder. "You don't have…" Damn it. My face heated. I'd showered before the party at Mom's, but that didn't make me any more comfortable with this.

"Want to." On the next pass, his tongue skated over untouched nerve endings.

I'd done this for him a time or two, and I wasn't squeamish about the act, but being the recipient was far different than I'd imagined, and I squirmed against the comforter. "Mase…"

"Let me." His voice was more authoritative now, making a shiver race up my spine. His mouth returned to that hidden place, torturing me with little flicks and nips before kissing my rim in earnest. It was wet and hot and dirty as fuck and I loved it. Acting on its own, my hand fisted around my cock, squeezing hard.

"Don't come. Not yet." His husky command had me moaning even before his mouth resumed its assault.

"God. More." I was shameless now.

"Finger okay?" He was already moving away from me, rummaging in his bag before tossing lube on the bed.

"I…uh…" Something in me had always resisted this path of exploration, not liking the weird quaking in my belly or the roller coaster in my brain. But as always, I was powerless to deny this man, so I nodded.

"I'll stop if you hate it," he promised, before returning to lick at my balls. Pretty soon he had me so worked up with his kisses there and lower that I forgot a good deal of my reservations. He added a finger alongside his tongue, and I moaned at the new, firmer pressure. Then the finger was back, slicker now, and I inhaled sharply.

"Just relax. It's not going to hurt," he soothed. And he was right—it was strange and slippery and intense in a way that nothing else had ever been, but it didn't hurt. Pressing in a little deeper, he used his tongue on my balls again, distracting me from the invasion.

"Oh, holy fuck. *Mase*," I babbled as he hit my prostate. I knew what it was, what it did, and Lord knew that I aimed for his often enough, but I'd never fully understood it until that instant when my spine turned to jelly and my insides went supernova.

Completely divorced from my brain, my ass rocked, riding back on his finger.

"Like that?" He sounded all smug.

"Uh-huh." I was beyond coherent speech. All I knew was I wanted more of that sensation. It wasn't like orgasm, exactly, and it wasn't like being drunk. Drugged, maybe. I certainly felt high enough and crazed, like I no longer knew my own body or my own wants. "More."

"Oh, yeah." He rewarded my shamelessness with a long lick up my cock. The second finger was a bit more of a pinch and burn, but it still wasn't painful and as soon as he started moving, the pressure against my prostate more than made up for any discomfort.

"Is this…what you…feel?" I panted. "This good?"

"When you fuck me? Oh, hell yes. It feels amazing." Mason's tongue danced all around my cockhead before he spoke again. "God, I want to fuck you, Nash."

There was a question there, and I knew he'd be fine if I said no—he wouldn't try to guilt me into it. But the raw enthusiasm in his voice got to me, made me want to try for him, even if I'd never really imagined myself in this position before. And frankly, although my mind was still trying to wrap itself around the concept, my body was one large nerve ending at that point and really liked the idea of a little more pressure inside me.

"Get…condom," I ordered.

"Seriously?" Mason looked up from my cock, smiling

widely. Something in my chest gave way, and I couldn't help but smile back. I'd been right to put my trust in this man. Withdrawing his fingers, he wiped his mouth on a corner of the bedspread before claiming my lips with an insistent kiss.

"Get on with it," I said as he pulled back to breathe. I'd always been the kid out at the lake who wanted to go first on the rope swing. Not because I had an excess of bravery, but because anticipation made me jumpy. Once I made up my mind to do a thing, I liked to do it.

Nodding, Mason took care of the condom, adding what seemed to be an alarming amount of lube. "Gonna make this good for you."

"I'm not going to break," I protested as he fingered still more lube into me. "Might be the first time, but I do know how this works."

"Nash." The look in his eyes was indescribable— tenderness and awe and something else, something new that I'd never seen before. It made me bold, made me open my legs more to him, pull them back to welcome him between them.

"This how you want it?" he asked, lining himself up.

"Yeah." I appreciated the consideration, but I wasn't tempted to flip over. Ever since that first time in my bed, I was more than a little obsessed with watching his face, and I wanted to see all this through his eyes. It should have made me feel exposed, but instead I felt surrounded in a way I never had. Safe. Protected, even. I couldn't say I'd ever felt precisely like this before.

He pressed in, and it was a decided intrusion—still not painful, but my body tensed all the same.

"Relax," he urged. "Breathe out. I know this part is tricky, but it gets better, trust me."

I did. I took a few rattling breaths and willed my muscles to soften—summoning whatever magic Mason always conjured to make this easier. He rocked forward again, sliding a little deeper, and I groaned. There it was, the pressure I'd never thought I'd crave, but hell, I *needed* this, needed him filling me.

"That's it. That's it." He stroked my abs, and sweat ran down his beautiful, straining face.

"More." I was still a little tense, but my body was far ahead of my brain, demanding more of that delicious torment his fingers had created, curious to see what the combination of pressure and fullness could do.

A lot, it turned out. I moaned as his cock brushed over my prostate, a steady rhythm of thrust and retreat that had me writhing against the bed.

"Fuck. You feel so good." Mason's head tipped back, his neck a tight cord of muscles, his chest heaving. God, he was glorious. "Nash…"

"It's okay. Go harder." I could tell what holding back was costing him, and grateful though I was, I really wanted to see him let loose, wanted to see him give in to his pleasure. Not that my own euphoria wasn't great—I wasn't close to orgasm precisely, more like I was riding waves of sensation, letting that pressure and fullness carry me to new places.

"Tell me…" His hips sped up, making lightning zoom up my spine with each thrust.

"Want it. Want you." I moaned when his hand found my cock.

"Need you." His eyes were glassy as they linked with

mine, and I knew he meant more than just the sex. "Need you so much."

"Me, too." My throat was thick, other words clamoring to get out. I'd never felt like this before. Mason had managed to rearrange everything I thought I knew about myself and my life in a matter of months.

"Please..." I wasn't even sure what I was begging for, just that I needed *more.*

"Not gonna last," Mason panted, hand speeding up on my cock. "You feel too good. Want you to come with me."

I wasn't sure that was possible, but I moaned my encouragement. I loved the franticness of his movements, the brokenness of his groans, the tension in his grip on my leg and my cock. Not losing rhythm, he added some lube to his hand, and, suddenly, coming became more than an abstract concept. I secretly loved it slick and messy, something that Mason had picked up on because he noticed *everything,* every part of me, even the things I thought I'd long buried.

"Mase...I need..."

"That's it. Let go. Let yourself go." His eyes squished shut, the way they always did when he was close, and watching him had me riding the edge. Felt different, the fullness of his cock in me adding a new dimension to familiar sensations. It felt like I was shattering, like I'd fall to pieces when I came, but Mason was right there, ready to catch me.

Trust me. Lord, I did. I trusted this man like nothing else. I added my hand on top of his, the last piece of the puzzle, and I moaned as the climax swamped me. My body—my whole body—tensed and that was new, the way my ass spasmed along with my cock. I came in long ropes, hitting my chin and chest.

Somewhere in there, Mason yelled like he'd been gut shot and went stiff as he came. His cock pulsed deep inside me.

"Oh, my God, Nash." He laughed as he pulled out. And, okay, that pinched. I tried to control the flinch, but he still must have noticed because he rubbed my chest. "Sorry. Too rough there at the end?"

"Nope. It was perfect." My words were slurred, and I felt pretty confident that I'd fail a DUI test right then.

"That was…incredible." Mason's hands continued to stroke my chest and arms. "You were so… *God*. And we should shower. Maybe find a new blanket in the closet—"

"Mason." I cracked open an eye.

"Yeah?"

"You fucked me stupid. How about you be quiet for a minute, let me pass out here."

"Isn't that my line?" He laughed and dropped a kiss on my cheek. "You sure you're okay?"

"I'm sure." I yanked him down next to me. "Just…be here."

I didn't really have to words to explain what I needed, but somehow he knew, wrapping himself around me, holding me close. "I'm here," he whispered.

And in that moment, all my questions about how much longer we could keep this going fled. All I knew was that I wanted more of this feeling of him surrounding me, more of these unfamiliar emotions that seemed to fill up long-empty spaces inside me. I wanted —*needed*—this man in my life.

TWENTY-ONE

Mason

"Hell." Nash's voice carried all the way into the bathroom where I was toweling off. He was understandably grumpy because it was after seven, almost eight actually, and this was a way later start than he'd wanted. I'd thought we both could use the sleep, and the early morning rubbing off we'd indulged in had been a nice bonus.

"What?" I grabbed a fresh shirt from my duffel bag.

"You paid for the drinks last night, right?"

"After all your manly man posturing, yeah." I smiled, trying to get him to lighten up. "Seemed only fair since you got breakfast."

"Hell," Nash repeated. "I don't have my wallet."

"Think it got lifted?" Fuck. That really would suck.

Nash groaned and paced. "Not sure...wait. I took it out at Mom's to put in new pictures of Trisha's kids. Probably still on her sideboard. Goddamn it. I am *never* this forgetful."

"Be easy on yourself." I patted him on the arm, but he shrugged away from me. "You've had a lot on your mind."

Like me. Like us. But I didn't say that, not wanting to remind him of the spectacular distraction that was this thing between us. Hell, I'd found myself distracted, too, staring off into space for no reason, thoughts of Nash invading when I least wanted them.

"We'll have to stop there on our way out of town." Nash reached for his phone on the nightstand. "Fuck."

"It'll be okay," I soothed him before pulling on pants. "We can make up time on I-5. And hopefully we'll miss the worst of rush hour, leaving now."

Nash grunted something unintelligible as he shoved on his shoes. Great. Grumpy cop all the way back to the coast. I couldn't wait to spend five hours in the car with *that.*

We checked out, and I grabbed a coffee from the carafe in the lobby, as I figured the chances of getting Nash to stop for breakfast were nil. He drove north through the downtown traffic to a trendy northwest neighborhood. I'd never been able to afford rent in this area when I'd lived in the city, but I'd worked at a few nearby restaurants and knew it well.

Circling several blocks, he finally snagged a spot near a large brick apartment building as someone zoomed out of a space. Pre-war, it was four stories high with a narrow courtyard separating the two halves of the building. While way more urban than I would have imagined for Nash's quiet mother, I could see the location being ideal for a retiree who wanted to walk to everything.

"I…uh…" He looked at the steering wheel, not moving to exit.

I sighed because I'd been expecting this all morning. "I can't go up with you. I get it."

I didn't, of course, not really. We were in Portland, not Rainbow Cove, and Nash's mother apparently knew he was gay. It made me feel all limp and small inside, like Nash was ashamed of *me* personally, not just uncomfortable with the world knowing he'd spent last night with a man. "There's a bakery two blocks over. I'm going to get myself a decent latte and you a muffin or something."

"Thank you." Nash gave me a tremulous smile, and I knew I wasn't imagining his relief.

I grumbled to myself the whole way to the coffeehouse—it was one of my favorite joints in the neighborhood, not quite as nice as their northeast location on Alberta, but I could count on the coffee to be hot, strong, and reasonably priced. I got Nash his usual black coffee and a marionberry muffin and myself a coconut latte and a scone. I figured we could flip for the food if the muffin wasn't to his liking.

I slowed up as I approached the car with the food and drinks in tow. Nash's mother had evidently walked him down—she was a tall, reed-slim older woman with ash-blond hair, and even though it had been years, I still recognized her almost regal posture. Another woman with the same hair and elegant mannerisms stood with them, probably one of her sisters.

Fuck. Fuck. Fuck. I couldn't go marching over there, couldn't do that to Nash, even if part of me wanted to, wanted to force him to deal with the reality of what this thing between us meant. I'd introduced him to Cat and would happily share him with the rest of my friends, but he couldn't even...

My phone buzzed in my pocket, but I didn't have a free hand to fish it out. Undoubtedly Jimmy or Dad needing something because God forbid I take forty-eight hours to myself. And there it was, the reminder that Nash and I both had shit that had to stay separate from each other, lines we weren't prepared to cross. Nash wasn't the only one unable to do the whole meet-the-family thing. I wasn't exactly going to bring Nash around for our weekly Monday-night dinner of tavern leftovers anytime soon. All I needed was Dad going off on one of his conspiracy theories or just outright blaming Nash for Freddy being locked up. Yeah. Not happening.

I could cut the guy some slack, even though I didn't want to. I headed back the other way. Made sense that he wouldn't want to be seen with a Hanks, anymore than I wanted to be associated with the law in my family's eyes.

God, this thing between us had gotten so complicated. Last night I'd been sure we'd turned some sort of corner, crossed a threshold to a new place where we weren't just fuck buddies who liked to cook and fish together. But it was all an illusion. We shouldn't even be messing around, let alone falling in—

No. I was not in love with Nash Flint. I absolutely refused to be. I collapsed in a vacant metal chair outside the coffee place. I dug out my phone where, sure enough, there was a text from Jimmy about Dad not taking his meds because he was low on money for the refill. I texted Jimmy that I'd cover the co-pay tomorrow.

I had no room in my life for loving Nash, except that

was exactly what I was doing. Somehow my life had rearranged itself around him, and that was dangerous, because what the hell was I going to do when he wasn't in it anymore?

Buzz. The next text was from Nash. *Finally free of family. Where are you?*

Hah. Neither of us was going to be truly free of family, not ever. After a fast text, I made the second trip to the car, this time with lukewarm coffee and a way heavier heart.

"Sorry," Nash said as I got in the car. It hadn't escaped my notice that he'd moved the car farther down the block. God, was that what this thing between us was doomed to be? Stealth meetings and spy-movie theatrics to avoid detection by the people closest to us? Nash's hard face and stiff shoulders shouted an unequivocal "yes." Yes, this was the way of things.

Thank God Nash wasn't a talker. He undoubtedly picked up on my black mood, but he didn't press. He flipped on a Portland radio station and we were treated to several ads. One for a meal-delivery service caught my attention. I distracted myself from thoughts of Nash and where this thing was headed by brainstorming whether it would be plausible for the tavern to begin delivering to more than just a few customers at City Hall and the police station.

Nash's tension seemed to increase with every mile after we passed Coos Bay. I tried to think of a good quip about dropping me outside town if he was so worried about someone seeing us, but every idea I had sounded too petulant to voice, so I just rode on in silence. We rolled into Rainbow Cove in the early afternoon, and it didn't escape my notice that Nash took Lakeview for the long way around town, using back streets to approach our neighborhood rather than cutting through downtown like normal.

He pulled into his garage, right next to his old truck. "Oops. Was on autopilot," he lied. "Should have dropped you off first."

"No worries," I lied right back. "I don't mind the walk. Need to stretch my legs anyway." I did wait a beat, see if he wanted to invite me in—neither of us had to be anywhere before the evening shift—but he just looked at the cracked cement floor of the garage as he gathered his things, not meeting my eyes.

"So…uh…I'll call you. Or text." Nash's neck was flushed. He was most likely having major second thoughts about everything, but I was having a hard time summoning sympathy.

"Sure. Whatever." I headed for the side door of the garage.

"Wait. Mason." Nash caught up to me, turning me to face him. He gave me a fast, hard kiss. "I don't like leaving things between us all weird—"

"Then don't." I kissed him back softer and slower, taking my time to reacquaint our mouths.

"I don't want to hurt you," he whispered.

But you did. I bit my lip, unable to let those words out. Hurt seemed inevitable here, on both sides, but I couldn't keep from holding him closer. He rested his head against mine. "I mean it when I say I'll call. We'll figure this thing out. Promise."

I nodded as I broke away. I wished I believed him, but I couldn't. My head was in a fog as I took the alley back to my place. I was unlocking my side door when a voice made me jump and nearly fall off the step.

"Where have you been?" Jimmy's tonewas hard.

"What do you mean?" I glanced at the driveway—why in the hell hadn't I noticed Jimmy's battered car when we'd turned onto the street? *Because you were too wrapped up in Nash. Too busy being miserable.*

"You weren't here when I knocked. I was about to drive off."

Why the hell didn't you? "I was...out for a walk."

"With your shit?" Jimmy gestured, indicating my duffel bag. *Fuck.* I'd forgotten I was holding it. "And your car's in the garage? Where the hell have you been?"

"None of your business."

"So you say, but Ringer said you was in Portland. I'm dealing with this crap with Dad on my own here and you're sneaking around—"

"You're going to lecture me on sneaking around?" I stared him down. "That's rich. When was the last time you did something on the up-and-up?"

"You don't get to tell me how to live my life." Jimmy kicked at a stray piece of gravel. "And all I'm saying is there's rumors floating around about you. Heard you and Flint get all cozy at the tavern. You and him buddies now?" He glanced down the street, in the direction of Flint's place, and Lord, the only thing I needed was Jimmy doing the math.

"My friends are my business, not yours. Why are you really here?" I kept my voice firm, trying to send the signal that my activities were off-limits, but Jimmy's eyebrows were knit together like he was thinking too hard.

"I gotta go to Coos Bay. Francine needs a ride back to town."

I groaned. The two of them back together in any capacity did *not* bode well for my sanity. "And this involves me how?"

"Dad's still doing badly. Leg's all swollen and his color ain't great. He won't listen to me about going to that urgent-care clinic downtown, but he might you. I can't even get him to run that blood-meter thingie of his."

"Fuck." The co-pay for urgent care was going to suck, as was convincing Dad to go in the first place. "Okay, okay. Let me throw my stuff down and then I'll head over."

"Good." Jimmy looked me over as if to size me up. I tried not to cower under almost three decades of being found wanting by him. "You fucking around with someone? With Flint? Told you I've heard—"

"What?" I didn't have to pretend my outrage. "What the fuck business of yours is that?"

"Better not. That's all I'm saying." He had a sour expression that made his thin face even more pinched than usual. "Or anyone else we know."

I forced myself not to shuffle or squirm. "I wouldn't fuck one of your friends if they paid me, if that's what you're getting at."

"Good. Not that they'd have your scrawny ass," he added sharply.

I clenched my jaw against the urge to tell him about the friend of his and Freddy's that I'd blown senior year. Fighting with him wasn't going to solve anything. "Shouldn't you be worrying about your own self? Are you taking Lilac with you?"

"Yeah. She misses her mama." Jimmy gestured back at the car, where, sure enough, Lilac was in the backseat, playing on Jimmy's phone. At least the windows were all rolled down. "You'll text me how Dad is?"

It was a rare moment of vulnerability from Jimmy. He might not care for me, but I knew he did love Dad. The two of them were a cranky pair of co-dependents who I didn't fully understand, but I nodded. At the last moment, I fished out my wallet and found a twenty. "Get Lilac some food on the way?"

"I can feed my own damn kid." Jimmy plucked the money from my fingers.

"You're welcome." I rolled my eyes at him as he headed back to his car.

Letting myself back into the house, I groaned. *Fuck.* What I really wanted was a nap, but instead I needed to text Adam and Logan that I might be late and then go deal with Dad. And wasn't that likely to be a basket of kittens?

I tossed my duffel bag onto my bed. And hell, I apparently couldn't see my bed without also seeing Nash in it. Last night, when it had seemed like we might actually have a shot at a future, felt so distant and yet the memories were visceral. God, the way Nash had looked when I'd pushed inside him...

It was humbling, the trust he'd put in me, and I knew in my gut that we'd both meant the words we'd said. This was more than fucking to both of us. Of that I had no doubt. But it didn't matter. Jimmy was perilously close to stumbling on the truth, and if he was, then everyone else was, too. And if I loved Nash at all, I needed to do the merciful thing and end this before he got hurt. It didn't matter how much it stung that he didn't want to come out. I wasn't going to be the one to wound him if I could help it. And even if he *was* willing to come out, my stupid fucking family was always going to be between us. Time to pay up and do the right thing—put Nash first, as much as losing him would kill me.

TWENTY-TWO

Nash

"You heading out?" Holmes asked as she came into the station. "Heard it was a rough day."

Rough was an understatement of biblical proportions. A father and his teenage son who lived south of the high school had gotten into an argument, both waving hunting rifles around. Now the father was dead and the son in critical care. I'd have to continue my investigation in the morning, but it was looking like a long week already, and my chest ached for the family and first responders who'd had to deal with the mess. Derrick Holmes in particular had looked torn up as they'd loaded the son for transport.

"Derrick okay?" I asked Candace. "You need some extra time or—"

"We're good." She gave me a tight smile. "Shootings always get to him, but I think he'd rather just sleep than have me fussing over him. I left him some peach cobbler for when he wakes up."

"That'll be nice for him." A weird pang resonated deep in my chest as I walked out after saying my good-byes. Derrick and Candace had each other, and, on days like today, that mattered.

Who do you have? Mason had asked me that weeks earlier, and I'd had no good answer at the time. It'd been a few days since our return from Portland—we'd both been busy, but I had the distinct impression he was dodging my texts. *I don't want to need you,* he'd said that night in Portland, and Lord knew I felt the same, but after the day I'd had, I needed him in a way that I'd never needed someone before, a way that I hadn't thought possible.

Before Mason, I'd head home, pour myself a double, take a long bath, and settle in for a sleepless night. But now, my feet had other ideas, walking directly from my garage to Mason's house.

Heart hammering, I knocked at his kitchen door. Mason must have been nearby because he opened the door almost instantly. Shirtless, he was down to jeans riding low on his hips, and he looked as tired as I felt, beard shadow and bags under his eyes making him look older than usual. "Nash? What's wrong?"

Everything. "Nothing's wrong." I hadn't ever shown up unannounced or straight from work, so who knew what he was thinking, seeing me standing there in uniform, probably more than a little frazzled looking.

"You're lying." He ushered me into the kitchen, where he had a mug of tea steeping on the counter. The air smelled vaguely like popcorn. I'd interrupted his before-bed snack.

"I should go—"

"Oh, no, you don't." Mason pressed the tea into my hands. "Drink something before you fall over."

I took a grateful sip. I couldn't believe how close I was to completely falling apart. I'd never been this unhinged around anyone. Mason's face stayed solemn. "Anyway, it's good you're here. We need to talk."

"Gene Hinkie's son shot him today, but not before Gene fired back." I gulped down the warm tea, welcoming the burn of the liquid. Had a feeling that wasn't the talking he had intended, but the words needed to spew before I lost my ever-loving mind.

"Oh, Nash." Mason took me in his arms, giving me some of his strength. My knees no longer seemed that close to buckling. "And you were there?"

"Got there too late to do a damn lick of good." I rested my head against his hair, breathing deep, letting the smell of his shampoo and skin drown out some of the day's stench.

"So glad you're safe." Mason held me close.

"Sorry for unloading on you."

"Never apologize for that," he said fiercely, steering me toward his bedroom.

Somehow, like always, he seemed to understand exactly what would help, helping me strip until we were both down to our underwear. Pulling the covers back, he crawled in after me then arranged the covers over us. It didn't matter that it was summer—my soul was freezing and only gathering Mason close under the comforter helped. I lay with my head on his chest, arms wrapped around his waist, holding him and listening to his beautiful, strong heart. Hands stroking my shoulders, he murmured soothing things that I hadn't known I'd needed to hear.

Gradually, some of the weight I'd been carrying around slipped off, leaving me depleted and sleepy. "Shouldn't sleep here," I mumbled.

"Already set you an alarm." Mason's fingers sifted through my hair.

"And you wanted to talk…" I ended with a yawn.

"In the morning. Sleep now." He pressed a clumsy kiss to the top of my head, and I gave in to my heavy eyelids and let sleep claim me.

Sometime in the night, our bodies found each other—solace in each kiss, comfort in each touch, each movement a vital affirmation that we were alive and okay, at least for the moment. I stroked both our cocks as I lost myself in his kiss. I wasn't so far gone with my own troubles that I couldn't sense his sadness or see the regret in his eyes. He was giving me this, giving me tonight, but part of him was saying goodbye.

And I sure as hell wasn't ready for that. I clung to him desperately, trying to chase away whatever was prickling at him with my kiss, trying to tell him how much I needed him with my touch, how I couldn't let him go, not ever. I tumbled over first, and when he followed, his face was damp against my neck.

"Nash—"

"Ssh. Sleep." I mopped him up as best as I could then held him until he drifted back asleep. In what had to be my most cowardly moment, I reset his alarm to his usual wakeup time and snuck out, leaving a note I scrawled on the back of a receipt saying that I'd call him. We *would* talk like he wanted, but later. Later when I'd had time to steel myself for it, time to come to terms with what was happening, what he wanted, time to get my head straight about my job. And maybe, part of me wanted time to come up with a counterargument, a reason to get him to stay, really stay, but not talk.

After a few restless hours back at my house, I showered and headed back to work—the place that had to be my first priority right now—in a fresh uniform. I was almost to the station when the scanner in the Jeep crackled.

"Chief? I've got Holmes requesting backup at a traffic stop on Lakeview and Butte."

"I'm on it. ETA three minutes." I flipped on my flashers and pulled a U-turn. Lakeview and Butte...

Please don't be a Hanks. Please. But of course, no one was listening to my paltry prayers. Sure enough, Jimmy Hanks's beater car was pulled up in front of Holmes's cruiser. And when I got out of the Jeep, Holmes had Jimmy over the hood of his car, cuffs on, and was reading him his rights.

He was cussing up a blue streak. "Why don't you arrest her? Stupid cow started it, hitting me."

"Oh, I intend to." Holmes's voice had no humor to it.

"Situation, officer?" I asked, hanging back slightly, both to give her room to work and for me to assess.

"Pulled them over for reckless driving and suspected DUI—car crossed the center line three times and skidded on the shoulder."

Oh, fuck. This was bad, and from Holmes's dark expression, this wasn't the worst of it. "He failed the sobriety test, I take it?"

"Fucker. I did not." Jimmy thrashed against the hood

of the car, working up a good lather. I let Holmes put a knee in his back, get him under control.

"Oh, yeah," she said to me over her shoulder. "But not before he got into a fistfight with his girlfriend in the front seat and—"

"She started it. She hit me! Just because you pulled me over. All I was trying to do was take Francine's stupid ass back to Coos Bay. Nothing illegal."

"And you hit back," Holmes said calmly, leading him to the cruiser. Jimmy sported the beginnings of what looked to be a hell of a shiner and had scratch marks all down one cheek. "Girlfriend's still in the car. With the kid."

With the kid. My insides dropped all the way down to the gravel shoulder. This wasn't just bad; this was a disaster. A disaster I was going to have to tread around very, very carefully.

Holmes got Jimmy into the back of the cruiser, door still open, as she said to me, voice lowered, "Between this and the shooting, we're not letting you recover from your Portland trip well, are we? But one of us is going to have to deal with CPS."

"What the fuck?" Jimmy made a wounded animal noise. Apparently Holmes hadn't been quiet enough for his ears. "You were up in Portland? Rumors are true, aren't they? I've heard about you cozying up to Mason. You're fucking my brother, aren't you, you sick fuck?"

"It's beyond time for you to get quiet." Holmes slammed the door as Jimmy continued his increasingly creative uses of the word fuck.

"Sorry," she said to me. "That's a new low from him, and that's saying something. Can I put the girlfriend in the Jeep after I arrest her? I don't think we want her and Jimmy in the same car right now."

"Of course," I said on autopilot, head still swimming. Jimmy *knew*. Suddenly I'd gone from needing to tread carefully to swimming in shark-infested waters. Holmes was acting like Jimmy was talking trash, which he was, but it wouldn't be long before her wheels started turning, too.

Holmes got Francine out of the car. She had a slap mark on her face and was as mad as a wet cat. I'd never much cared for the woman, and she proved my dislike more than valid as she spat on the gravel. "It's true, isn't it? Jimmy told me them rumors about Mason. I said no way was you all friends. But you fucking around with Mason? I know my rights—that's a conflict of interest right there. You can't arrest us."

"*I'm* arresting you," Holmes corrected her. "And you watch your mouth. Now, you have the right to remain silent…" She went into the whole spiel as she cuffed Francine.

A soft sobbing came from the backseat of Jimmy's car. The kid. I knelt beside the door. This wasn't the first time I'd been in a situation like this, but every time I had to deal with a child I was extra cautious. I wasn't great with kids, and I was very aware that sometimes the sight of a uniform could make children skittish. "Hi, there." I tried to remember her name. I'd heard Mason use it often enough. "Lila—Lilac, right?"

"Uh-huh." She gave a big sniffle. "Mama hit Daddy."

"Was that scary?"

"Uh-huh." Another big gulp. "Can you call Uncle Mason? He'll know what to do."

The sharks swimming through my life took a big bite out of my ass—and my heart. I was about to hurt the person I cared most about. Calling Mason was the one thing I could *not* do, especially not with Jimmy and Francine spouting their venom. I was going to have to do everything by the book, line by line. And that meant a call to the county CPS, getting them involved, especially since this wouldn't be the first report for Jimmy and Francine. Child endangerment had happened here, and I couldn't just sweep it under the rug.

I wasn't going to have to worry any more about Mason and his request to talk—he was going to skin me alive when he found out about this.

"It's all going to be okay," I said lamely to the kid, wishing like heck I could do more, could promise her that I'd get Mason.

"You want me to move the kid and her booster to the Jeep?" Holmes returned to my side. "I figure CPS is more used to dealing with you, and I can handle with the bookings. If that's fine by you."

"Sounds good. Let me search the car before we head out." It was a routine thing, another by-the-book necessity.

"I'll settle the kid then help."

That was what I needed. I needed Holmes's involvement here, especially if things went south. She moved a still-tearful Lilac to the Jeep then came back. I checked the glove box and under the seats, while Holmes popped the trunk.

"Uh, Chief," she called from the back of the car. "You're going to want to see this."

I was fresh out of prayers for divine intervention as I

walked over to her, but all my muscles went tight at the look on Holmes's face. I peered down into the trunk.

Not drugs, thank God, but a dozen or more cans of spray paint, all colors, and some dirty rags.

"Think he could be our vandal?" Holmes asked.

Oh, fuck, I hope not. "You'll have to do some careful questioning," I allowed. "And bag all this as potential evidence. I'd get a call in to that friend of his, see if you can make him squeal."

"I'm taking lead on the investigation?" Holmes's head cocked to the side, her eyes wide and thoughtful.

"You are." I nodded. *By the book, by the book, by the book.* That was going to have to be my mantra to get me through the next few days. And I had to think minute to minute, task to task, not get too far ahead of myself, not think what was going to happen when Mason found out, or what he'd do if Jimmy turned out to be our vandalism suspect. I'd already sent one of his brothers to prison for pranks gone way out of hand. What would he do if his other one ended up serving time? And what the fuck was he going to do when he learned that Jimmy suspected we were seeing each other?

My gut hardened, stomach turning to cement. *We need to talk.* Had he already known? Had he wanted to warn me? He'd said no one knew about Portland, but that was clearly a lie. I was torn between guilt and anger and frustration at the whole damn situation. There wasn't any possibility where this didn't all blow up in my face in the worst possible way.

TWENTY-THREE

Mason

I woke up to Nash being gone, which honestly wasn't that huge of a surprise. He'd come to me a wreck, and I hadn't been much better—getting teary during sex had to have freaked him out as much as it had me. So it was no wonder that he'd skipped out on my request to talk.

And it wasn't like I could go track him down. I had to get to the tavern, get the bread started, then beg more time from Adam and Logan to go see my dad in the hospital. I hadn't told Nash about that last night because he had more than enough on his plate. But when I'd taken Dad to urgent care, the doctor had taken one look at his leg and his blood sugar levels and sent us on to Coos Bay for admission. I didn't even want to think about the bills, and the stress of trying to run the restaurant and dealing with Dad and whatever the hell was going on with Jimmy and Francine had been weighing on me long before Nash had shown up last night.

But Nash had *needed* me, and that had broken my

heart even as I thrilled in seeing him with all his defenses down. He'd finally allowed me in, just like I'd craved, right as I had to let him go. Irony was a cruel bitch.

I was working a batch of sourdough rye into buns when my phone went off. Unknown number, and I normally wouldn't answer it, but a niggle in the back of my mind said it could be about Dad.

"This is Mason," I answered formally, bracing myself for bad news. Across the kitchen, Logan gave me a quizzical look.

"Mason Hanks? This is Sylvia at the county jail. Do you accept a call from James Hanks?"

Oh, fuck. Jimmy, what the hell did you do? "Yeah," I said, temples pounding before Jimmy even came on the line.

"Mason?" Jimmy's voice sounded broken, same it always did when he got in more trouble than he could handle. "You've gotta help me, man. It's bad."

"What happened?" I really, really didn't want to know, but playing ostrich wasn't going to help the situation any.

"They took Lilac! They took her from me and Francine."

"Wait. Slow down. Who took Lilac?" I dropped the dough scraper onto the metal work table with a clatter. Not giving me the pretense of privacy, Logan's eyes went wide.

"That rat bastard you're sleeping with. Flint. He took Lilac."

"What? Why?" Oh, this was bad. I didn't doubt that Flint had had a reason, but why the hell was I having to hear this from Jimmy? Shouldn't he have called me straightaway?

"A stupid traffic stop. Something about my driving," Jimmy said vaguely. His words were just this side of slurred, the way he got when he was coming off a drunk.

"Were you drinking? Jimmy, you can't get another DUI—"

"Think I don't know that? You're as bad as Francine. That bitch went and hit me in front of that chick officer and now we're both in jail and they've got Lilac—"

"You were drinking and fighting with Francine and you had Lilac in the car?" I went from concern to white-hot anger. How dare he endanger Lilac? Sadly, I wasn't shocked. I'd been half expecting a stunt like this since I'd come back to town. And judging from Logan's hard expression, so had he. He started putting finished rolls on a baking tray while I stepped away to pace.

"Don't you go all high and mighty on me. I figured out your dirty little secret—you're fucking around with Flint." Jimmy's voice was as nasty as I'd ever heard it.

"You be quiet." I was painfully aware of the fact that half the jail could probably hear this conversation. "I'm not fucking Flint."

The lie rolled off my tongue easy enough, but it left an acid burn in my throat. *Not anymore, at least. Not ever again.* The baking tray clattered against the counter as Logan dropped it, gaping at me. He wasn't going to believe me anymore than Jimmy did, but at least he wasn't a fucking gossip like my brother.

"You're a damn liar. And now you've got to convince him to drop these BS charges, let us out of here."

"I'm not gonna be able to get you out of a DUI." That much I knew for certain—no way did I have that kind of pull over Flint. If he couldn't even warn me that this was going down, no way was he being swayed by anything I said.

"Then get me a damn lawyer. They can't take my kid." Jimmy's voice cracked. "You can't let them have Lilac."

"Who's them? Who has Lilac right now?" I paced away from Logan and the work table, fighting the urge to race for my car straightaway, fetch Lilac, protect her from this awful mess.

"CPS. That's what they said at the station. They were calling the county DHS office, getting her in the system."

Oh, fuck. *Nash, why didn't you text me?* This was super bad. Bile rose in my throat at the thought of Lilac in foster care. "I'll call them. See what I can do about making them give her to me, but I'm going to have to wait on the lawyer—"

"What the fuck? Why?"

"*Jimmy.* I've got to make my priority Lilac. And I can't be sure that they'll release her to me if I'm paying for your lawyer. I need to talk to some people, sort this out."

"You can't let Francine's folks get her. They're nuts."

"I know." With Dad in the hospital, I was pretty much it for Lilac. Francine's family was a mess, worse than my family, and no way was any social worker with half a brain giving Lilac to one of them, even if Francine's folks agreed to take her. "Let me see what I can do. You're going to have to trust me here."

Jimmy made a scoffing noise. "Trust you? You've been sneaking around, making fools out of the whole family, fucking the damn chief of—"

"*James Nolan Hanks.*" I channeled every bit of my

father's stern voice, the I-mean-business one. "You stop spouting nonsense where anyone can hear. I'm not helping you, not one bit, if you can't be quiet and listen."

Not that it would make a difference. The damage was inevitably done. If Jimmy thought he knew, then that probably meant Francine did, too, and that woman had never learned to keep her mouth shut about anything. She was undoubtedly telling anyone who would listen in the holding cell.

"Whatever." Jimmy's tone was the verbal equivalent of an eye roll. "Just get me out of here. Get me my kid back."

"Stop with the orders. You fucked up here. And now I've got to clean up your mess."

"I'm sorry." Jimmy's voice broke again, and we ended the phone call with some sloppy tears and apologies from Jimmy that I didn't delude myself into thinking he meant. Only thing Jimmy was truly sorry for was that he'd been caught.

"I've got to go," I said to Logan as soon as I hung up.

"I figured. What the hell did Jimmy do anyway?"

I gave him the condensed version. "Do you know anything about CPS? How I can get Lilac back?"

"You'll have to ask them to be an emergency placement." Logan's childhood best friend was a social worker of some ilk in Portland, so I knew he'd have good info for me. "And you should brace yourself for it taking some time."

"*Fuck.*"

"Mason? Are you really sleeping with Flint?" Logan shook his head. "Because if you are...that's going to complicate things in the worst way."

I groaned. I wanted nothing more than to unload the whole truth on my friend, but I had to think of Lilac. The lie slipped off my tongue easier the second time. "Nope. Nothing going on with Na—Flint."

"You're a terrible liar." Logan came over and gave me awkward pat on the shoulder. "Just watch yourself, Mason. This could all go south in a hurry."

"I know." I ran my hands through my hair. God, I hated this. Hated how powerless I felt. "And my dad's still sick. All Lilac has is me." I could hear my brother's desperate helplessness in my own voice, and it made my stomach churn.

"And you'll do right by her." Logan sounded way more convinced than I felt. "Adam and I will hold down the fort here. You focus on your family."

Focus on my family. That was what I should have been doing all along, not fucking around with Nash in an affair that had been doomed from the very start. And now, because I hadn't kept my head, I might lose the most important piece of that family, and I'd only have my stupid self to blame.

Nash

My day was shit. First there was booking Francine and Jimmy, then the trip to the county seat to dump them in jail pending an arraignment and bail setting. While there, we'd had to meet up with the social worker at the county DHS office and deliver a still-sobbing and scared Lilac.

My ribs felt kicked in, heart bruised and battered,

and I couldn't fully look at the kid. I'd gotten her a blanket and some books from the box we kept for situations like this, but she hadn't touched either. I knew the social worker, Maureen, a kind, middle-aged woman who'd gone to high school with Easton, and I knew she'd do right by Lilac, but that didn't make me feel one lick better about this whole mess.

"You'll investigate relative placement?" I confirmed as we took care of all the details in her office while Lilac glanced stone-faced at the toys in the corner.

"Of course. You know we always start there. But this family…" She shook her head. "Well, we'll have to see. There's a history here."

I wanted to stick up for Mason, put in a good word, tell her to not lump him with the rest of his family, but I couldn't, not without endangering his case before it even got started.

"Make her call Uncle Mason." Lilac threw herself at me right as I was about to leave.

"Now, now." Maureen soothed as she pulled Lilac away. "I've got lots of calls to make. And I promise you, we'll find you the *perfect* place —"

"I want Uncle Mason. And Mama. And Daddy."

God. My chest ached with each teary onslaught, bringing fresh guilt.

"I know you do. Let me tell you about what's going to happen. Step by step." Maureen hugged her tight, making a shooing motion for me to go.

Each step as I walked down the hallway killed me, the tears echoing in my brain. Jimmy might have brought all this on himself, but it was Lilac who would pay the real price, and that was eating me up, more than it usually did in these cases. And Mason. He'd pay the price, too.

I ached for him, needed to go to him. Needed to warn him what was about to come down on his head, but of course I couldn't risk that. We'd have to talk soon enough, but not while I was on duty. Not when I was walking this by-the-book tightrope of making sure I handled any conflict of interest the right way.

God, I'd known this day was coming. The thing between us had always been destined to blow up in a career-and-life-threatening way, and still I'd walked down this road, knowingly. Happily, even. I'd have to live with that a long, long time.

But I didn't have the luxury of stewing on it. Back at the office, I had the Hinkie shooting to tend to, and it was late before I headed home, the long day pinning me down like cement pylons on my shoulders.

I left the back gate unlocked, and I wasn't surprised one bit when the knock sounded on my back door ten minutes after I got home. I abandoned my microwave meal on the counter and opened the door.

"What the ever loving fuck, Nash?" Mason burst in, without any preamble. He looked like shit—still hadn't shaved and his clothes were all rumpled, flour on his pants, grease stain on his T-shirt, and eyes were as tortured as I'd ever seen them.

"I know you're mad—"

"Mad. Mad? Mad doesn't even begin to cover this." He paced the length of my kitchen. "You couldn't give me a heads up? A text? 'Hey, I'm pulling over Jimmy.' Something."

"You know I couldn't do that. And it was Holmes

who pulled them over. It's her investigation. I was just backup—"

"Bullshit. You're the freaking chief of police. If you don't want them charged, they don't get charged."

"You're asking me to not charge your brother with a DUI after he failed a sobriety test? To let him off because...of what exactly?"

"No." Mason yanked at his hair. "I don't know. I thought I'd at least merit a call. Something. And you could have brought me Lilac. No need to involve CPS—"

"You're asking me to break the law, Mason." I slumped into one of the chairs at my kitchen table. "They endangered the welfare of a child. That's a chargeable offense. I wouldn't be doing my job—"

"And it's always about the job for you, isn't it?" Mason didn't slow his pacing.

"You knew that. Before we ever started this thing. You knew that. The job has to come first," I said dully, hating myself more with each word.

"You're tearing my family apart. Don't you care about that, even a little?" Mason's voice broke, spearing me as surely as a bullet piercing the Kevlar I wrapped my heart in.

"Of course I do." My voice was rough.

"Do you care about *me*?" Mason stopped pacing and whirled to face me.

"You know I do. But Jimmy made his choices, not me."

"Lilac has to stay with an emergency foster placement overnight, did you know that? She's alone and scared and with a strange family, and the most they let me do was bring the social worker some clothes and her bear. There's going to be a hearing."

"That's standard procedure, yes." I knew it was the wrong thing to say and not at all soothing, but it was all I had.

"Fuck standard procedure. You know me, Nash. You know she'd be better off with me than some stranger, and you couldn't even tell the social worker that? Couldn't get them to—"

"Are you seriously asking me to pull strings for you? Call in favors?"

"*Yes*. Okay. Yes." Mason all but threw himself into the chair opposite me.

"I couldn't do that. It would be a violation of every principle—"

"Fuck your principles, Nash. Fuck them." As fast as he'd sat down, Mason was up again.

I'd been working hard at staying calm, but now I felt my anger building. "My principles are all I have—"

"Fuck that. You had *me*."

Had. Past tense. My heart cracked a little more. "What happened today with Jimmy has nothing to do with us and what we have—"

"What we have? You won't introduce me to your mother, even as a friend. You're ashamed of me. Ashamed to be fucking a Hanks. And you don't think I'm worthy of—"

"I'm not ashamed of you," I said firmly, even as I knew my guilt was a real, palpable thing. But I couldn't have him thinking like that. My guilt and shame were my own deal. "You knew going into this that I wasn't coming out."

"Of course not." Mason's voice was bitter as three-day-old coffee. "If it's not me you're ashamed of, it's *you*. And either way, there's nothing between us, not now."

"I know." I rested my face on my hands, unable to look at him a second longer. "Jimmy thinks he's figured it out."

"That's really why you didn't call me, isn't it? You were pissed at Jimmy, so you punished—"

"Don't be ridiculous," I said sharply. "But if there's even a whiff of conflict of interest..."

"Here come your damn principles again." Mason shook his head.

"I'm trying to save your ass." I rubbed my eyes. "Last thing I need is them thinking your case for the kid is tainted. Or them declaring a mistrial against Jimmy—"

"Can't have that," Mason snarled. God, I wanted to hold him, wanted to soothe his ruffled edges. This wasn't like him, and I knew it was the stress speaking, but it still *hurt*. "You won't be happy until my whole damn family's behind bars."

"Mason—"

"Don't tell me it's not like that. That's the real reason you've held back—not because of the age difference or you not wanting to come out. It's because I'm a Hanks. And that'll always mean I'm trash around here."

"Mas—"

"Don't *Mason* me. I saw how that social worker looked at me. Same way you always look at my brothers. Like trouble's just around the corner. She doesn't trust me. She let me fill out all the paperwork and stuff, but I could tell. And you could fix that, but you won't."

"I can't." I couldn't believe he was asking this of me.

Unable to sit any longer, I pushed away from the table, strode to the opposite side of the room. "I'd be turning my back on everything I am, everything I've been for twenty years in law enforcement. I can't do that. Not for you, not for anyone. And trust me, if there was ever anyone I'd compromise myself for, it would be you."

"But it's not me, is it? Not ever going to be. You'll deny it if Jimmy spews any rumors about us, of course. Can't have a hint of tarnish on your shiny halo. And you'll end this thing with me because it's the *right* thing to do. Well, screw right, Nash. And screw you."

"I'm not telling you to lie," I said roughly. "If they ask you point-blank—"

"Of course you're not asking me to lie. You're not asking me for a damn thing." His voice was tortured, and I no longer had a clue what he wanted to hear from me.

"I'm not." I had a feeling it was the exact wrong words, but I didn't know what else to say. "You're the one who's asking for impossible things—"

"Not anymore. Not asking you for jack crap now." Mason's eyes narrowed as his face hardened. "I thought you had a heart, Nash. I was wrong."

I do. And it's breaking. But I didn't say that. Didn't stop him when he stalked to the door. Didn't call him back with an offer to talk to the social worker. Didn't tell him I'd go easy on Jimmy if only he'd stay. Didn't tell him that I loved him and that it was killing me to see him like this. Didn't cry when the door shut behind him, even as my eyes burned. It was better that I'd left the words unsaid, not told him the truth in my heart.

I knew how to be a good cop. I knew how to do my job. I knew how to be a respectable man, but I wasn't sure I knew how to be the man Mason needed. He needed someone proud to walk down the beach with him, someone unencumbered by this job, this past, this pressing sense of responsibility that I just couldn't shake.

Disgusted at myself, I threw my long-abandoned dinner in the trash and poured myself a shot. Not to get drunk—I had to be back on duty too soon for that—but to feel the burn, to feel something, to remind myself that I wasn't the hollow, cold man that Mason thought I was.

He thought I had no heart, but the truth was that he was it. He was my heart, my world, my everything. And hell if I knew how to walk around, do my job with that heart missing. Hell if I *wanted* to. I'd never thought of myself as lacking in courage, but I was going to have to find some extra in hurry if I wanted a chance to make this right.

TWENTY-FOUR

Mason

"I told them. I'm ready to go home. You need me."
Wheezing with the effort, my dad sat up in the hospital
bed.

"And the doctor said another day or two. You're
lucky you're not losing the leg. Yet." I slumped in the
visitor's chair in his hospital room. My everything hurt
and I was beyond tired, to the point that the empty bed
on the other side of Dad was pretty tempting.

"I've got to talk to Gunnar. See if we can scrape
together the bail money for Jimmy, maybe do a deal—"

"There's no money." I rubbed my head. I'd had a
nonstop tension headache since Jimmy's first phone call,
made worse by my argument with Nash. "None. I
balance your checkbook. You had to borrow twenty
from me for the prescription co-pay. Gunnar doesn't
have it, either."

"But you—" He had that wheedling tone that I hated,
and I held up a hand, cutting him off.

"Everything I have is sunk into the tavern. I had to do some creative rearranging to find the fee for my lawyer—"

"Your lawyer?" He made a dismissive noise. "Your poor brother is rotting over there in the jail. That public defender has it out for us."

"The world is not out to get the Hanks." I was weary, so damn weary of being a Hanks. How did I manage to share DNA with Jimmy and Freddy? It was like Jimmy had learned absolutely nothing from Freddy's crimes, letting Chester and who knows who else talk him into vandalizing businesses. And oh, yeah, it was all just allegations right now, investigation pending and all that, but I knew in my gut that Jimmy was in on the vandalism. It might come down to whether Chester tattled on him, but the spray paint in his car was damning enough for me. "And yes, *my* lawyer. They're not giving me Lilac fast enough. I need a lawyer for this hearing tomorrow."

The morning after I'd lost my freaking head at Nash's place, there had been a scrap of paper shoved under my kitchen door.

Call Julie Turner. Family lawyer. Decent person. Local. She'll help.

The note wasn't signed, but I recognized Nash's blocky writing. I'd said some pretty awful things. We both had, really. But he'd thought enough to give me a recommendation for a lawyer, and that counted for... something. What, I wasn't sure, but it was *something*, and Julie's rate was far better than someone from Eugene or Portland. Hiring an attorney from out of the area was what Brock and Logan had wanted me to do.

I'd recognized Julie from Pride Night at the tavern—

she was our librarian's partner, an older woman with a calming demeanor. She'd managed to arrange for a visit with Lilac hours after our first meeting and thought I had a decent chance of getting the emergency placement. She'd immediately become my favorite person in the world. But, of course, Dad would begrudge me her fee.

"If I could leave this damn bed, they'd give her to me—"

"Dad." I didn't have it in me to sugar coat the truth. "You're sick. You can barely get around these days. Your place is a wreck. They're not giving you custody. Like it or not, I'm our best shot."

"I wish your sainted mother was here." His eyes filled with tears, not the first time since this ordeal had begun.

"Me, too." God, how I wished that. The social workers might have looked askance at the house, but they would have given her custody, and she would have known what to do to keep Jimmy and Dad in line.

"Or that you had a...*someone*. Single, young guy...like you..." Dad stumbled for words.

"They're not denying me because I'm gay." The social worker seemed to have far more issue with me being a Hanks than being gay, and Julie was convinced that it was just a matter of jumping through all the right hoops for DHS.

"Of course not." Dad wasn't going to confess to any bigoted assumptions, and he bristled like I was accusing him of something. "Jimmy's the one who's...hard on you, not me. I promised your mother..." Another big sniffle.

I seized on his emotional reaction. "She'd want me to do this. Want me to step in and do what's right for Lilac."

"She would." Dad looked at me through bleary eyes. "God, I loved that woman. Didn't deserve her."

"No, you didn't." I laughed, trying to break up the mood. My parents had been far from perfect, but they'd loved each other almost ferociously and been intensely loyal to each other. I'd always wanted a love like that, albeit a saner one, with a partner deserving of my affection. I'd wanted to know how it felt to love that deeply.

And now I knew.

And it sucked.

I'd lit into Nash because I was hurting, because nothing in my damn life made sense anymore, and because I wanted *someone* to be there for me, and I wanted it to be him. And it wasn't ever going to be him. So I'd lashed out.

I knew deep down that he'd only been doing his job. I didn't want special treatment. I just wanted...him. Us. A future where we dealt with crap like this together. But a future where we were a couple wouldn't ever happen, and rage over the unfairness of that had made me say a lot of shit, most of which I didn't even remember. All I knew was that I loved Nash and he didn't love me back and the timing of that realization was absolutely worthless.

"Don't see why you can't get Flint to drop the charges."

"Jimmy's gotten to you, I see." I wasn't sure when Jimmy had been allowed a phone call to Dad, but it didn't matter. Gossip traveled fast around these parts, and I'd known that Jimmy and Francine wouldn't keep their traps shut in jail.

"It's true, then? You and him…" Dad pulled a wounded face, begging me with his eyes to deny it.

But I was tired. Very tired. So I shrugged. "Does it make a difference? He's not going to drop the charges. He can't do that."

"Does it make a difference? Of course it makes a difference!" Dad's face turned purple, and he gestured wildly. I needed to calm him down or I'd have a nurse in here on my case. "That Flint has had it in for our family since before he was an officer. His father did, too. Their whole family looks down on us. He's just using you."

And there it was, the gut punch I'd figured was coming. Nash hadn't used me, or at least, no more than I'd let him. But my dad's words still tickled the back of my brain, an itch I wasn't ever going to be free of. *Had* this been just sex for Nash? It had slid way past that for me, but maybe it had always only been physical for him. He'd let me go, after all, let me rant and rave and storm off and hadn't come after me, hadn't texted. He'd left the note, but that was the sort of neighborly kindness he might do for anyone.

"No one's using anyone." My voice was rough and shaky.

"I get that you don't want to…be alone. But why not Adam? Someone closer to your age?"

I had to laugh at that. "Adam's like my third brother. The good one. We're never going to hook up."

"Flint won't ever give you a future," Dad said firmly. And I knew he was correct. There'd been no future here, right from the start. "This is one more strike against us, one more thing to hold over our heads—"

"Take a breath," I ordered. "It's not like that. He's not

like that. You and Jimmy and Francine need to stop spouting stupid conspiracy theories, especially if you want me to be able to help Lilac."

And that was where my focus had to stay—on helping Lilac, on saving what was left of my family. Much as I wanted to go to Nash, fight for a future together, I couldn't allow myself the luxury. Family had to come first, just like his job did for him. Dad was right about one thing—there was no future here.

Nash

My phone rang ten minutes before I needed to drive to the station. My heart galloped. It wouldn't be Mason —hadn't been Mason since our argument in my kitchen, but hope was a stupid thing. And it wasn't like I would know what to say even if it was Mason. I didn't have the right words for him yet, wasn't sure if there even was a way to fix things between us.

And sure enough, it was my mother's number flashing on my screen. I leaned against the kitchen counter, taking my time to hit answer.

"Nash. Sweetheart. How *are* you?" Something about the strain in her voice told me this was more than just a welfare check.

"I'm good. Heading to the station in a few, so I don't have much time—"

"That's fine. I just wanted to talk about me coming down, end of next week."

Oh, hell. I'd forgotten about my father's birthday. She always liked to put flowers on his grave and Easton's, treating the occasion as some sort of macabre holiday. My neck tightened at the thought.

"Is Trisha driving you?" I didn't like her making the long drive on her own, and public transit wasn't a realistic option way out here. No way was she suffering the bus to Coos Bay.

"Yes, her and the kids, too. You'll...have room?"

That had never been a question in the past, and the hesitation in her voice had me on edge. "Of course. Guest rooms for you and Trisha, and the kids can do the slumber party in the living room again."

"Oh, good. I wasn't sure you'd be free..."

"Work's a bear lately." I deliberately misunderstood her. "But I'll make the time to take you out to the cemetery."

"That's not what...I shouldn't have to tell you this..." *Then don't.* I braced myself for her next words. "...but there's awful rumors swirling about you. Terrible things. About you and a Hanks. I said there was no way, of course. You wouldn't take up with...someone. Not again. You wouldn't risk your career like that. Not for a Hanks."

Oh, I would. And I did. And I'd do it again. "Mom, you know I'm gay."

I'd never said the words before, not directly anyway. We'd danced around the issue when she'd been set on moving up to Portland, and we'd always couched any further discussion in vague terms that weren't doing either of us any favors, not anymore.

Her sigh could have sliced the county in half. "Yes, but I thought you learned your lesson with that teacher

—your preferences can't be public knowledge. You know that, Nash."

She made it sound like a taste for rhubarb pie over apple. I sighed right back, because I shouldn't have to explain this to her. "It's not something I can just turn off. Steve was a good man. Better than I deserved. And I'm tired. Tired of skulking around in secret, hiding people I care about because of the job."

"So it's true? You and this Hanks kid? Oh, *Nash.*"

"He's not a kid." The age difference might still be something I was coming to terms with, but I wasn't going to let her dismiss Mason that way. "He's twenty-eight. And he's nothing like his family—"

"They're all the same. Users and losers, your father always said. Oh…what would he say about this? Have you thought about that at all?"

Only every damn day. "Mason's not a loser. Or using me." If anything, I'd done the using—keeping him at arm's length when I knew he'd likely wanted something more, something real, letting him tell me as much in Portland and then still hurting him. "He's a business owner. Upstanding citizen. And he's trying to stand by his family, best he can. There's a kid involved. I like to think Dad would respect that."

He wouldn't, of course, not even a small amount. He'd been a hard, grudge-filled man who thought his judgment was the be-all and end-all. But I liked imagining a world where he could see someone like Mason turn their life around, become more than what they'd been raised to be, and see beyond labels and assumptions. But that hadn't ever been my father.

Mom's answering *tsk* said she knew it, too. "He'd

want you to do the right thing. Break this off, whatever it is. Try to salvage your reputation. You can deny the rumors. People will believe you."

Yes, yes, they would. I knew that. Holmes hadn't asked me whether Jimmy's venom was true, and I knew she'd back me up if I said he was full of shit. Whole department would, really. But that wasn't the issue. Mason would still be the one hurting. And I wanted to go to him something awful, to comfort him, to protect him from any gossip. I'd thought that denial was the best way to protect us both, but the more I missed him, the less I thought that. Denial was selfish and would only end with me alone, more bitter than ever.

I liked who I'd been with Mason. Liked the man who was learning to cook, who laughed and smiled at the end of the day, liked the man who could show his favorite places to his guy, share his hobbies and his life and be richer for the effort. I liked Mason here in my house. Liked the sound of his voice in my big kitchen, liked him hogging space in my shower and coaxing me into a crowded tub. Simple truth was—I liked that version of myself too much to let Mason go, regardless of whether it was the smart option.

"Maybe I don't want them to," I said at last. "Maybe I don't want to grow old alone. Maybe you're okay with that future for me, but I'm not, not any longer, not since I've seen what I could have if I tried."

"You don't have to be alone. You've got your family, your job."

I couldn't believe the next words that came out of my mouth, but they tumbled out all the same. "The job's not enough. Not anymore. I'm not like Dad. I can't have it be my entire life. I don't want to be old before my time, stroking out because I never took a minute away —"

"You watch your mouth. Your father gave everything he had to that city —"

"Yes, and nothing left over for us. For you. I want something more for my life." As soon as I said it, I believed it. I did want something more. Someone more.

"But a Hanks? Really?" My mother's tearful voice awoke an ache behind my ribs and a tightness in my throat, but it didn't loosen my resolve.

"He's more than his family." Guilt washed over me. I'd done a piss-poor job of convincing Mason of that. Made him think I was ashamed of him. Made him feel not worthy and hadn't really corrected him, hadn't stood up for him. For us.

And that had to change. Starting right now.

"Oh, Nash. I hope you know what you're doing." My mother sounded weary and resigned, but I'd never been more determined. For the first time in a very long time, I knew *exactly* what I was doing. My only worry was whether it would work.

TWENTY-FIVE

Mason

The county seat was forty-five minutes south of us, with the courthouse right next to the jail. I'd had far too much experience with this drive in my life as well as with both buildings. Dad was still up at the hospital in Coos Bay, and cranky though he was, I really wished he'd been able to come with me to the hearing. Despite our argument in the hospital room, he'd given a statement to the social worker supporting my bid for custody, and I supposed that was as much as I could hope for.

This building felt too big for me, the day too momentous. The courthouse was an old stone building full of wide, drafty hallways lined with long, wooden benches. I wore my best clothes, the ones I'd worn in Portland to make the presentation to Brock's investors, tie and all.

"This is most likely just a formality," Julie said, patting my arm. We'd done all the paperwork, met with the social workers more than once. They'd even been to my house, looked at my car. We *should* have everything they wanted, but my life had shown me that *should* had a way of not working out. My mom *should* be alive. Freddy *should* have been smarter than to listen to his friends. Nash *should* love me back. Nothing went as it *should*.

"I'm nervous," I admitted outside the courtroom. We were early and another hearing was going on before ours.

"Well, don't be." She gave me a warm smile. "This judge is nice. Compassionate. She'll listen fairly, and that's all we can hope."

Actually, it wasn't. I didn't only want a fair hearing. I wanted Lilac with me. Anything short of that was going to be a crushing defeat, but I nodded anyway. No sense in unloading on Julie.

"I'm going to duck into the restroom. I'll be right back."

I sank onto the nearest bench as she walked away, her brown heels clip-clopping on the marble floor.

"This seat taken?" A familiar voice had me glancing over. *Nash*. He wasn't in uniform, but he was dressed up in a crisp white shirt with a gray tie and gray pants.

"What are you doing here?" Unable to keep the suspicion out of my voice, I still slid over to make room for him. "Are you testifying at the hearing?"

"No, I told you, I can't do that." Deep lines of regret creased Nash's face, and it felt like I had similar ones on my heart. So nothing had changed, not really. "Not that they'd ask me to, anyway—this one is likely to be mainly procedural."

"So why come?" My voice was cold, not something I recognized.

"I'm not here on official business. I took the morning off. I came for *you*."

"For me?"

"I thought you could use a friend today, whichever way this goes. And I want to be that friend." His eyes seemed more green than usual, deep pools of sympathy, and I wanted to touch him so badly it hurt.

"But what about your conflict of interest? People are going to talk, more than they have been, you showing up here."

"I'm working on the conflict of interest." Nash sighed. "Holmes will handle the investigation, and I'm talking with the county and the state board on other steps—I'm not the first cop to end up with a conflict of interest, and there are procedures in place."

"So you told them? About us?" I gaped at him.

"I had no choice."

That wasn't exactly what I wanted to hear, but Julie came back over. "Chief, how lovely you could make it."

"I'm not the only one." Nash gestured down the hall. Walking through the double doors were Logan and Adam, and Adam's mother and sister. Dolly from the donut place and a number of our servers and regular customers followed. Even stuffy Everleigh from the visitor center was there.

"What the… I don't understand."

"We thought it might help the court to see that you're not alone," Julie said gently. "That you've got a whole community to support you."

"Thought you weren't going to pull strings," I hissed at Nash.

"I didn't. They wanted to help. And I can't testify, but I can be here. For you."

He didn't get a chance to reply because the crowd was upon us then, everyone offering words of support. I hadn't realized how big an impact our business had made in just a few months—to have so many people ready to go to bat for me was very humbling and had my sinuses burning.

A clerk informed me it was time to enter the courtroom. Julie and I sat in the front of the small room, but I was painfully aware of Nash right behind me, a warm but highly confounding presence. What was he doing? What did he want? Was this merely—

"All rise." The bailiff summoned our attention, and I had to drop my endless questions as my heart hammered faster. Nash and I would have to wait. This was it. Lilac's future was on the line.

The attorney for DHS spoke first, answering some questions the judge had about where the case stood. Neither Francine nor Jimmy had made bail. Francine was facing charges of assault, child endangerment, interfering with law enforcement, and possession of a controlled substance—she'd been found with drugs when they'd searched her at the jail, adding to the trouble she was in. Jimmy was similarly up a creek without a paddle —assault, child endangerment, DUI, and the ongoing investigation into potential vandalism charges.

Finally, it was Julie's turn to speak on my behalf. She made an eloquent little speech about how my request for emergency placement should take priority under the law as I was a relative, the only one to come forward. Then she indicated all the people behind me. "And Mr. Hanks has the support of his community. I know this court may have concerns given his age and childlessness, but Mr. Hanks won't be doing this alone."

For the first time in days, I felt my shoulders relax. I wouldn't be alone if the court gave me this chance.

I'd been so damn alone all week, all the hours spent on the highway between Rainbow Cove and the hospital and the county offices. It had been like shoving a huge boulder up a cliff. But sitting there, with my friends behind me, pillars of the town there, too, I realized for the first time that it wasn't just me against the world. The whole town wasn't simply waiting to see if I failed. I had roots here. Connections. A network to hold me up. And it was staggering, realizing that they were all there, had made the drive for me and Lilac, that I was that important to them.

The judge asked Julie about the home study—that was still pending, and I had a checklist of things to do around the house before a second visit from the social workers. My heart sank. Maybe none of this mattered— maybe the court was going to find me lacking even with a small army behind me.

"This court always gives first priority under the law to relative placement. However, this is not absolute."

Oh please, oh please, oh please. I squished my eyes shut, unable to watch.

The judge continued, "In this case, though, I think it is clearly in the child's best interests that temporary custody be granted to Mr. Hanks and that the state work with him to quickly complete the home study and get the placement ASAP. The next hearing on this matter will be..." She discussed the next steps in the case, the many steps ahead for Lilac and me, depending on what happened with Jimmy and Francine. But I couldn't think about that, could only rub the bridge of my nose and exhale noisily. I'd done it.

Nash leaned forward and squeezed my shoulder. "See?" he whispered. "This will all work out."

I still wasn't sure I quite believed him, and I had no idea whether I had that certainty where he and I were concerned, but in that moment I was profoundly grateful he was there. I was getting Lilac. Everything else could wait.

Nash

I'd been around the legal system long enough to know that Mason and his niece had a long, long road to travel, but my heart was still light as I headed back to Rainbow Cove. There had been too many people around Mason after the hearing for us to talk, and that was all right. I hadn't come hoping he'd take my sorry ass back, but rather to lend moral support, regardless of where we stood. The talk we desperately needed to have could wait until we didn't have an audience.

So I had nodded at him, trying to tell him with my eyes that I'd be around later, after I settled a few things at the station. I was already leaping ahead to "later," though, rehearsing what I'd say, when Holmes came into my office.

"Chief?" She stepped inside, closed my seldom-shut door. "I just had a phone call from the ethics board. Are you sure you want to formally recuse yourself from the Hanks case?"

"I am." It didn't matter what Mason and I presently were—I knew what I hoped we'd be, and that was what mattered. This was the right thing to do, even if my mother and others might not see it that way.

"Is this because of what Jimmy Hanks is saying? Because you know I've got your back—I'll say that there's nothing going on between you and that family other than a lot of bad will on Jimmy's side." She crossed her arms.

"I know you've got my back, and I appreciate it." I took a deep breath. "But it's true. I'm...seeing Mason Hanks."

To Holmes's credit, she didn't flinch. Didn't look all that surprised, actually. She nodded. "Mason seems like a good guy. I heard he's getting custody of the kid. That's a big job."

"He'll be up for it." My confidence in our future might be shaky, but I'd never believed more in Mason as a person.

"You sure *you're* ready for that? For all of it, I mean." She leaned against my desk. The room was small to begin with, and the conversation had me feeling like the walls were inching toward me.

We weren't particularly close, Holmes and I. I'd hired her, trained her, respected the hell out of her, but we didn't share confidences or offer more than passing friendship. Thus, I was tempted to lie and more than a little surprised when the truth slipped out. "I'm not sure. Guess we'll all find out."

"Well, you have my support. And Derrick's, for what it's worth. And I know an out officer up in—"

"I'm not looking to start a club," I said more gruffly than I'd intended. I took a breath and backed down. "Thank you, though, for the support."

"You let me know if there's anything I can do. And not just about the Hanks case." Her brown eyes were full of compassion I wasn't quite sure I deserved.

"Will do." My throat felt strangely tight.

"You heading out soon?"

"In just a few." I finished up my latest round of notes on the Hinkie shooting and headed home, making sure to drive by the tavern. Not surprisingly, Mason's car wasn't there. On my way home I spotted it in his driveway, so I gathered up some things at my house that I'd set out that morning and walked to Mason's place. Down the sidewalk even. I was done with stealth.

I could have texted him, but I didn't want to make it easy for him to shut me out. Still, my heart pounded as I waited for him to answer the front door.

"Nash?" His eyes went wide when he saw me standing there, holding the two overflowing shopping bags. "What's this?"

This had gone much better in my head. I coughed. "Figured you might need some things."

"Things?" He eyed the bags like they might contain live grenades.

"I went through a bunch of our stuff in the attic. Pink sheets and some other bedding from Trisha's old room. A doll. The bear, though, used to be mine…" I was rambling and didn't seem able to turn it off.

"I'm building the bed right now, actually." Finally,

Mason ushered me in. "Adam's mom had a spare twin bed, so it's just a matter of putting together the frame. Adam's working my shift at the tavern or he'd be able to help me. I've got a long list of stuff to get done before the social worker comes in the morning for a final check."

"I can help." I swallowed hard.

"Can you?" His eyes were guarded. "Isn't that going to cause issues for you? I mean, it was nice of you, coming to the hearing, but I don't want you losing your job or outed over this. The gossip will die down if you let it."

"I don't want it to." That wasn't the complete truth— I hated knowing that people were talking about us, and that probably wasn't going to change, but I'd take the gossip if it meant having a shot at Mason. "And I'm not losing my job. I'm doing everything above board. Declaring the conflict of interest and all. There are rules in place, guidelines for things like in-laws."

Mason's laugh was more than a little bitter. "My family's not your in-laws."

"Better safe to treat it like that than be sorry." I quoted the person I'd spoken with at length at the ethics board. "I don't want to hide, Mason."

"Maybe I do." He studied the scarred hardwood floor of the living room. "I didn't stop and consider how bad the gossip could be—people are saying I roped you into something. Like, I don't know...like I corrupted you. Maybe you don't want to be tied to a Hanks."

Setting the bags on the couch, I took his shoulders, made him look at me. "I want to be tied to *this* Hanks. You're worth more to me than some gossip."

"My family hates you." Mason's voice was pained.

"My dad thinks you're just using me —"

"Is that what you think?" I asked sharply.

"No." He shook his head. "Not really. But this thing, it got complicated hella quick. You deserve a better coming out than this. Someone with less baggage."

"I don't want someone — I want *you*. And we've all got baggage. And I'm not coming out for you."

"You're not?" Looking understandably confused, his eyes narrowed. The lone lamp in the room cast deep shadows over his face, but it was the shadows in his eyes that made me ache.

"I'm coming out for me. Because I'm almost forty now, and it's beyond time that I stop running from my father's ghost. Because I'm worth it, every bit as much as you are. Because I deserve to be happy and not be alone. It took you to show me that, but I'm doing this for me. It's time I was free."

"Yeah." Mason's voice was husky. "Your family isn't going to be any more understanding than mine, though."

I thought back to my conversation with my mother. "Nope. But I can't live my life by their rules. And I think deep down my mother *does* want me to be happy. And you — you make me happy."

"I do?" He tilted his head to one side, considering me. "For real? Because it's not just sex for me, Nash. There are some serious feelings involved here, feelings I didn't count on, but I can't ignore them."

"I don't want you to. It's not just sex for me, either." Unable to stop myself, I stroked his arms.

"But you've never been out before. Maybe you don't want to tie yourself to me —"

My laugh echoed through the nearly bare room. "You

seriously think I want to play the field?"

"Maybe." He worried his lip with his teeth.

"You're the best man I know. I'm sorry I didn't tell you that before, that I made you think somehow that you're not worthy. There's no one else I want to be with because I know you're it for me."

"I can't change that I'm a Hanks. I'm always going to be related to Jimmy and Freddy, and chances are that I'm going to have Lilac for a while."

"It's all a part of you. I get it." I wanted to kiss him so badly, but his face was still wary. "I'm still going to be the police chief. Late nights. Lots of stress. It's not going to be a picnic being with me, either. But I want us to try. For real this time. No hiding."

"You want to date?" Mason lifted an eyebrow.

"You could call it that," I allowed. "I want more cooking lessons and more fishing and more late lunches. But yeah, if you want dates, like movies and whatever else it is people do, I'm game."

Mason finally laughed. "Cooking and fishing and eating sound good to me. I want that, too. Not like I'm going to have much time for the dinner-and-a-movie kind of dating." He shook his head. "God, I have so much to do. I'm not sure I'm ready for this, Nash."

"Then let's tackle your list. Together."

We still had a long ways to go, but when he nodded I finally felt like I had my footing after days of treading through wet sand and sharp rocks. Maybe it was going to take more time than I'd like, but this was a start, a really good one. The next step was getting Mason to truly believe that I meant what I said. He was the guy for me, no turning back.

TWENTY-SIX

Mason

Nash was saying all the right things, the things I'd waited all summer to hear, but I wasn't quite ready to throw myself into his arms. I was damn tired, and I was afraid I might not get back up again if I let myself collapse against him with the relief coursing through me. I needed to get the room together for Lilac, and maybe I needed to stew over everything that Nash had said.

I stepped away from him, approaching his bags on the couch. It was a sweet peace offering, bringing me stuff from his childhood and from his nieces and nephews. "Let's take this to the spare room," I said with more decisiveness than I felt. "Then we can put the bed together."

"All right. Mind if I take off my uniform shirt?"

I wasn't ever going to turn down a chance to ogle Nash in a white T-shirt and his uniform pants, so I nodded, watching as he undid his buttons and set the shirt carefully on the couch. Things still seemed very tenuous, like we were feeling our way out of a dark sea cave.

Ready for building, he followed me to the spare room, and we worked in near silence setting up the bed frame and getting the mattress on it. Then I made up the bed using the sheets Nash had brought instead of the plain white that Adam's mom had donated. Lilac would like the pink, I thought. My throat went as tight and fuzzy as a shrunken sweater as Nash arranged the doll and bear against the pillow.

Fuck. This was *real*. I was about to get a kid. And Nash. And I wasn't sure how to cope with either. A choked noise escaped my throat.

"Hey, now." Nash drew me to him. "It's been a long day, yeah?"

"Yeah." I gratefully seized that excuse as I finally let myself be held by him, relaxing into his grip.

"You go take one of those long showers you're so fond of. I'm going to put the outlet covers on and stabilize the dresser like they want, get the last of your list done."

"You don't have to do that." My voice was thick. God, he was so *nice* to me. Nicer than I deserved after all the things I'd said. "Nash, I'm sorry —"

"We can both say sorry later." He steered me out of the room and into the small bathroom. "Right now you're exhausted and running on empty. Let me help."

It was a sign of how weary I was that I nodded. I stripped off my dusty work clothes and turned the spray to super hot as Nash backed out of the room.

His suggestion that I shower had been a good one. The hot water worked its usual magic, and I stayed in until the water ran tepid, trying to get a grip on my roiling emotions. It *had* been a day. Nash. Lilac. Everyone's support. It was almost too much.

Enjoying the puttering sounds coming from the front of the house, I slipped on a pair of flannel pants. I had a strong feeling about where this night was headed, but walking out in a towel or less felt a bit...presumptuous. There were still things I needed to say, even if Nash wanted to wave them off.

I found him in the kitchen putting the finishing touches on two grilled cheese sandwiches.

"Well, look at you." I grinned at him. "Guess I did teach you something after all."

"You taught me a lot." Nash's face was serious. "More than you know."

Throat like sandpaper, I nodded.

"And I didn't burn anything." He slid me a plate across the counter. "Did the shower help?"

"Yeah. There's still so much to do—"

"I did the outlets, the dresser, swept the room, and made sure the lamp was far enough from the bed. I think you're ready, Mason. They're not going to turn you down. You heard the court. The judge wants you to have custody."

Afraid that if I spoke I might cry, I nodded again.

"You're going to be terrific at this. Really. I believe in you."

I hadn't realized how much I needed to hear that until right then. My eyes burned and I scrubbed furiously at them. "I treated you like shit, and you still believe in me?"

"Of course I do." Nash gathered me up in a hug.

"You were hurting. I get that. And you were right about one thing—I did spend all summer denying that I had a heart. I didn't treat you like you deserved."

"I'm sorry I asked you to pull favors. I didn't really want you to. I was just so scared and angry and alone—"

"You're not alone now, not any longer." Nash pressed a soft kiss to my forehead.

"Thanks." I brushed a kiss across his mouth. "For everything."

"You're welcome. Now eat." Instead of deepening the kiss as I'd expected, Nash steered me to the table then sat opposite me with his own sandwich.

"I missed this," I admitted.

"Me, too." He gave me a tentative smile, one that I felt all the way to my bare toes.

"Tell me where the good early fall fishing is," I said, still not able to handle heavy conversation but needing some sort of goalpost to look forward to.

Nash took the bait, and we spent our meal talking rivers and fishing and the type of ties he might make me. It was only after I'd washed our plates that my heart started fluttering again.

"Do you want me to go?" Nash asked, looking at the door instead of my face.

"No," I said honestly. I dried my hands then pulled him toward me. "I want you to stay." *For always,* my heart added, even if my mouth wasn't up to such fanciful declarations.

I pulled him to my bedroom where I threw back the covers and helped him strip off the T-shirt and his pants. "I should shower," he mumbled. "You're all clean—"

"Not caring." Getting him naked had become my top

priority. I pushed my pants down, and then we tumbled onto the bed in a heap of limbs and bare skin. I pulled the covers up around us, both because I knew he loved that and because I needed it, too, needed to be surrounded by his warmth and closeness every bit as much as I needed sex.

Tugging him over me, I lost myself in his kiss. His lips were as tentative as his smiles had been, gently seeking and questioning. That wasn't going to do, not at all. I growled before taking over, chasing his tongue, claiming his lips.

"*Mason,*" he sighed against my mouth. "Slow down. We've got all night. Don't want this over—"

"It's not." I was starting to believe that, believe that we might actually have a future beyond tonight, but that didn't make me any less desperate for him. I ran my hands down his sides, thrilling to his warm, strong flesh under my palms.

He gasped when I reached his ass and pulled him firmly against me, letting him feel how turned on and needy I was.

"Missed you," I whispered.

"You've got me." He kissed me fiercely, stroking my face. "You've got me."

"Good." I surged up against him, hard cock dragging against hard cock, making me shiver. "Fuck me."

"You sure? This is plenty for me. And you've had a day—"

"Which is why I need you." I bit at his neck. "Want to feel you in me. Want to feel you tomorrow, know that I've got you."

"I'm not going anywhere." Nash reached over to the

nightstand, got the stuff I kept there. He kissed his way down my torso, but I yanked at his shoulders.

"Nuh-uh. Don't want to wait."

"I do." He pinned me to the mattress before engulfing my cock in his hot mouth. As usual, he didn't tease, just started a hard and fast rhythm that had me chanting his name. I wasn't ever going to get tired of Nash doing this for me, even if I did want him inside me in the worst way.

"Nash. Come on." Fumbling for the lube, I shoved it at him. "Don't want to shoot yet."

"Bossy, bossy." He clucked at me as he opened the tube. After taking care of the condom, he slicked us both up. He knew exactly the fine line between teasing and torture that I liked and knew that what I really needed was him.

Groaning, he pressed inside in a long, slow stroke. I shuddered beneath him, still gobsmacked by the intensity of this, even after all these weeks together. It felt like the first time all over again, my mind struggling to adjust every bit as much as my body. Being claimed by Nash was seriously the best head trip in the world, one that pushed everything else from my brain.

All the events of the last week or so fled until it was only us, moving together, my legs hitched up around his waist, his abs rubbing against my cock with each thrust, and us kissing. Always kissing.

"Mason...God...you...incredible." Sweat dripped down Nash's face, and the covers were long since tossed aside. He managed to hit my gland on each upward thrust, making me moan.

As much as I wanted to watch him, my eyes drifted shut. "Need to come."

Shifting his weight, Nash got a hand between us, started a leisurely stroke. "So impatient."

"Missed you. Missed this." I rocked up into his touch.

"Me, too. I need you, Mason. So much." His tone was tortured, and I believed him, really believed him, for the first time all evening. I wasn't in this thing by myself. He needed me as much as I needed him. I still wasn't precisely sure what I had to offer him, but in that moment, I was determined to be enough.

Back arching, I fucked up into his hand. "Love this." *Love you.* I didn't want the first time I said the words to be in the middle of sex, but I was thinking them, *owning* them. Someday soon I'd be brave enough to say them aloud, brave enough to truly believe in a real future between us.

"Come for me." Nash's thrusts picked up in intensity, rattling the headboard.

"More. Harder. Please."

Mercifully, he tightened his grip on my cock, stripping it faster as he hammered me in quick, deep thrusts. "That's it. So good for me."

His praise was every bit as potent as his hand, and I moaned as my balls tightened. His muscles tensed, tendons in his neck standing out, and his cock spasmed inside me. That was all it took before I was coming, too, shouting his name and thrashing back and forth on the bed.

"Oh, fuck." Nash's voice was so dismayed as he pulled out that I glanced down to make sure the condom hadn't burst.

"What?"

"We cracked your headboard." He pointed above my shoulder where, sure enough, a long hairline crack marred the dark wood.

"Finally." I grinned up at him. "Bed breaking achieved. We're awesome."

"Yeah, we are." He flopped next to me. "Fuck, I'm tired."

"I'll set the alarm—"

"I'll do it." He stayed my hand. "No more middle-of-the-night sneaking out. I do have to go home in the morning and change, but I meant it when I said I wasn't going anywhere. I'm in this now. All of it."

"You sure you're ready for this?" Propping myself on my elbow, I peered down at him. He looked sated and sleepy, eyes half-closed, not like a conflicted man who was about to run, but I still had to ask.

"Yup." He tugged me close enough to kiss. "Not saying it's going to be easy, but I want to face this together."

"Together," I echoed before I kissed him back. "That sounds nice."

Later I'd need a second shower. Later he'd have to go home, have to go back to work, face whatever was waiting there. Later I'd have the social workers. Later we'd both have family drama. But right then, we had each other, had that kiss, and it was more than enough.

Nash

I woke with the sun coming through the windows of

Mason's room—a novelty. And I won't lie, walking home in broad daylight wearing yesterday's uniform was a bit…unsettling. But it felt right in a way that little else had all week, barring last night's reunion with Mason. I'd left him a note wishing him luck with the social worker and inviting him to update me later. I whistled softly as I turned into my drive. Maybe I'd get around to asking Mason if I could keep some clothes at his place, avoid such a blatant walk of shame. But there wasn't that much shame. I loved Mason Hanks, and the truth lifted me up. Of course, I hadn't exactly told him yet, hadn't wanted to spook him. But we were getting there.

A new lightness in my heart, I showered and shaved and drove to the station. For the first time, I was looking as forward to the end of the day as I was to the start—I couldn't wait to head home, find out how things had gone for Mason, maybe cook together again. Just knowing I might have those simple things added balance to my day that I hadn't known I needed.

My other officer, Locklear, was getting ready to head out as I came in. He gave me an appraising look, one that said he'd probably heard the rumors. But he only nodded at me. "Chief. Hope you have a slow day. God, knows we need it after this week."

"That's the truth." I gave him a slow and steady look back. He was older than Holmes, more old-school, more set in his ways. I was prepared for…*something*, but the confrontation didn't happen.

However, as soon as he left, Marta coughed from over at the dispatch desk. "So is it true, Nash Flint? You breaking your poor father's heart?"

I sighed. Should have known this day wouldn't go

smooth. "He's been dead a long time. Think he's lost the right to an opinion."

"Don't you go getting fresh with me. I've known you since you were riding around on his shoulders. And you're a good man. He raised you right. Better than this."

"You've always been a friend to the family, Marta. And I'm sorry that me being with Mason Hanks is troubling you, but it's a done deal." I was proud of how firm my voice was. I loved Marta like an aunt, but I was done taking judgment about my relationship with Mason.

She made a sour face. "Trouble isn't the right word. You've worked for the city decades now. There's a good pension with your name on it if you can't abide this."

"Why, Nash Flint, are you forcing me out?" She put a hand to her heart.

"Nope. You're the best I've got," I said honestly. "Best damn dispatcher in the county, really. But my personal life's not up for discussion. Or judgment."

She made a clucking noise but returned to her monitor screen. "If that's how you want it..."

"It is." I'd spent years being concerned that Marta and people like her might turn away from me, and now that it had finally happened, I was surprised by how little I actually cared. What mattered was what Mason and I had together, not what a few narrow-minded people thought. I only wished I'd been able to come around to that way of thinking sooner. The people who truly loved me would accept me for who I was, not some mythic ideal of the local police chief that even my father hadn't been able to fulfill. Sure, he'd been the quintessential officer, but at what price?

All I knew was that it was a price I wasn't willing to pay.

As the day dragged on, I started to think about food and was considering a walk over to the tavern when the City Hall receptionist banged on the wall. "Chief? Your lunch is here."

I couldn't help my smile as I made my way to the front. I didn't miss Marta's snort as I walked by, but I also didn't pay her any mind.

"This okay?" Mason stood by the receptionist's desk with two white takeout containers. "I had good news, so I thought I'd bring you lunch before I relieve Adam at the tavern."

"Of course. And I want to hear your news." I wasn't going to risk ushering Mason past Marta and her foul mood, so I led him out into the sunshine to one of the benches lining the town square.

"You sure about this?" Mason looked around. "For a guy who doesn't like feeling exposed, this is pretty...open."

"I'm not ashamed to be having lunch with my..." I trailed off, not sure exactly what we were now. I knew what I *wanted* to be, but that didn't mean he wanted the same thing.

"Boyfriend?" Both Mason's eyebrows tilted skyward. "Adam and Logan are never going to let me live down snagging Sheriff Sexy."

"I'm too old to be a boyfriend," I grumbled, already hating that nickname. "I always liked the word partner, though I know it's a bit old-fashioned."

"Kind of like you." Mason leaned in and patted my

cheek. "And seriously, you're going to stop it with the 'old' business."

"My father was fifty when he had his first stroke. That one was mild, but—"

"You're not your dad," Mason said firmly. "And I fully intend to stuff you full of healthy food and see you live to a hundred, so none of this 'I could die first' bullshit."

"Okay." Duly chastised, I opened the food container. Mason had packed my burger, no tomato, and a side salad, exactly how I liked it. "God, I love you," I said without thinking.

"How about you love me for more than my ability to make Logan throw together a lunch?" He laughed but there was a seriousness there.

"I can do that." Not caring who might be watching, I reached over and squeezed his hand.

"You mean it?" His eyes were liquid and full of hope.

"I do." I wasn't quite ready to kiss him on the town square, with traffic rolling by and kids playing in the fountain on the other side of the grassy expanse, but I was sorely tempted and I tugged him closer. "Now, you said you had news?"

"Yup." He grinned at me. "Home-study approved. I have to drive to the DHS office to pick her up in a few hours. I get her *today*."

"That's fabulous." Oh, screw it. Screw everyone. I leaned in for a fast kiss. Let people talk. His answering smile was worth it.

"And tomorrow, Dad's likely to be discharged. Lilac can come with me to pick him up, and I know that will cheer them both up."

"Glad he's doing better." I forced myself to be charitable. He was important to Mason, so that made him someone I needed to respect, no matter my official dealings with him. "Is it going okay with your friends, you missing so much work?"

"They're being really supportive. I'll be back to normal soon, I hope. And I think they're stoked that Brock called with great news—the investors for the resort are looking at moving ahead. That'll mean more than enough business to keep us going."

"Good news all around," I agreed, basking in the sunshine of his happy mood.

"Is it okay if I tell them? About us, I mean? They've heard the rumors, but I haven't confirmed anything—"

"Tell them I love you." This kiss was longer and my cheeks went hot before I pulled away. "And to drop the stupid nickname."

"I can do that." Mason was as pink as I felt. He didn't say it back, but it was okay. He'd had a huge day. I had no doubt he did love me back, and that was what mattered. The day was sunny and full of promise, and I was happy and grateful to be there in the center of town, sharing it with my guy.

Mason

The lunch rush had almost passed, and I had about an hour before I needed to pick up Lilac from the summer day camp I'd enrolled her in. My dad was helping where he could, but it was going to be a while before he was back to full strength.

"Well, look at that. Sheriff Sexy brought a crowd," Adam called back to the kitchen where I was prepping salads for a group of female tourists.

"Stop calling him that." In the week or so since we'd started openly seeing each other, Logan and Adam had been merciless with the teasing.

"Would Grandpa work better?" Logan asked, his eyes dancing.

"Shut up." I grabbed the finished salads and delivered them to the table of ladies in the back before heading to the front to see who Nash had brought. He and Curtis had been in a few nights ago, Curtis teasing me as much as my own friends, which was strangely nice.

Whoa. I pulled up short when I got a good look at Nash's table. I'd momentarily forgotten in the rush of the morning that today was the day his mother was coming to town. But there she was, sitting across from Nash, and looking none too happy about it. Trisha, Nash's sister, was there along with two kids who looked around Lilac's age. The adults had menus, and the kids were spitting straw wrappers at each other.

"You want me to take the table?" Adam came up behind me. Fuck. I was standing there staring, and that wouldn't do.

"No, I'm going," I grumbled. "Could have warned me better."

"Aw, come on," he whispered. "And miss all this meet-the-family fun? You wanna keep sleeping with Sheriff—"

"Be. Quiet." I gave him a death glare as I grabbed crayons and two of the new kids' menus that Lilac had helped me design. I'd done the menus on the library copier when I'd taken her to stock up on books.

"Mason." Nash's smile was a bit more tense than the one he'd given me last night when we'd stolen a few kisses after Lilac fell asleep. "I've been raving about your food the last few hours. This is my family. Mom, Trisha, this is Mason."

Trisha gave me a polite smile and offered me her hand. Like Nash and his mother, she was tall and had hazel eyes. She had very Portland soccer mom vibe with highlighted hair, sandals, and utilitarian clothing that looked like it was from an REI catalog. "Nash said you can handle food allergies? The naturopath has Jeff off gluten and eggs right now."

"Of course. I've got gluten-free burger buns, and I'll make a note about the egg allergy, too."

"It's not just your food that Nash can't shut up about." Her eyes twinkled, and my shoulders unkinked a bit. At least some of Nash's family wouldn't be openly hostile. I could deal with an interfering sister much easier than the glare coming from his mother. "He says you've got custody of your niece? Think she'd want to play with Jeff and Andrea later? I could use someone to run them ragged so they actually sleep tonight."

I hadn't expected the offer and my sinuses burned. Too many freaking emotions the last few weeks. "That would be nice, thanks. She'd love that."

"And I can grill you while they play." Her tone was light, and I found myself looking forward to getting to know her—she'd been older than me in school by several years and went Portland for college and then stayed there after, so I didn't have many memories of her younger self.

It would be nice for Nash to have an ally, too, especially given his mother's sour expression. She kept glancing around like a drag show was about to bust out of the kitchen.

"You want your usual?" I asked Nash while glancing at her. *See? I know him. Know what he likes and doesn't and how to take care of him.*

"Yep." Nash's smile this time was more genuine. "But throw on an order of fries — I'll split with the kids. It's a good day to splurge."

Yes, yes, it was. I smiled back at him, happy to finally be able to let some of my affection show.

Trisha ordered gluten-free burgers for the kids and the Cobb salad off the specials board for herself. His mother very grudgingly got hot tea and a side salad, no dressing, still not meeting my eyes. Oh, well. Maybe eventually that ice would thaw. I hoped so, for Nash's sake, but I was prepared to deal either way. My own family was hardly warming to the idea of Nash, my dad acting like I'd decided to join the circus for all the support he was offering. He'd undoubtedly be happier if I took up with a Hell's Angel instead of a law-enforcement guy, but whatever.

I was done putting my family ahead of myself — I had to make Lilac and my future my priority. If anyone had a problem with that, too bad.

Hours later, I sat on Nash's back porch step watching the kids play some complicated game involving a magic ball, a pile of stuffed animals, and a lot of running around. It was a gorgeous late-summer night, warm with a strong breeze off the coast and a pink sunset in the distance.

"I'm getting more iced tea." Trisha pushed herself off the swing. Nash's mother had long since gone to lie down, pleading a headache. "You guys need anything?"

"Nope," we answered at the same time, and I laughed.

"You okay?" Nash asked as soon as the door closed behind her. "This isn't too weird."

"Not weird at all." I scooted closer to him on the step. "I like her. And the kids. And she clearly loves you."

"Yeah. She does." Nash rubbed his face, eyes not quite convinced.

"And I love you, too," I added lightly, but my heart still pounded. "We've got that in common."

"Do you now?" A wide smile broke across Nash's face, and his eyes promised a thorough kissing as soon as we didn't have the pint-sized audience.

"I do. Sorry it took me forever to say it. This all feels so much like a dream. Like I can't believe we're actually here. Together."

"Doesn't feel like a dream to me." Nash shook his head. "Feels more like this was inevitable, even from our first conversation. Like we've been building to this, and now here we are. And it's nowhere near as scary as I'd feared."

"I'm glad." Taking a chance, I reached for his hand. Neither of us had exactly trotted out the PDA all day, and I was desperate to touch him. He took it, squeezing my fingers tightly.

"I want more of this." With his free hand, Nash

gestured at the yard. "More nights like this. More time with you and Lilac. I want the long haul, Mason."

"Me, too." I had to bite my lip to keep from getting all emotional again. Our eyes met, and I swore I could see our future—not smooth and calm, but bumpy and unpredictable and *ours*. We'd face whatever it brought, together.

TWENTY-SEVEN

Four months later

Mason

The wind howled and whipped the tree branches outside the house, rattling the windows in the sort of late-fall storm I'd actually missed a bit in my years away from the coast. The sea had been roiling on my drive back from the county seat with Lilac earlier.

I was digging in the bedroom closet when the sound of the front door and heavy footsteps cut past the wind noise.

"What are you doing?" Nash came up behind me.

"It's cold tonight. I've got an electric blanket in here somewhere." I reached past my dress clothes, the spare uniforms Nash kept here, and the stash of holiday presents we already had going for Lilac. Nash had proved to be even worse than me, arriving twice recently with "a little something for Christmas." Lilac was going to be thrilled with this year's Santa haul, and I couldn't wait for Nash to share it with us. "Here it is."

"I can keep you warm." Nash wrapped me up in a hug, pulling my back to his front.

"Oh? You staying?" I tried to sound disinterested and not pathetically grateful. Lately, he'd been here more nights than at his place, and no blanket was a match for Nash's warm bulk in my bed.

"Yeah." Nash plucked the blanket from me, tossing it on the bed before turning me to face him. Deep lines bracketed his mouth, and I could tell from his cloudy eyes that it had been a long, hard day. "That okay?"

"Always." I gave him a slow kiss. "There's food for you in the fridge—"

"Later." He broke away enough to start unbuttoning his uniform. Yup, it had been a long day indeed. And maybe later he'd tell me about it, but I knew what he needed now. I spread out the blanket and plugged it in while he stripped down to the black boxer briefs I'd gotten for him on my last trip to Portland. He looked damn sexy, but I reined in my ogling as I locked the bedroom door before removing my own clothes.

He was already under the covers when I slipped in, and he gathered me close, burying his face in my neck, breathing deep.

"Bad day?" I whispered.

"Not so bad now." He squeezed me tighter, his shaky words calling him a liar. "Okay. Maybe a little. But this helps."

"I'm glad." I snuggled closer, trying to give him the contact he needed to re-center himself.

"Tell me about your day," he ordered, still breathing me in. "Business good? How was the DHS meeting?"

"Business is slow with tourist season done, but we're

doing okay. Logan's got white chili on the menu tomorrow. You might like that."

"If it calms down, I'll stop by." His hands smoothed down my ribs. "And the court stuff?"

I sighed. I knew he wanted a distraction, but I wasn't sure if this was it. "DHS is still working on the concurrent plan with me. There will be a review hearing in the spring. Jimmy's still waiting for trial. Chester, too. Chances are high that Chester takes a plea deal on the vandalism charges to testify against Jimmy if Jimmy won't plead guilty." At least with the two of them off the streets, the vandalism had stopped and businesses had been able to relax, focus on the good news about the resort and the success of our group ads. I wasn't ever going to be okay with Jimmy's behavior, or the fact that we shared blood, but moving forward with my big plans felt like the right path. Maybe Jimmy couldn't appreciate what we were trying to build here, but plenty could. "Francine's plea bargain was accepted, but she'll be in prison at least the next two years. So it looks like Lilac's with me for the foreseeable future."

"Excellent." Nash's voice was firm. "You're good for her. That's the best outcome right now, and I know the court will agree."

"You don't mind? I know getting me plus a kid wasn't exactly in your plans—"

"You're a package deal. I get it." Nash squeezed me closer, dropping a kiss on my shoulder. "And I've been wanting to talk to you about that, actually."

"Oh?"

"Think the social worker would work with you if you wanted to file a change of address?"

"Change of address?" My heart thudded against my ribs, and I was sure he was able to feel it.

"Yeah. My place is bigger, and it's empty most of the time. Seems a shame. It's less drafty than this place, and I've got the wood stove for winter. And my bathroom's better."

"That it is," I managed to say around holding my breath.

"I was thinking we could look at Trisha's old room, have Lilac pick out the paint colors, maybe get her some new furniture for it. Then we can let the social workers come have a look, see if they're good with the move."

"I'm sure they would be." My voice came out all rough. "But is that really what you want?"

"More than anything." He pressed another kiss to the back of my neck. "I'm too old—"

"Nuh-uh," I corrected him.

"—for this back-and-forth business. I want you in my bed every night. Want you in my life. I've waited too long for someone like you. I don't want to wait anymore for a life with you."

"I do like your kitchen." I had to make a joke before the moisture in my eyes escaped.

"And it likes you." Rolling us, Nash looked down at me with serious eyes. "Way I figure it, it's past time to turn the old house into a real home again. And that's going to take you. And Lilac."

"You sure this isn't just a bad day talking?" I reached up and stroked his face. "We can take it slow—"

"No day is truly bad when I've got you at the end of it." Nash brushed a fast kiss across my lips. "And I took it slow for forty damn years. As long as you're on board, I'm ready for this."

"I'm on board," I whispered. "I love you."

It was still hard for me to get the words out, to trust that I was really here in this place with this man, that this was my life now, but there was no greater thrill than when he answered me. "Love you, too, Mason. So much."

And then we were kissing, and I didn't even bother trying to cover my damp cheeks. It had been a hard few months—all the stuff with Lilac and my family certainly hadn't helped. And Nash was still deciding what it meant to be out. I'd been right that most people didn't care, but a few did, and I knew that rankled him more than he liked. But we were here now, closer than ever with this next phase to look forward to.

I hoped we could get the social worker's approval quickly. I wanted a Christmas tree in Nash's front room, wanted to teach him how to make gingerbread in his big kitchen, wanted to move Lilac into a room we'd made perfect for her. I wanted it all, and I wanted it with Nash, and for the first time I really believed I was going to get it. We really were stronger as a couple, and as our kisses heated up and my cheeks went from wet to flushed, my heart surged ahead to that shared future. Our bodies were making promises that I knew our hearts would keep, and I couldn't wait to watch it all unfold. Together.

~The End~

Want more Rainbow Cove? Next in the series is Curtis and Logan's book, TENDER WITH A TWIST. Adam gets his book in HOPE ON THE ROCKS. If you enjoyed TRUST WITH A CHASER, I'd be honored if you'd consider leaving a review, as reviews help other readers find books.

Want ficlets, contests, and updates on other favorite characters? Make sure you're in my Facebook fan group, Annabeth's Angels, for all the latest news, contests, and freebies. And newsletter subscribers always get the latest news on releases, freebies, and more!

http://eepurl.com/Nb9yv

Want more books like the Rainbow Cove series? Be sure and check out my other series and single title books!

ACKNOWLEDGMENTS

Rainbow Cove is a fictional town on the southern Oregon coast. Any resemblance to real places, people, or events is entirely coincidental. Some readers may wonder why Nash is the chief of police instead of a sheriff. In Oregon, sheriffs are county wide offices while police usually handle law enforcement for each city. Many thanks to those who helped with my research in Oregon law enforcement, family courts, coastal living, and other matters. A special thanks to my editor, Edie Danford, for her tireless work and her help in pushing me to go deeper into Mason and Nash's journey. My proofreader, Jody Wallace, does amazing work and deserves huge kudos as well. Wendy Qualls, Karen Stivali, and Layla Reyne keep me on track with writing sprints and support. My Facebook group, Annabeth's Angels, has been so supportive of this project, and I treasure all my readers. Thank you to everyone who has reviewed, tweeted, shared, and cheered me on—your support is priceless. My family puts up with my crazy hours, and I love them for their understanding. Writing and publishing is a journey, and I'm so grateful to everyone who has helped me along that journey.

Arctic Sun

Arctic Wild

Arctic Heat

Hotshots series

Burn Zone

High Heat

Feel the Fire

Up in Smoke

Shore Leave series

Sailor Proof (September 2021)

Sink or Swim (February 2022)

Perfect Harmony series

Treble Maker

Love Me Tenor

All Note Long

Portland Heat series

Served Hot

Baked Fresh

Delivered Fast

Knit Tight

Wrapped Together

Danced Close

True Colors series

Conventionally Yours

Out of Character

Single Titles

Better Not Pout

Resilient Heart

Winning Bracket

Save the Date

Level Up

Mr. Right Now

Sergeant Delicious

Cup of Joe

Featherbed

AUTHOR BIO

Annabeth Albert grew up sneaking romance novels under the bed covers. Now, she devours all subgenres of romance out in the open — no flashlights required! When she's not adding to her keeper shelf, she's a multi-published Pacific Northwest romance writer.

Emotionally complex, sexy, and funny stories are her favorites both to read and to write. Fans of quirky, Oregon-set books as well as those who enjoy heroes in uniform will want to check out her many fan-favorite and critically acclaimed series. Many titles are also in audio! Her fan group Annabeth's Angels on Facebook is the best place for bonus content and more! Website: www.annabethalbert.com

Contact & Media Info:

- facebook.com/annabethalbert
- twitter.com/AnnabethAlbert
- instagram.com/annabeth_albert
- amazon.com/Annabeth/e/B00LYFFAZK
- bookbub.com/authors/annabeth-albert

Made in United States
Troutdale, OR
01/26/2024

17202468R00184